CW00432827

Rosemary Ingham

WHERE THE
TRUTH LIES

MACMILLAN NEW WRITING

First published 2007 by Macmillan New Writing,
an imprint of Macmillan Publishers Ltd
Brunel Road, Basingstoke RG21 6XS
Associated companies throughout the world
www.macmillannewwriting.com

ISBN-13: 978–0230–01962–1 hardback
ISBN-10: 0230–01962–5 hardback
ISBN-13: 978–0230–01963–8 paperback
ISBN-10: 0230 01963–3 paperback

10 9 8 7 6 5 4 3 2 1
14 13 12 11 10 09 08 07 06 05

A CIP catalogue record for this book is available from
the British Library.

Typeset by Heronwood Press
Printed and bound in China

*To my children Alison, Caroline and Mark
for all the happiness they bring me and
to Helen Dennis for the support only
another writer could provide.*

Chapter 1

May 1981

'All right, Isabel?'

A moment of shock before I find my voice to respond to the fifteen-year-old boy. 'Fine, thanks.' His intention is obviously friendly. One of my earliest decisions as Head of Thomas Paine High was to be on first-name terms with everyone. Why is there a gap between theory and practice? Recovering, I add, 'How about you?'

'Okay.'

'Where are you off to?' Carefully casual language, to remove any hint of aggression from the enquiry.

'Max sent me to fetch summat from his room.'

Ignoring the mild disapproval this prompts, I nod smiling consent to his errand. I don't plan to be the sort of headteacher who goes round disapproving of things. Though it's less than two hours since I agreed with Max to have a blitz on wandering students. (Got it right this time. I must banish the term *pupil* even from my thoughts.) I walk on down the corridor, ordering myself to focus on the positive. The management technique I've vowed to practise. Which seems as natural to Max as breathing. Anyone could forget something vital to the lesson.

Not at all the same as a failure to exercise proper control. Perfectly acceptable to send a student. (Right again!) Not that I could. I lack Max's easy confidence. I have this compulsion to do everything perfectly. Natural enough when I've only been in post four weeks. Except I'm always like that. Finding it almost impossible to forgive my own mistakes. Marriage made it worse. Much worse. Twelve months since I separated from Richard. I ought to be in recovery. Only divorce still seems like admitting to the ultimate unforgivable mistake. Negative thinking. *Focus on success.* I got my dream job, didn't I? Even though it seemed presumptuous to fill in the application forms, implying I saw myself as a worthy successor to Will Fullwood. Will, one of my heroes. It's a year since I put my name down for that conference he was running. But the cancer had already started and he was too ill to come so we never met. It didn't stop the sense of personal loss when he died three months later. I used to imagine working with someone of his vision. Instead of being Deputy to poor old Albert, the Head at Moorlands, who was out of his depth with any development later than the 1944 Education Act. Thomas Paine High is the vision made real. And I'm the school's new Head. When the governors offered me the job, I was almost too astonished to accept. I still can't quite believe it.

I'm doing the Head thing at the moment. Management by walking about. And there's no way I can ignore the horrendous racket coming from that classroom. Tricky to do it well but I have to intervene. I wrestle with the brass doorknob, and stand still in the doorway. An uneasy silence spreads outwards from me. The chattering ceases and the lounging students adopt postures suggestive of at least an intention to work. A white-haired teacher is peering at me over his half-moon spectacles, his face flushed. So many names to learn. I retrieve his with relief. Trevor Bennett. I smile a bit, aiming for friendly but not ingratiating.

He's stepping forward in an apparent attempt to seize the initiative. 'Mrs Lincoln, what can I do for you?'

'I'd like to join you, if I may.' It must be obvious to every student in the room that I'm here because Trevor's lost control, but I can't say that, can I? So I improvise. 'I'm trying to get direct experience of all areas of the curriculum.'

He's clasping one hand in the other as though he's wringing them. 'You're welcome, most welcome. It's not a particularly good moment though. I've just been running through the causes of the Civil War and we're about to start on the written work. Perhaps another day?'

I hang on to my smile. 'Not at all. The routine is what I want to see. It doesn't need to be anything special.' If I take that empty chair across the room he can scarcely eject me. He ought to be grateful. My arrival has restored order.

He's seized a piece of chalk and turned his back on the class, to write a question on the board. Is that wise, in the circumstances?

A voice from the corner behind me. 'Causes of the Civil War? Is that what you've been going on about, Mr Bennett? I 'aven't 'eard any of 'em.'

He swings round. His chin drops to his chest as he contorts his face to look over his spectacles. I tighten the muscles around my mouth against the tug of a grin.

'Your failure to listen is your problem, boy,' he snaps.

A swelling chorus, all insisting on a matching ignorance.

'Shut up, shut up.' Trevor Bennett pauses to remove a fleck of spittle from his lip before repeating the same command, which everyone's ignoring.

I can't let it go on. 'Mr Bennett.' Lucky I have the knack of being audible without shouting. Thank goodness the class is growing quiet to listen. 'There seems to be general support for some further discussion. I'd find it interesting. The religious arguments, for instance?'

He glares, looks grudging, but at least he's answering the question.

I'm setting myself up to fail here. Somehow I have to make the topic real or I'll never engage the students' attention. I can't afford to get it wrong. 'How much does religion matter to you? Is there anywhere where it's a burning issue now, in 1981?' I make myself wait for someone to respond, though it's a temptation to prompt again.

'Northern Ireland?' An uncertain voice.

'Israel.' A more confident contribution.

'Jews against Muslims,' someone says.

'Zionists,' a dark-haired girl corrects. 'We're Jewish, but my dad doesn't agree with the Israeli government.'

'Israel brings religion into it. All that crap about God giving Palestine to them. Anyone could claim that, couldn't they?'

'It's part of the argument then,' I say, not taking anyone's side.

The melting pot of North London. Students identifying themselves as Irish, Jewish, Muslim, Greek and Turkish Cypriot. Lift-off. An animated discussion developing. 'So lots of people are still fighting about religion.' Why on earth doesn't Trevor Bennett seize the opportunity and feed in a few facts about Archbishop Laud or Puritanism or something, instead of standing aloof, radiating disapproval? As pleasantly as I can manage, I say, 'Do help me out with some information about the religious arguments in the seventeenth century.' He's bound to answer.

He does, though with a notable absence of enthusiasm.

What was that management technique again? Here the positive seems to have dwindled to invisibility. Left with no choice, I continue teaching on his behalf until he cuts in with an abrupt dismissal several minutes before one o'clock, when the lunch hour officially begins.

There are no bells at Thomas Paine. They're at odds with the philosophy of personal responsibility. I'm regretting their absence, fuming that he's skiving out of four minutes of responsibility for the class, but nothing could diminish the glow I always experience from a successful lesson. Especially after putting myself on the line like that. The students are still debating the issue as they leave, saying, 'See you, Isabel.' 'Thanks,' the dark-haired girl says as she passes me. 'That was great.' Though no doubt it's only in contrast to the dire tedium of other history lessons.

The teacher's voice cuts in. 'I'd like to talk to you. Now.'

'Of course.' He'll want to offer an explanation or apology after his disastrous performance. Not that I can see anything conciliatory in his manner. 'Let's go to my room.'

He marches one pace behind me through the crowds flooding out of classrooms. Will Fullwood rejected the tyranny of uniform along with the rest of the grammar school baggage, but the students have imposed their own norm of sweatshirt and jeans. Wherever possible in the narrow corridors, they part good-humouredly to allow me to pass.

'Out of the way! Let Mrs Lincoln through.' Trevor Bennett's intervention, as strident as it is unnecessary.

I refuse to have any part in it. 'You're doing your best, aren't you?' I say to a girl who's trying to flatten herself against the wall. I press on without glancing back at him. A look from me would only point up my disapproval.

Once inside my office, he closes the door and hovers near it.

'Have a seat,' I suggest. I'm disconcerted by his air of belligerence. Though that might be pure defensiveness.

'No, thank you. I wish to protest in the strongest possible

terms about your appearance, without invitation or even notification, in my classroom. I warn you I shall report the matter to Douglas Blake, my union representative.'

My heartbeat rises. I'm sure I was entirely within my rights, yet I can't prevent a rush of guilt, as though I'm a child caught out in wrongdoing. Playing for time, I sit down near my desk. Not behind it. I've moved it against the wall so it can never be a barrier. I manage a bland response. 'Which union is that?'

'NAS,' he replies.

Not reassuring. I know from Max that NASUWT members lead the opposition. 'How long have you been a teacher?' I ask.

He looks puzzled. 'Thirty-one years.'

'Then you will have recognised as I did that your class was out of control. As the Head, I couldn't ignore that. I had to restore order.'

'There is no order in this school. No respect. No discipline. Those of us who attempt to maintain standards are constantly undermined. As you undermined my effort to demand basic courtesy just now.'

I avoid this attempt to sidetrack me. 'We may argue about the reasons, but you accept that the class was misbehaving?'

'Will Fullwood's airy-fairy notions have turned the school into a bear-garden. You can't expect me to fight against the anarchy which prevails here. I fear for my personal safety, let alone my sanity. We are forced to compromise to survive.'

The phrase 'spitting out the words' has never seemed so apt. A white froth of saliva lingers on his lower lip. Horrid fascination draws my gaze. Yet to look away would suggest a failure of nerve. I say, 'I found no difficulty in securing appropriate behaviour.'

Trevor Bennett laughs. It's not a pleasant sound, combining as it does sneering contempt and dwindling self-control.

'Appropriate behaviour! Is that your name for it?'

A blatant challenge to my authority. Unexpected. Maybe it happens to Heads all the time. How would I know? 'Yes.' I struggle to keep my voice steady. 'Once I intervened, the students' behaviour was entirely appropriate.'

'God knows what harm you did, bringing simmering tensions to the surface like that. War may already have broken out in the playground.'

For an instant I seem to be looking at the lesson through those ludicrous glasses of his, seeing it as he saw it. Alarm makes my breath flutter in my chest. One month in the post and I may be responsible for a riot. Should I rush out and check?

'Nonsense,' I say aloud. Needing to persuade myself, I put as much conviction as possible into the word. Trevor Bennett seems increasingly agitated, shifting his weight from one foot to the other. I've mishandled the situation. I should have insisted he sat down before I began. Nothing positive can come out of such a fraught encounter. 'We disagree.' I hope the admission may calm him. 'The suggestion of involving your union rep is an excellent idea.' More soothing stuff. Plus it secures a postponement. 'Speak to my secretary. She'll tell you when I'm available.'

'I have every intention of doing so.' It's delivered as a threat. At least it's his parting shot.

On my own I do my best to make an objective assessment of the incident. As an example of personnel management it has little to commend it. In my defence I can claim that the combined charisma of Will and Max has failed to secure Trevor Bennett's allegiance to the school's founding principles. And the lesson worked, even though I'm no historian. At least, I thought it worked. Was it a risky strategy? According to the Thomas Paine mission statement, differences are enriching, not threatening. My pleasure in the contact with students is fading, the doubts growing. Maybe I should go and talk to Max. What for? Advice? Consolation? He has a knack of putting any incident in a good light. Taking the doubts away. Odd that it makes me feel uncomfortable sometimes.

Max is an amazing person. He's got every reason to feel resentful of me. The outsider who took the job which was rightfully his. After everything he'd done. Running the place single-handed through Will's terrible last illness and during the nine months it took the governors to appoint a successor. Having to adjust to the role of my Deputy. Giving me ungrudging support from the moment I got the job. Which must have been the hardest moment of all for him.

The disquieting thoughts buzz insect-like in my brain. Why did it take the governors so long? When they appointed me it was the second time they'd gone through the whole process. Offering it to me after hours of discussion. Not reassuring, that. As though I was the choice of last resort. The Chair and Vice-Chair will be here in thirty minutes so we can interview candidates for the post of Second Deputy. Something I've never done before. I have to be calm and confident. Part of proving to them they got it right after all. Max was trying to save me from disappointment when he warned me Will only ever secured his choice after endless wrangling, if at all. I'd like to demonstrate I can manage the governors. I had a reputation for plain speaking in my previous schools. Today I need to be as silver-tongued as Max. Irresistibly persuasive. I've made all the arrangements so I shall at least appear competent. As long as Trevor Bennett doesn't waylay the governors to complain about me. As long as they don't have to struggle through rival gangs of warring students as a direct result of my impromptu history lesson.

❏ ❏ ❏

The fourth and last candidate. Jack Redfern. I watch him come into the room. Tall, broad-shouldered, quite heavily-built. A contrast to Max, who has the compact elegance of a gymnast. There's an awkwardness about the way Jack moves and takes the chair placed in front of the interviewing panel. Habitual or the result of nervousness? An interesting face. Not good-looking though – his features are too strongly-pronounced. I focus all my attention on him, desperate to get this one right. Even if I make the correct judgement, I may not manage to convince the governors. Say too little and it may go by default. Argue too strongly and they may dig their heels in. They want a hard man, someone to help me clamp down on what they despise as an absurdly liberal regime.

Gordon Lindsay, the Chair, is asking the first question. 'Your entire teaching career has been spent at Thomas Paine High School. How do you propose to overcome the handicap of such limited experience?' A question of the when-did-you-stop-beating-your-wife genre, asked with a disapproving frown which is deepening as Gordon listens to the response.

Colin Blaine, the Vice-Chair, wants to know how he proposes to counter the school's laissez-faire culture. Jack begins to sketch a gesture with his right hand and truncates it. His answers are hesitant. More questions, all hostile. He should have been prepared for that. Max backs him but I'm already disappointed. Now the Inspector, Robert Swift, is asking about changing student behaviour.

At once Jack's animated, leaning forward in his chair. 'A school can impose behaviour, using rules, regulations, punishments. Or it can take the more rigorous approach of seeking to change hearts and minds. Which demands much more of teachers and students, but makes a lasting difference. At

Thomas Paine, there's no culture of "them and us". It's the school's greatest strength. Allies can influence one another. No one embraces the ideas of those they regard as the enemy.'

I'm smiling and nodding agreement when Gordon cuts in. 'Is this your attempt to justify "friendly" relationships between teachers and pupils?' The quotation marks are audible and contemptuous. 'Have you no appreciation of how dangerous they are?'

There's the briefest hesitation before Jack meets the accusation head-on. 'Exploiting our position of trust is always unforgivable. We don't build up the mystique of teachers at Thomas Paine. We're honest about our shortcomings. That offers a level of protection. But you're right. The danger exists and we have to be vigilant here, as in every other school.'

I can't interpret Gordon's grunt. He looks towards me and says formally, 'Mrs Lincoln.'

My turn to ask a question. 'Six weeks ago I was a Deputy myself. I know what a tricky role it can be. Even more tricky when it's an internal appointment. Whose side should the Deputy be on? His colleagues' side? Or the Head's?'

'It's the Deputy's responsibility to make sure there are no sides.' He corrects himself. 'That's too glib. The staff here divide along various fault-lines, though we're more united than most. I'd try to see everyone's point of view and work for reconciliation. Even when there seems to be some advantage in fostering divisions, it's always a mistake.' Jack smiles. 'You want to know what I'd do if it came to the crunch. Absolute support for the Head. Reserving the right to say what I think in private. And to be heard.'

It's obvious enough interview-speak. What candidate would be foolish enough to suggest he'd let you down? Yet as his gaze meets mine I recognise someone I can trust.

The exchange is continuing. I will myself to listen with total concentration, trying to see the person behind the words, the expressions, the body language, and at the same time to gauge the panel's reactions. If Jack is my preference, I'll have a struggle on my hands. But I'm not sure. Not at all sure. I want my two Deputies to work well together. Only isn't Max a little too enthusiastic about Jack? I don't want to find myself an uncomfortable outsider whenever the three of us meet. As an interviewee, I believed the stress was all mine. Now I'm longing for that easy option of being at the mercy of others' decision. Far too much seems to hang on my ability to get it right. To opt for the right person. To find the right arguments to sway the governors.

With a brisk, 'Thank you, Mr Redfern,' Gordon is drawing proceedings to a close.

There's a moment or two of bustle as the tea and biscuits I've ordered are set out on the table.

'Very civilised. Never had this with Fullwood, did we, Gordon?' Colin comments.

'Certainly not. He thought afternoon tea was bourgeois. Never offered anything except that disgusting home-brewed beer of his.'

The comments and accompanying male laughter leave me wondering if I'm conforming to some womanly stereotype. I tell myself the discussion matters more than my feminist hang-ups. At Gordon's invitation the Inspector is summarising his impressions of the four candidates, giving me time to organise my notes. Is he neutral? I listen attentively. It's easy enough to use emphasis and omission to promote a favourite. When will I have a chance to say what I think? What shall I do if Gordon doesn't even ask me?

'Isabel, who do you want?'

It catches me off balance, as though my foot's come down

upon a familiar step only to find it missing. The query is too straightforward, leaving me no space for strategy. Besides, who do I want, if any attention is to be paid to my wishes? I live through seconds of silence, before I answer. 'Jack Redfern.' Did I say that? It sounds like someone else's pronouncement rather than my own judgement. Which the governors probably intend to ignore.

Gordon leans forward to take another biscuit. 'Sure about that?'

Better to sound decisive even if it's disastrous for Jack's chances, so I say, 'Quite sure.'

Gordon hunches his shoulders. A trick he has. He's exceptionally tall and seems never to have come to terms with his height. 'No point in prolonging the discussion then. We've all got better things to do.' He's finishing his shortbread.

My lips seem stiff with astonishment, making words hard to form. 'You mean, you're happy to appoint Jack?'

'I'm happy to appoint the man you want. Seemed a bit of an awkward customer to me. Might help you in your battles with Max Truman. His pernicious influence has had free rein for far too long. He'll be a tough opponent. If it's Redfern you want, we accept your judgement, don't we, Colin?'

'Absolutely.'

As I murmur my thanks I'm struggling against a new uncertainty. I'll be able to report a triumph to Max. But is it my triumph? Or his?

Chapter 2

Jack Redfern, Deputy Head. It takes some getting used to. He feels like he's trying on a different personality. Someone older than thirty-two, with more gravitas. Who you are. Who you intend to be. Does everyone suffer from the same uncertainty? Out of school he's never managed it. Actions always falling short of intentions. Too inclined to live up to his name. Jack the Lad. Self-disgust tugs his mouth into a grimace. That wasn't how he'd meant it to be. Him and Maggie living together. Buying the three-bed semi in Enfield. Betsy and then Matt. It was supposed to be forever. As far as anything could be. The business with Jill wasn't serious. But when Maggie found out, that was it. Not that he blamed her. She'd forgiven him twice. And he'd promised. Both times. Never again. Thinking of his children brings the familiar twist of pain. The shiver of guilt. He'd meant to stay close. Meant. That word again. But it was awkward, now there was a stepfather on the scene. At his age he'd like to be settled. Or he imagines he would. Perhaps it's only wanting what he hasn't got.

At school he's always taken himself more seriously. Ever since the day he turned up, six months out of his art degree at Central, half-convinced by his teacher training course that it wasn't for him, and met Will Fullwood. And that was it. No more doubts.

Thomas Paine High was his future. Swapping schools to climb up the ladder of promotion never interested him. He became Senior Tutor of Lexington House because it was the job Will needed him to do. A conversation only days before the cancer was diagnosed. It was the one thing he had to offer his hero. Being the best Senior Tutor he knew how to be. He feels the heat of embarrassment because it sounds sentimental even though it's the truth. The long pain of Will's dying was agonising. No one could want to see such suffering prolonged. It had all fallen on Max. The sheer hard slog to get the work done. And resist the governors' sabotage. And keep up everyone's morale, even at the most hopeless moments. He was the heir apparent. But he didn't get it. They appointed a woman instead.

It fell to Max to announce it at staff briefing the next morning. 'Isabel Lincoln is our new Head. She takes up her post on April the 23rd.' And to cope with the buzz of astonished dismay which greeted the news. The indignant protests against such injustice. Though they ought to have guessed. Max was far too loyal to Will to please the governors.

Jack felt bound to seek Max out afterwards though he didn't know what to say. What could anyone say? 'Tough on you,' was the best he could manage. 'You'll be looking for another job.'

'No,' Max said. 'It's not about me. Never has been. It's about the students. I need to stay.'

So Max remains a Deputy. Despite the promotion, Jack can't see himself as an equal. He looks up to Max almost as much as he looked up to Will. When Isabel allocates responsibilities he hopes he gets Pastoral. To begin with at least. Knowing he has a gift for managing students, he'd feel more confident. With him it's instinctive. Something he'd never thought about until Will pointed it out. It's like a posthumous blessing on his new job. If he can be Pastoral Deputy. He'll find out when they meet tomorrow – him, Max and Isabel. The strangeness of it still possesses him. Her gender ought not to be an issue. Only it is. At Thomas Paine men are in charge. Why has he never noticed that before? He reckons up. Two-thirds of the teachers are men and they hold all the senior positions. Plenty of young women in their first year or two of teaching. They find it tough. As Jill did. He came across her in tears after a disastrous lesson. That brief flare of sexual excitement he was too self-indulgent to resist. And then she moved on. Not many stayed and none of them had major responsibilities. Take Joan. Second in PE when he arrived. After nine years they're on their third Head of Department – Graham, male like his predecessors. Though he's generous in his praise of Joan. Says she does all the paperwork. He doesn't know how he'd manage without her. Like Rosie, Jack's assistant in Lexington House. She never even applied for the Jefferson House job when it came up.

He feels a touch of shame when he thinks of Valerie Stephens. Whose job he's taking. Except she never really had it. One of the governors' appointments. Made to thwart Will. Not her fault though. He used her as Head of Modern Languages. With a few token extras, like preparing agendas and minutes. Under Will it all happened without comment. Isabel brought it into the open. Said at a staff meeting she needed two fully-functioning Deputies – Christ, he hoped he could be that – and she'd tried to persuade Val to change her role but she'd preferred to stay in charge of languages and very generously insisted on reverting to the appropriate salary grade. Which created the internal vacancy. Isabel's first change. It's everyone's fear. That nothing will stay the same, not now she's got the job, instead of Max.

A face appears around his door. 'Congratulations!' And disappears.

'Max,' Jack calls after him. 'Come in.' He stands up to clear a chair for his visitor. As usual the room is cluttered with his students' art work, at various stages of completion.

Max obeys the summons. 'Didn't want to interrupt anything,' he says. A smile lights up his face, crinkling the skin around his dark eyes. 'It's brilliant news. I couldn't be more delighted.' He seizes Jack's hand, presses it and shakes it warmly.

Jack finds himself grinning. There's a glow about Max that's catching. In his presence the world seems a brighter place. 'Thanks. I'd never have put in for it if you hadn't persuaded me.'

'You were the obvious choice,' Max insists as they both sit down. 'Mind you, for that very reason I doubted the governors would have the wit to offer it to you. They always took a perverse delight in buggering up Will's plans.'

Stretching out a long leg, Jack slams the door shut with his foot. There are things to say which shouldn't be overheard. 'Am I Isabel's choice?' It's important to him to know.

Max looks serious. 'Absolutely.'

The seriousness carries conviction. But a question remains. 'How did she swing it with Gordon and Colin?'

'Honeymoon period. Doesn't make sense to thwart her so soon after appointing her. No telling how long it will last.'

'She's a good listener,' Jack suggests. Something he noticed in the interview.

Max is beaming again. 'Yes, isn't she?' His voice is warm with praise.

'But she strikes me as having a mind of her own. Though I hardly know her,' Jack adds apologetically. 'You've spent much more time with her.'

Max spreads his hands in an all-embracing gesture. 'Heart's in the right place and all that. But there's so much she doesn't know. We're going to have to work hard at supporting her.'

Jack nods his understanding. He wants to ask Max why he

thinks the governors chose her. Only it's delicate. 'When she was interviewed, did she fool the governors or what?' he asks, not sure how tactful he's being.

'Good question. She must have done.' Max is laughing. 'The candidate they were seeking would make Norman Tebbitt look like a bleeding-heart liberal.'

'They've made a mistake then.' A statement of fact. He couldn't have said why he sounded so certain.

'If she has any doubts, we have to convince her. And really,' Max points out reasonably, 'she can't be expected to feel the way we do. We worked with Will. He left his school in trust to us.'

'There'll be stuff she wants to change.'

'Bound to be.'

'You don't mind?'

'Jack, change was Will's lifeblood. He was the last person to want the place to ossify. It's hanging on to the principles of Thomas Paine High that matters. Putting the students first, valuing every one of them equally, no hierarchies of subjects or people. It's up to us to back Isabel's innovations. That way we can make sure they're true to the TPH ethos.'

The words are comforting. The prospect of conflict recedes, as it always does when Max explains things. Yet a misgiving lingers. Like the itch of an insect bite, it won't be ignored, even though scratching it will make it worse. He remembers what he said in the interview. *When it comes to the crunch.* Something specific. 'Supposing she tries to impose a uniform? The governors are bound to lean on her to do that.'

'So, what would we do?'

'Talk it through, the three of us?'

'Exactly. Look at enforcement. Endless negative encounters with students and parents. The triviality of it. Tutors distracted from their core responsibilities: enhancing students' self-worth and developing their potential to the full. At the end of our discussion, Isabel will be as determined to defy Gordon *et al* as the two of us are.'

'I guess so.' Palms uppermost, Jack slides his fingers between one another. Looking up, he asks, 'What will you let her change?'

The laughter bubbles up again. 'Isabel's in charge, for Christ's sake. Not me. You make me sound like some sinister puppet-master. Don't put that on me. I'd be hopeless at that kind of subterfuge.'

'You must have some idea,' he persists. 'What would Will have done next? Everything's been on hold for more than a year.'

'There's something she can do, which he would never have done. All our systems creak. Once it fell to me, I realised that within days. I didn't have the space to do anything about it. She's got a flair for organisation, like a lot of women. We ought to encourage it. Will didn't think it was worth bothering with. But the attacks on us are bound to intensify now the Tories are in power. We can't afford an Achilles' Heel.'

Jack's impressed. Impressed by the analysis, because it's not the kind of thing he does well himself. Impressed by Max's generous identification of Isabel's strengths. He's looking forward to it now, the three of them working together, helping Thomas Paine to flourish. 'Not sure how much use I'll be,' he says. An honest assessment, not a plea for reassurance.

But Max exclaims, 'Balls! You'll be brilliant. We must celebrate. How about a few jars this evening?'

They fix a time and agree the usual place. The Sutton Arms, the school's local, where they gather to hatch schemes, mourn defeat, toast success.

Jeremy is lounging against Jack's desk. 'Honestly, Jack, it's not humanly possible to behave well in Trevor's lessons. He is *so boring.*' Both o's are stretched to accommodate the extent of the tedium.

Jack continues to assemble the paraphernalia he requires for the first lesson of the morning. 'You're on course for top grades in every subject. Except history. You've got O-level next year. If you continue to fool about, you'll mess up your chances. I know you can be a first-class clown. I know you get a thrill out of making everyone laugh. But use a bit of self-control.'

Jeremy picks up a pen from the desk and presses the top, concentrates on watching the end flick in and out. 'I don't mean to be big-headed but I think I could scrape it however much I mess about.'

His senior house tutor laughs. 'You're probably right. The trouble is, the rest of the group would rather be entertained by you than do the work. And not all of them will scrape it. Besides which, I'm fed up with filing the complaints Trevor bombards me with. Not to mention the forests which are being sacrificed to provide the paper for them. We've tried talking with him. I've sat through his lessons—'

'You know how dire they are,' the boy interrupts.

'You said that. The point is, I can't change the situation. You'll have to change. I'm asking you to cut it out. As a favour to me, if you like.'

'Okay, Jack. I don't want to give you hassle. I'll do my best to behave like the ultimate swot.' He puts the pen back on the desk. 'Rumour has it you're our new Deputy. Great stuff.'

'Thanks. Get off and register now.'

'See you.'

Jack considers the tactics he's just used as he checks he's got fifteen pairs of scissors. Should he have wrapped it up more? No, Jeremy's too bright to be fooled by teacher-talk.

Hearing his name, Jack looks up. 'Valerie,' he says. He's

been wanting to speak to her but he didn't see how he could take the initiative.

'You're busy.'

'No. It's all sorted.'

At that she comes in, closing the door behind her and taking the chair he cleared yesterday evening. 'I wanted to wish you well.' She smiles. 'I can't offer you any useful advice, since I never did the Deputy job.'

'Thanks. A pity about the advice. I need as much as I can get.'

She laughs. An attractive laugh. Mid-forties. Sensible blue cotton skirt which, his art training notes, picks up a colour in her Liberty flower-print blouse. Dull as ditchwater, of course. His colleagues' verdict, which he's never questioned. Whatever, she's a good teacher in a difficult area. No avalanche of complaining notes from her cluttering his pigeonhole.

'Max knows it all,' she says. 'He'll be happy to put you right.'

A little sharp. Any resentment is perfectly understandable. 'It feels as though I'm taking your job.'

'No way. It's what I came to say. If it was bothering you at all. Isabel gave me the choice. It was my decision. Finally.'

He's curious. 'You must have wanted it when you applied.'

'Oh I did. Thrilled to bits when I got it.' She leans back in the chair smiling. 'Before I understood the way things were.'

'You mean, the ongoing row between Will and the governors?'

'That amongst other things.' She doesn't elaborate but she doesn't get up to go.

'You didn't want to work with Isabel?'

'I was tempted. She's straightforward. And tough. I hope I can be some use even in a more lowly role.' She hesitates. 'I said no for her sake, more than mine.'

'For her sake?'

'I want her to succeed. To make TPH the school it ought to be. I wasn't going to handicap her.'

He starts to deny she'd be a handicap, to insist on her strengths, but she cuts in. 'Two women out of three in top management? Here? Be realistic. With all the machismo there is around? They'd have found some way to destroy us both.' She frowns. 'Can't think why I'm telling you this. Only you're not part of the worst of it, are you?'

'I don't mean to be,' he says, though he's not clear what she's talking about. She's divorced. Maybe it's made her anti-men. He's not sorry when she checks the time and jumps up. For seconds her words jumble in his head, like a code he might be able to crack. But she can't know more than he does – Will always excluded her from anything significant. Gathering up his stuff, he strides off to his lesson, the class he's about to take occupying all his attention now.

The door's open. Jack likes that. 'Hi,' he says, as casual as he can manage. It was unexpected, seeing her alone. But Isabel had said she wanted to talk before their meeting with Max at two o'clock.

She swings round on her desk chair to face him. 'Jack. Thanks for coming in your lunch hour.'

'Should I close the door?' he asks, and then feels awkward he's suggested it.

'Please. When it's open, it's an invitation to drop in and I don't want us to be interrupted.'

He sits down, stretching out his legs. It seems too relaxed so he sits up straighter, planting both feet on the floor.

'Have I stopped you eating?'

It's not a question which would ever have occurred to her predecessor.

'There's coffee,' she says, waving towards a filter machine. He could smell it as soon as he came in, making the room un- expectedly homely. 'And biscuits.'

He watches her as she gets up to fill a mug for them both. Her movements are fluid. He wonders how he'd convey them in two dimensions. A line drawing, maybe? Like Valerie, she's wearing a skirt and blouse, but somehow hers – black linen and coral pink silk – give a very different impression. Then he's afraid he's staring at her, so he studies his shoes until he accepts his coffee with grunted thanks. He's a bit intimidated when she picks up a pad and pen from her desk. He hopes nothing he says will be used in evidence against him.

'I was never lucky enough to meet Will Fullwood. I've read his books, of course. I envy you, working with him.'

'Yes,' he mutters. He knows it's inadequate but he has no words to express what Will and the death of Will mean to him. He accepts the jug of milk she's offering and pours from it.

'He said everything I wanted to say. I read the books, saying *yes, yes, yes!* And he put it all into practice, here at Thomas Paine High.' She pauses to add milk to her own mug. 'I could never be so uncompromising.'

Unwise, he thinks, admitting to a weakness like that. 'Will never compromised. He didn't know how to.' It's a compliment to his hero's total commitment.

She nods. Sunlight from the window gilds the blond lights in her hair. 'Have you spoken to Val?' she asks.

The abbreviation takes him by surprise as much as the change of subject. 'She came to see me this morning.'

She ticks an item on her pad. 'I'm glad. Despite everything, she's genuinely happy about your appointment. As I am.' She laughs. 'If only because I like to get my own way.'

With her laughter he relaxes and helps himself to a biscuit.

'Thanks.' He can't quite see where all this is leading.

'Val was a casualty of Will's war with the governors. I understand why he fought them. From what Max tells me, they want a school modelled on the fantasy boarding establishments of Thirties fiction. The ultimate hierarchical set-up. Uniforms, prefects, caning. I have every intention of resisting them just as strongly as he did.' There's a pause while they both drink coffee. 'But differently.'

He's wary. 'Differently?'

'Fighting takes a lot of energy which could be put to better use. And as you pointed out in your interview, who was ever persuaded by an enemy? I want to change the governors' minds. And give peace a chance.' She quotes the words, the familiar chant at every anti-nuclear demo.

Going head-to-head with students is a nonsense. Never works. How many times has he told colleagues that? But it's different with governors. She can't know better than Will. 'They're not persuadable,' he tells her.

'I have to do it my way,' she says. 'It's harder for Max. For years he's been fighting Will's battles, first at his side and then on his behalf. You're not part of that, any more than I am. I need your backing. Over time, we can get Max to see things our way.'

Our way? How much is she taking for granted here? 'Max and I work well together.' He's warning her off, making it clear where his allegiance lies.

'Exactly. And all three of us want the same end. It's only the means which are in question.'

She seems to rate him as an ally. Which is flattering. But he won't let that seduce him. 'Why can't the three of us talk about it together?'

'We're going to. But you feel a great loyalty towards Max. He's done a wonderful job, keeping things together under such appalling circumstances. He's an amazing person. He has every reason to resent me and yet he's been supportive from the first moment, which must have taken some doing.' She hesitates, does a little cross-hatching on her pad. 'I need you to be your own man, Jack. Will rated you. He promoted you. Accept his judgement. Don't assume Max must always know best.'

The analysis is so shrewd it's uncomfortable. He can't imagine ever having Max's self-confidence. So he has to argue with her. 'I make my own mind up.'

'Excellent.' Another tick on the pad. Looking up, she meets his gaze. 'I can't do management Will's way either. He seems to have been a natural autocrat. I'm sure he valued Max, but not as an equal partner. Now I'm here the three of us will be in charge. Providing we make it work, it will triple our strength. We'll share everything. No secrets. No games-playing. Because I have no gift for playing games.' The laugh comes again. 'How does that sound to you?'

He finds himself matching her extraordinary honesty. 'Scary. Good, but scary.'

'Right.' Until that moment she's looked pleasant, half-smiling, the way you expect a woman to look. Now her expression hardens, so that he sees for the first time how stern her mouth and chin can be. 'If it all goes wrong, the blame will be mine. Naturally. I'd never try to wriggle out of that.'

Jack believes Isabel. Believes her and trusts her, though he scarcely knows her. And with all his heart he wants it to go right for her.

Chapter 3

'You're not to blame,' Max says.

It's the second time he's said it. I hear it as a double negative. Meaning I am to blame.

'Trevor Bennett is trouble. Always has been and always will be. Him and his mates.'

I stifle uneasy speculation about why Will did nothing, which suggests some snag I'm too naïve to have noticed. 'Like Douglas Blake, his union rep, you mean?'

'Him and at least a dozen others. Wreckers,' Max says. 'They fought against everything Will stood for. You'll bear me out, won't you, Jack?'

Jack mutters assent.

'They had to recognise he was too tough for them. When I took over they had a go at me. Invoked the union and tried to cause all sorts of trouble.'

'You had to back down on the residential week,' Jack reminds him.

'Oh, that.' Max dismisses its significance with a gesture. 'They realised fast enough they hadn't a snowball in hell's chance of making me move away from the TPH ethos. But with someone new they're bound to try it on. They see your appointment as their big opportunity. A chance to get the changes they want. They're on the governors' side.' He pauses as though to point up the betrayal. 'This business with Trevor is bad news.' He studies the pen he's holding. Looks up to say in a low voice, 'It'll be seen as a provocation.'

It's out of character. Max is never alarmist. He must think I've mishandled it disastrously.

He launches into anecdotes about the opposition. Demands for rigid streaming. Threats of mass detention if a culprit won't own up. Inappropriate sanctions like writing a thousand lines. Petitions to bring back corporal punishment. Jack joins in.

It makes me uneasy to hear the two of them, linked by experience I don't have, excluding me. So I cut them short. 'I'm not sure this is helping.'

'Isabel,' Max says. As usual his soft drawl makes me feel I've been abrupt. 'I know you want to treat everyone like a friend, but it helps to know who your enemies are.'

Am I being ungrateful? Resentful, because as always my Deputy understands the set-up better than I do? So I accept the copy of the Staff List he's brought and let him go through it. I listen to his analysis, trying to sort out one kind of truth from another. I'm learning something, if not altogether what he intends.

Well down the alphabet we reach Valerie Stephens.

'You persuaded her to give up the Deputy role.' Max smiles at me, his gaze holding mine. 'I can't tell you how grateful I am to you for that.' He turns towards Jack, making the smile a compliment to him, then back to me again. 'Could you work some more magic and persuade her to apply for promotion elsewhere? Tell her she's clearly management quality, it's a waste of her talents, etcetera.'

'Why?' The single word is Jack's.

Max looks from me to Jack, from Jack to me again. 'Help me

out. Why do I have this nagging uneasiness about Valerie Stephens?'

'Where would we find anyone half as good to run Modern Languages?' Jack grins. 'Don't know what it is about learning another language. It destroys the capacity to communicate with kids. Valerie is an honourable exception. The students rate her.'

The way Jack says it I know it's high commendation.

Max is looking contrite. 'You're absolutely right. She does have some good qualities. I guess she's bitter because Will excluded her from management. The job didn't work out for her. Tough on such an ambitious woman.'

'There's nothing wrong with being ambitious, is there?' I say.

'Not as such, no. But there's something a bit strident about her, don't you find?' When there's no immediate agreement from Jack or me, he seems about to say more. Then he appears to think better of it and moves on through the list.

My thoughts linger on Val. Bitter? I haven't detected it. But Max may be a stern judge. No trace of bitterness in the way he acts with me.

It's after six by the time we've finished. Jack makes a rapid departure with the air of a man who has somewhere to get to. Max lingers.

'Are you busy tomorrow evening?' he asks.

Friday. Time for Laura and Daniel and for myself. Here at school it's Youth Club and a full programme of community activities. I've stayed on the last two Fridays, taking an interest. I give up the self-indulgences I'd planned for this week. 'I could be free,' I say. Half-hearted. So I add, 'Easily.'

'I thought we might have a meal together. A chance to chat and get to know each other a bit better.'

I flip into panic mode. Why is he suggesting it? I'd prefer to help out with the Youth Club. If only we were the same gender. Or I still had my married status to protect me. Telling myself divorce has made me absurdly over-sensitive, I say, 'Good idea.' And sort the details with appropriate casualness.

Friday evening. We're sitting out on our small paved area, taking advantage of the warm May evening, unwinding with mugs of tea. Daniel is complaining about the hours of work he has to do. His O-levels start within days so it's not surprising and I'm not too sympathetic. I agree to discuss *Henry V* with him. 'It'll have to be tomorrow,' I tell him. 'I'm going out later on.'

Naturally neither of my adolescent children has any intention of spending the evening at home. We usually have a meal together around seven. Nothing in their world happens much before ten o'clock. Tonight they'll help themselves from the supplies I grabbed off the supermarket shelves on the way home.

I watch my tall blond son as he walks through the open patio doors into the kitchen. He looks unnervingly like his father. He hacks off hunks of bread and cheese to carry off to his room.

When Laura asks if I'm going somewhere nice I turn to smile at her. 'Probably not,' I say. 'I'm meeting Max for a meal.'

'Don't you want to go?'

'Not particularly.'

'Couldn't you have said no?'

'I'd prefer not to spend my precious Friday evening with him but I need to find out more about him. About everything. Becoming a Head de-skills you. I'm trying to teach myself how to do the job and at the same time discover exactly how the place ticks. There's no one who knows as little as I do. Max is at an advantage because he has it all at his fingertips.'

'Interesting. I never saw it like that when our new Principal came. I took it for granted he was all-knowing from the moment he arrived.'

'If only! Until I have more information, I can't be properly in charge. So I can't pass up a chance to pump Max about Thomas Paine High. And learn more about him at the same time.'

'He'll learn more about you,' she warns me.

'Snag,' I acknowledge. 'I shall have to assume a mask of sphinx-like impenetrability, while putting him through the third degree.'

'Don't you like him?'

'It's impossible not to like him. He's invariably pleasant and helpful.'

'Suspect,' she says darkly.

'Rubbish. Besides, you have to trust people until they prove they're untrustworthy.'

'So you're always saying.'

There's a silence, in which I think of Richard, the husband I trusted for years, against all the evidence. Trusted or pretended to trust. I imagine Laura wondering why I haven't learnt from experience.

Finally she says, 'Does Max have children?'

'None in evidence, though he could have a wife and quads, for all I know.'

Laura leans back in her chair, stretching out long bare legs. She's still wearing her travesty of a school uniform: the shortest possible skirt and the clumsiest shoes she could find. 'He could invent whatever he wanted. So could you.'

'I'm tempted to invent a husband.'

'God, Mum, why?'

'To make me more respectable. People make all sorts of assumptions about divorcees.'

She looks down her nose at me. 'It's 1981. Not 1881.'

'Even so.'

'Don't have regrets,' she says fiercely. She springs up to give me a hug and a kiss before she too disappears indoors.

We can't come any nearer to speaking about the divorce. I swirl the dregs of tea in my mug, ashamed of my inability to discuss it. I've failed my children, robbing them of the normal family they both deserve. It adds to the guilt that they've been incredibly supportive. I don't know how I'd have survived the past eighteen months without them. It was their pain which convinced me the marriage couldn't continue. I'd set up this crazy game of deception. Me pretending their father was working late when I knew he was out with his latest woman. The children pretending they believed the pretence. Until the day when I found Laura in furious tears. Which was when I had to accept I'd invented a game with no winners – not even Richard, since carte blanche to behave like a complete bastard can't be good for anyone's long-term mental health. At least I bought out his share of the house so we could stay here in Islington. The thought of the vast mortgage I've taken on gives me the familiar prickles of alarm. It has to be worth it. Daniel and Laura need the stability.

I find something else to worry about. What shall I wear? A familiar preoccupation. Tonight a particularly delicate decision. Not dressed up. Not the formal stuff I wear to school. Not too casual. Ruling out almost every garment I possess. I dump our three mugs in the dishwasher and go upstairs, hoping a glance in the cupboard will disclose the perfect outfit which has somehow slipped my memory.

'Relationships,' I tell Max. 'If I have to choose just one thing, it has to be relationships.'

Across the table, he smiles at me, a smile which dances in his brown eyes as well as curving his mouth. It's impossible not to smile back so I do, accepting the astonishing truth that I'm enjoying myself.

'Absolutely,' he says. 'The key to everything else.' Then he stops short. 'School.' He snaps his fingers. 'Sorry.'

When he suggested an embargo on work I felt bound to agree. It's lasted until now, halfway through my spinach and ricotta cannelloni and his cartwheel-size pizza. We've talked childhood, university, teacher training – both at the London Institute by coincidence, though he was five years after me. Seizing my opportunity, I say, 'No, no. I'm happy to talk school. We can break our own rule, can't we, since neither of us believes in rules?'

That makes him laugh, the nonsense of rules being TPH dogma. Then he grows serious. 'You understand, Isabel. It all hinges on relationships.'

Flattering to have my insight acknowledged. I take a few sips of the Valpolicella we're drinking. 'Everything does,' I suggest. 'Where would I be if you'd behaved the way most men would and frozen me out?'

His eyebrows lift in astonishment. A young man's fine-arched brows. Richard's are starting to go old-man-bushy. 'Why should I give you shit because you were the governors' choice? Where would be the logic in that?'

'Oh, logic. Kicking the cat is never logical, only human.'

'It shouldn't have been a surprise.' He hesitates. 'Yet it was. That was my failure of logic. To dream they'd offer me the job, when they knew my scale of values was the inverse of theirs.'

I hear the depths of regret in his voice. Such an honest admission of vulnerability touches me. It encourages me to match it. 'I wanted it desperately. I'd have been horribly disappointed after five hours in the place. But for you, after five years ...' I let the words trail away.

His hand reaches out and rests briefly on mine. 'Thanks.' At once his smile's back. 'Imagine if the governors had found the hatchet man they were looking for, someone to undermine everything TPH stands for! That would have been the real disaster. What matters is that we're both on the same side.' He raises his glass. 'To our partnership.'

I clink my glass against his, though the hubbub of Friday night in a busy Italian restaurant almost drowns out the tiny sound. We both drink. We eat for a bit before Max says, 'It's an interesting moral dilemma. I guess we both believe it's a Deputy's first duty to back up the Head. But what about the Head who's the enemy of everything that matters to you in education?'

I think of Albert. Too spineless surely to rate as an enemy. Though maybe someone more principled than I am would have resigned. I feel a twinge of retrospective guilt.

'Could it ever be right to stay and sabotage?' Max asks.

'Only if you could make enough difference. And to do what? To reverse the process? Or to make the Head's life such hell she walks out?' We both laugh at the unlikely scenario.

Max looks into the distance. 'I could. I think I could do it.' His gaze meets mine again and he grins. 'But I can't tell you how glad I am not to have the problem.'

As I smile my acknowledgement, I shift the conversation to something more productive. 'What's the history of the governors' hostility? Whoever appointed Will Fullwood must have had some idea what sort of school he'd run.'

'Thirteen years ago everywhere was going comprehensive and excited about it.'

I sigh, remembering the excitement. 'Our chance to change children's lives, and through them our world.'

He nods. 'There'd been a messy start in this area. Split-site schools. Amalgamations where nothing altered except the name. The disaster of cosmetic change. Irate middle-class parents on the politicians' backs. A reforming Chief Education Officer—'

I interrupt. 'James Greville?'

'Hardly. He's antediluvian. His predecessor. He convinced them that only radical solutions worked. A school that was purpose-built. A whole new concept of education, under an inspirational Head.'

'Even the name,' I say.

'Exactly. 1968, the year of the revolutions. Thomas Paine, writer and revolutionary. *The Rights of Man*. Three years later, the building was finished and the High School was open for business.'

I share the nostalgia with him. 'Before the backlash. The Thatcher clampdown.'

'The backlash began almost at once here. I guess it was a failure of imagination. The governors were incapable of imagining how it would be. One look at Thomas Paine High in action and they were pissing themselves in alarm. No uniform. No list of rules with dire penalties for any infringement. No hectoring teachers barking out orders. Where was the authority? How would the staff clamp down when there was trouble? As there would inevitably be if you treated kids like human beings.'

'But when there wasn't—' I begin.

'When did facts ever change a bigot's mind? They knew the whole set-up was a disaster so the harmonious reality had to be an illusion.'

'And in ten years there's been no convergence?'

'Will knew he had to be one hundred percent consistent. He said only toddlers believed you could take away the bright red brick in the middle of the tower without the whole structure collapsing.'

The comparison – instantly recognisable to a parent – makes me laugh. I'm curious to know what it means to Max. Unless he actually has the multiple offspring I playfully attributed to him. 'Forceful and accurate,' I say, 'if not tactful.'

'Will couldn't afford to be tactful.' Max sounds vehement, though he was laughing with me seconds earlier.

I doubt anyone who wants to influence others can afford not to be tactful, though I don't argue the point.

'He had to protect the integrity of his vision of education. It all connects. Take uniform. How can you build a relationship with anyone when you're nit-picking all the time about what they happen to be wearing? As though it matters, for Christ's sake!' He stops short and grins, as though half-embarrassed by his own passionate intensity. He's gazing at me in a way I find mildly disconcerting. 'Except I do like that top you're wearing. The colour really suits you.'

'Thanks,' I mutter. I glance down at the flame-coloured blouse I finally dug out, wondering whether the neck's too low.

A frown creases his forehead. 'Women are reckoned to pre-fer negotiation to confrontation, aren't they?'

I hear it as a challenge. I won't fall into the trap of claiming to be as aggressive as any man. 'I certainly prefer negotiation. It works, if you're tough enough and clever enough.'

The frown deepens. 'High risk,' he says. 'Offer one con-cession and they'll demand another.'

I spread my hands. 'If negotiating can make us a few allies, I'll do it. The Tory government is certainly not on our side. How many enemies do you want?'

'Enemies.' He repeats the word musingly. 'I've been arguing

with myself since yesterday. Wondering whether or not I should speak out. I hate being negative about anyone.'

'Yes?' I say. I can't keep the question mark out of my voice. I've heard the way he talks to colleagues, full of warm praise, but there was plenty of negativity in yesterday's meeting.

'I've come to the conclusion it's only fair to warn you about Valerie Stephens. She is pure poison.'

'In what way?'

'She's the most malicious woman I've ever met. Spreads the vilest rumours. Never, ever, take anything she tells you at face value.'

I've no evidence one way or the other. Yet I have an impulse to defend her. 'Why didn't you say this when Jack was singing her praises?'

'I said as much as I could. It's tricky for him at the moment. He thinks he owes her, because she gave up the Deputy job.'

'Which was generous of her.'

'Maybe. Take care, Isabel. She's going all out to make a favourable impression on you.'

It happens. I've already had plenty of friendly overtures from colleagues determined to get me on their side. But Val? Val seems so straightforward. It needs more than innuendo to make me condemn her. 'These vile rumours. What exactly has she said?'

Max looks graver than ever. 'No, Isabel. I'm not about to give them currency by repeating them. I admit she had me fooled. It never crossed my mind she'd invent something so despicable. So I investigated. There wasn't a word of truth in her allegations.'

'What could she hope to achieve? Especially since you had no problem disproving what she alleged.'

'You know how it is in teaching. A breath of scandal can finish someone's career. If I'd been less punctilious about total
confidentiality she might have destroyed—' He breaks off, tan-
talisingly short of the name which was apparently on the tip of
his tongue. 'I've come down on the side of warning you. But
you must see how tricky it is.'

Dissatisfied as I am, it seems voyeuristic to press for further
details. I tell him I won't forget what he's said.

There's an awkward silence. It's Max who breaks it. 'We have
to work together,' he says. 'It's bound to be one of the strategies
the opposition will use, trying to drive a wedge between us. Will
and I knew we could depend on each other one hundred percent.
It made all the difference.'

'I think the three of us will work well together, you and Jack
and me, don't you?'

'I hope so.'

Hope. It makes it sound less than certain. 'Why shouldn't
we?'

'It bothers me that you're prepared to negotiate with governors. You know what that means? Compromise.' The tone of voice
leaves no room for doubt. To him it's a dirty word.

I'm dismayed. He's the last person I can afford to alienate
for all sorts of reasons. 'I'm as loyal to TPH principles as you
are. There must be room for manoeuvre though.' I can see from
his expression I'm not persuading Max. I pick up his word. 'I'd
never agree to compromise anything we stand for. Never. But
you said it yourself. There's endless myth-making about the
school and the terrible things that go on there. We have to open
their eyes. Honesty will win our case. Once they understand the
truth about Thomas Paine High School, they'll see how much
we're doing for our students.'

It's like my words have a slow-burning fuse. In the pause

before Max answers, the background noise of the restaurant is suddenly loud. I watch his sombre face, trying to read his thoughts.

'The truth about what goes on ...' Then there's that irresistible smile again. 'Of course. If they could see the truth, that would change everything.'

Chapter 4

July 1981

It's the Parents Evening for new students, in the last week of term. Jack's final appearance as Senior House Tutor of Lexington. They're sitting in a circle. A question and answer session in groups. Isabel's bright idea. Safer all round than a plenary in the Assembly Hall. The woman is sitting directly opposite. A couple of times she's shifted in her chair as if she was going to speak. Now the words burst from her. 'You hear so much about what goes on here.' Her face is creased with anxiety. 'I hope Amy's going to be all right.'

'Amy will love it. I can promise you that. Did you talk to the second years who were showing you round?'

'Yes. And you're right. They were really enthusiastic.' She hesitates. 'Only that's not exactly what I meant. I mean, it's part of the problem. You don't just want children to enjoy them-selves at school, do you?' Her glance appeals to the rest of the circle for confirmation.

Before Jack can speak, Tim Mayhew, his successor, leans for-ward. 'You don't want your daughter to be miserable, do you?'

Hard to accept someone else moving in, doing it their way, even with a new job waiting. Jack's already had some insight into how it must have been for Max, admires him more than ever for not carping on the sidelines. But in anyone's book Tim's answer is crass, making light of genuine concerns. He has to intervene. 'We all want happiness for our kids, don't we? I know I do.' He's playing the parent card. They're not to know he's an absentee father. 'But we also want them to fulfil their potential. As Isabel said when she spoke to you, in the next seven years we have to make sure that children are transformed into confident, independent adults, able to flourish whatever they choose to do.' He thinks he's quoting her verbatim. 'We all have this feeling that education's like medicine. Unless it's unpleasant it can't be doing you any good.' There's a ripple of laughter. 'Yet looking back I realise I did my best learning when I was enjoying every moment.' It's a relief to see a few nods of agreement.

'But it's tough out there.' It's a guy whose casual clothes proclaim his middle-class credentials. 'Can a pleasant life really be a good preparation for the future?'

'Yes, if my daughter's experience is anything to go by.' It's Rose, one of 'his' parents, Jack's relieved to see. 'Janey came as a maths-phobic. I don't know how the teachers here have done it but there's been a transformation. It's her favourite subject now. She chose her options this term. Mainly sciences because she wants to carry on with Maths and Science in the sixth form.' He might have planted her it's such a perfect answer. Then she adds, 'Providing she gets the grades.'

'A necessary proviso,' says Mr Middle Class. 'Your exam results were poor last year. Will they be any better this time around?' There's a supportive murmur.

It's fair comment. Don't attempt to cover up, Isabel said. Be honest. 'You're absolutely right, Mr—?' He pauses for a name.

'Chamberlain. Michael Chamberlain.'

'We don't know about this year yet, Michael, but last year's grades weren't good enough. Our new Head agrees with you one hundred percent. She's made it her top priority and got us all to sign up to that.'

Michael Chamberlain remains sceptical. 'And is that likely to make a difference?'

'According to the latest HMI report, *Ten Good Schools*, the single factor which makes most difference to a school's performance is the Headteacher. You've heard Isabel Lincoln speak. I don't know what impression she made on you but after just one term I've learnt she's a very determined lady.' The parents are grinning, as though they're fellow-sufferers, coping with strong-willed women. Breakthrough. 'I'd back her to achieve any goal she sets herself.'

'What do the children call her?'

The speaker's right next to him. Overweight. Crammed into a shiny suit. For a moment Jack's thrown. Is the chap implying some insulting nickname? Then he realises. It's the old chestnut: using first names. He produces the standard explanation. No, it's not cheeky, because Isabel's invited them to call her that. The discussion becomes general, most parents with older kids defending the practice, while first-timers remain doubtful. He glances at Tim, expecting him to join in. Looking mildly interested would help, but Tim's got his head down, staring at the patch of floor between his feet.

Jack puts the case for mixed-ability groups. Treating each child as an individual. Can't we all remember those moments of boredom, when we'd 'got it' and had to wait for the rest to catch up? Or struggling because the rest were there ahead of us? He risks asking who's unhappy about the system because they'd prefer their son or daughter to be placed in the A-stream?

After some hesitancy two thirds of the parents raise their hands. The more savvy smile ruefully, seeing where this is leading.

'And who would prefer them to be in the D-stream? Or the J-stream, I guess, since we have ten first year groups.' Laughter, in which one brave mother puts her hand up.

'Barry's not very quick, I'm afraid. Won't he struggle, amongst all the cleverer children?'

He explains the school's Learning Support system. He must make sure he gets her to talk to the LS teachers. The group moves on to uniform. Or the lack of it. And what about this residential week in Dorset? Tricky to handle, that one. Isabel did her best in her speech. Knowing it won't happen. Needing to go through the motions of consultation. He feels on safer ground with bullying. The discussion circles round, coming back to what goes on at Thomas Paine High School. He's not sure what they're on about. Some panic over moral laxity? Safer not to probe too far. He issues an invitation to spend time in the school. He thinks he's swung it.

Until Shaun Brett cuts in. 'All this chummy business. Toby said this, that and the other. What the bloody hell does Toby know about anything? And then you realise it's their teacher they're talking about. You can't tell me that's right.' His loud, aggressive voice dominates the group.

He's a policeman. Two kids in the school already. Why send the third, if that's how he feels? It wouldn't help to say that. Instead, Jack asks, 'Are we back to first names?'

'We've heard the party line. We don't need that again.' The group's body-language suggests the rudeness is alienating some, emboldening others, who lean forward, keen to join in. 'Christian names are just part of it. Kids and teachers all pals together. It's bloody *dangerous*.' The last word is harshly stressed.

It's no longer Jack's audience but Shaun's, and a good half is offering an instant reaction. Just as well teachers are used to bringing unruly classes to order. 'One at a time, one at a time,'

Jack says. A shout, half-humorous. And as the noise-level falls, 'Let's give everyone a chance to be heard.' It's a gamble, letting them argue it among themselves, but he needs time to come up with something which will satisfy Shaun Brett. Who almost certainly is still smarting from their last encounter, when Jack called him in because his son Jason had 'lost it' in a science lesson.

'Got to be dangerous,' says the parent who raised the issue of first names before.

Michael Chamberlain takes over. 'Dangerous? We need to be more precise about our concerns before Jack can respond.' He's become an ally then. 'Is it a general sense that without a distance between teachers and pupils it's hard to maintain order?'

His language has lost some of the parents.

Rose, Janey's mother, says, 'It's just the rumour-mill, isn't it? Thomas Paine High has a different approach from most schools and it makes some people nervous. From our experience, the approach works, doesn't it?' She turns to her husband for confirmation.

Janey's father says, 'Definitely.' Brief but unhesitating.

Shaun sticks his oar in again. 'I don't know what it does for discipline. Not much, I suspect. In my house my kids know who's in charge. Me.' He gives a triumphant glance around, as though he deserves applause. Mrs Brett, on his left, nods and smiles obediently. 'It's worse than that though. You don't want adults getting too close to kids. I'm a policeman and I know.' His glare challenges anyone to argue against his professional opinion.

Jack can't ignore the challenge. 'If you're talking improper relationships between our staff and students I can tell you categorically that there hasn't been a single case in the ten years since the school opened.' He hesitates. Should he leave it there? No, Shaun's drawing breath to say more. 'And in your job you'll be well aware that there are cases in schools which are run on the most authoritarian lines.' Safer not to suggest a connection, though he's tempted.

Shaun sits back, muttering to his neighbours. One or two others take up his accusations. Jack asks which of them has children at the school, confident he'd recognise any parent, unless it's a new step-father or -mother.

No one claims an existing student except Rose who comes to his aid again. 'Like I said, it's all rumour.'

There's the predictable claim – no smoke without fire. Michael Chamberlain points out that if anyone had any evidence they'd be duty bound to report it. Without evidence, the comments are slanderous.

It seems to silence them though it's not exactly satisfactory. Parents need to go away with something positive. Jack thanks them for the wonderful support he's had as Senior House Tutor. He'll miss the job even though he's looking forward to the new one. He gets a few congratulations. He reminds them Tim will be taking over and grins across at him. At last Tim finds his tongue and says a lot of tactful stuff he seems to have prepared in advance.

Don't they have homes to go to? The July evening is stifling and he complied with Isabel's request to wear a formal shirt and tie, though jeans and t-shirt have always been the norm.

At last the group decides the session's over. He singles out Barry's mum. Knots of parents remain, still wanting his attention. After what's gone on, it's a pleasant surprise that a lot of it is supportive, even complimentary. Tim seems to be doing a good job too, getting friendly laughter.

Outside the classroom windows the sky has deepened to dark blue before they're left on their own. Jack abandons a half-formed intention of finding out how it's been for Isabel. She won't want him holding her up.

'Christ! I need a drink after that,' Tim announces. 'I bet Max has been in the Sutton Arms for hours. Coming?'

'Try and stop me,' Jack replies as he tugs off his tie.

The Sutton Arms is a bog-standard pub. Nothing so fancy as tables on the pavement. But on this warm evening people have spilled outside, perching on steps, or leaning against railings. Max has spotted Jack and Tim through an open window and is giving them a shout. By the time they edge their way in, he's at the bar, buying pints for them and another for himself. He gestures towards his table. Jack squats on a stool which is a good six inches too low to accommodate his long legs. The pints arrive, dribbling froth, and he gulps gratefully. High School staff have taken over the place. Mostly male. Isabel's not there, a glance shows him. Two or three young women, Steph amongst them, in the far corner to his relief. He hopes she's got the message. In future, relationships are strictly an out-of-school activity. With his new job he can't risk the complication. Fifty conversations are going on at once. Everyone unwinding.

Tim punches him on the arm. 'You were brilliant, Jack. God, I don't know how you do it. I was useless.'

He shrugs off the praise. 'Practice. And it wasn't that brilliant. More a case of *Could do better*.'

Tim appeals to Max. 'Forty parents, Max, all firing questions, and Jack never once lost his cool.'

'I always say no one can touch you with parents.'

Jack doesn't want to hear it. He's not sure why. Some implication that he lacks the higher-order management skills? No, Max is too generous for that. Jack's recycling the parents' awkward questions. His inadequate responses. Memories which grate, the way the shriek of chalk down a chalkboard grates on the ears.

'It gets to me when they start criticising.' Tim again. 'I want to shout at them, "You ignorant bastards! You don't deserve a school like Thomas Paine High." When I think of the crap they dish out at Blenheim School or the Grove and the parents lap it up. How can they be so stupid?'

Jack recognises Tim's problem. He needs to justify his failure to perform. He won't let go of the subject until he feels better. 'Their kids only have one chance,' Jack says. 'It makes them anxious.' He takes a long drink, thinking of his daughter Betsy. Starting school for the first time in September. When he rang two weeks ago, Maggie was surprised. Or pretended to be. Fair enough. His contact isn't as regular as he intends. He'd suggested going to the session for new parents. Maggie said it would confuse everyone, including Betsy. She had a new dad, one who was around all the time. It wasn't fair to drop in and out of her life. He ended the call before the rage burst out of him. He slammed around the room until he cooled down. Being pushed out would be a lot easier to bear if he hadn't brought it on himself.

When he tunes into the conversation again, the inquest is still ongoing. Except they've moved on to Isabel's speech. He shifts on his stool, to ease his cramped legs.

'Will Fullwood she isn't,' Tim says.

Max springs to her defence. 'She said the sort of stuff parents want to hear.'

Jack agrees, though not out loud. What did parents make of Will's brilliant utterances? He suppresses the heresy. Will inspired the staff, Jack included, didn't he? Keeping their missionary zeal alive was what mattered. He gets up to fetch three more pints. As he stands waiting his turn, he sees Tim's smooth dark head close to Max's dark curly one. He doesn't know why it bothers him. The pub's so noisy you can hardly hear yourself speak. Even the most ordinary exchange looks like conspiracy.

When he gets back, Tim is still leaning forward across the table. 'That's what worries me. Can we trust her?'

'It's a tough job,' Max replies. 'She's doing her best.'

'But you'd have done it so much better.'

'Balls, Tim. I never think about that now and nor should you.'

Could it be true, Jack wondered? Could anyone be so ungrudging? Even if there wasn't a hope in hell of the governors appointing Max, he'd had a raw deal.

'The way she dresses too.' Tim sounds disapproving. 'That skirt and jacket she was wearing.'

Jack couldn't see anything wrong with it. Almond green. Cool-looking for a hot evening, the silk swirling as she moved.

'Be fair,' Max says. 'Formal dress reassures parents. Besides, Will wore a suit all the time.'

'He never suggested we should dress up. Quite the opposite. He thought conforming to some middle-class dress code was the professions' way of distancing themselves from their clientele.'

'Wearing a suit himself was a bit of a contradiction then,' Jack says. But Tim ignores the comment, waiting for an answer from Max.

Max mainly dresses casual but he's the type who looks elegant whatever he wears. Now he glances down at his pale blue shirt and dark trousers. 'It's not important. She's new. Give her a chance.'

'Do you think she knows what she's doing? She may be trying to keep everyone happy but you can only do that for so long. In the end, she'll have to choose. Then she'll find she's up shit creek without a paddle. No one will trust her.'

'I trust her,' Jack says. It comes out too quietly to qualify as a ringing endorsement.

Max takes it up. 'Of course we do. We're her Deputies, for God's sake. If we couldn't trust her, we'd resign.'

'Who're you kidding? I know you better than that. You'd stay and fight.' Tim's green eyes narrow. 'Wouldn't you?' There's something close to alarm in the question.

'I guess I would,' Max says slowly.

'You wouldn't walk away. You couldn't,' Tim urges. 'Not after taking on the governors the way you did.'

'This would be harder. The enemy within ...' There's a pause while Max seems to muse silently. 'But it won't come to that. Isabel wants a triumvirate. The three of us managing together. That's what she said, didn't she, Jack?'

'Yes.' Better to leave it there, only he can't. 'She said it and she wants to share decisions. When it comes to the crunch, though, she'll do it her way. She's not a natural autocrat but she's tough.'

'Tough?' Tim is incredulous. 'How come she's not fighting to keep the residential week for first years then?'

'Tim,' Max says, his voice a sharp warning. He glances around and Jack's gaze follows his. Everyone seems intent on their own conversations. 'What gave you the idea anything was decided?' Max goes on. 'You heard what Isabel said to parents.'

Jack would like to be convinced but he isn't. It sticks out a mile that Max has been leaking confidential stuff. He's always been close to Tim. Perhaps it doesn't matter if it's gone no further. Don't they say every secret is passed on to just one other person? Which makes confidentiality a joke.

Tim leaps up. 'Time for one more, if we're quick.' He shoulders his way through the crowd to the bar.

In Tim's absence Jack considers tackling Max about talking out of turn. The seconds pass and he says nothing. Max may be at fault but who isn't? Christ, if you have to be perfect to be a Deputy he'd better resign at once. He made heroes of Will and

Max, heroes who could do no wrong. Up close, you can see the flaws. Maybe it's like an Impressionist painting. Peer at it closely and you see a confusion of brushstrokes. From a distance, the way you're meant to look at it, pure light.

Chapter 5

As Laura sets down three mugs of tea, I settle deeper into the armchair. A gust of wind drives the rain against the windows with a staccato rattle. Dan puts more coal on the fire he's lit. The warm, lamp-lit room seems like a good place to be on this wild October evening. Time to draw breath at last, after the usual frantic week. 'I can't believe it's Friday again,' I say.

My daughter offers her own cliché. 'Time flies when you're having fun.'

Daniel makes a derisive noise. 'Flies? Bet it feels like you've been a Head forever.'

'It's not a prison sentence, Dan. But I wouldn't describe it as having fun.'

'You enjoy it really,' Laura insists. 'All the manoeuvring and manipulating.'

I'm about to protest it's not the way I am. Other people may be devious. Never me. But being straightforward has its risks. How straightforward shall I be with Max this evening? So I admit to occasional manoeuvring but without any intent to manipulate.

'You like it better than being a Deputy, don't you?' Daniel asks, as he offers me one of the crumpets he's toasting in front of the fire.

Laura answers for me. 'That's because Albert was useless. No one would want to be his Deputy.'

'No one would want to be a Deputy, full stop,' Dan declares, stabbing another crumpet and holding it towards the flames. 'All three of ours are robots. In the dim and distant past, someone threw the switch to start them shouting and they carry on whether there's anyone there to shout at or not. At the end of the day they're trundled into a cupboard. The next morning they wheel them out again, still shouting.' He makes a premature examination of the limp and pallid crumpet. 'They've got to be robots. No human vocal cords could stand the strain.'

I grin at his nonsense while Laura says, 'Max and Jack aren't like that, are they? I can't imagine Max shouting at anyone.'

Max. The name makes my heart race but my answer is carefully casual. 'No way. Not TPH style at all. Too disrespectful.'

'You certainly run a weird school, Mother. Respect is strictly for teachers at Windlesham, isn't it, Laura?'

'You're exaggerating, as usual. How about Jack? We've never met him. Does he shout?'

I'm not sure why this second question should disconcert me, but it does. 'He doesn't need to. He's brilliant with students.' I half-regret saying it, even though it's what I think.

'Better than Max, I bet,' Dan says.

'What have you got against him?' I ask. I could ask the same question of myself.

'Arrogant. Thinks he's God's gift.'

There's a bit of me that knows just what my son means. But I say, 'He's been totally supportive when he could have made my life hell.' And still could, so I can't afford to make an enemy of him.

Laura declares her brother is jealous. He denies the charge.

'Are you having a meal with Max this evening?' Laura says.

'Yes,' I say. 'I'm going round to his flat.' At the prospect my heart starts to race again.

'Cosy,' Laura teases, while her brother pulls a face.

When they've both disappeared upstairs, the imaginary conversations start up in my head. Max won't mind. He won't mind a bit when I ask him about it. He'll be glad of the chance to explain. Though the circumstances make it awkward.

I have a perfect right to be in the library. And libraries have bays. Audibility without visibility. I couldn't help that. Was I supposed to bounce out and announce myself?

I'm making too much of it. Why bring it up at all? Because the uneasiness won't go away. The doubts will grow between us if I stay silent. There's nothing personal in my wish to get on well with my Deputy. With both my Deputies if possible. Being at odds is bad news for Thomas Paine High. It's not Isabel Lincoln but the Headteacher (if I can separate the two) who needs to be on good terms. Everyone looks to Max to give a lead. Still. Despite my best endeavours.

I try to compute the risks of challenging him. As against convincing myself it never happened. Or not in the way I think it did.

Know it did.

The fire startles me with a sudden flare of blue gas and a collapsing in on itself.

Hair blown every which way, I speak into the panel of the entry-phone. There's a buzz and the door opens to my touch. Do I want to be here? Last week when Max suggested it I was pleased. Now, as I wait for the lift, curiosity battles with apprehension. I've never been inside his flat before. I step into the metal cell and hear a faint pneumatic hiss as I'm enclosed. The doubts begin to scurry like mice. My appearance. Mirrored in the gleaming walls,

I smooth my ruffled hair. Clothes are okay. Black jacket over white polo-neck. Dark red trousers. White trainers. It's what I wore to the Women's Group. Max won't know that. It wouldn't matter if he did. They shouldn't feel like opposite sides. I don't have to choose between them. Secrets. Val's invitation to the Women's Group in my pigeonhole after that Heads of Department meeting where we got all the unaware male chauvinist stuff. Which Val, the only other woman in the room, confronted. My support was less than forthright. But I accepted her invitation. And I had a meal with Val. Which I won't mention. Challenging Max has nothing to do with feminism. Any responsible Head would do it. How? When? The awkwardness that it's his space. His uniquely. Whereas I share the house with Dan and Laura. All this in the time it takes to glide from the hall to the fourth floor. And there is no chance to resolve anything. Because Max is standing in the doorway to welcome me.

It's exotic. Dark blue carpet. Several patterned rugs which look expensive to my inexpert eye. Two dark red sofas, heaped with velvet cushions. On the walls, Indian mirrorwork hangings. Framed posters, Picasso's peace dove and Che Guevara among them. Two lamps, their crimson shades gold-lined. A spicy scent. Incense sticks, I hope.

Max is taking my jacket. As he turns away to hang it up, my gaze settles on a shelf crowded with potted plants, dripping luxuriant foliage. I won't avoid. I'll challenge him straightaway.

But he's beside me, smiling. 'See my view.' Palm in the small of my back, he leads me across to the window.

Beneath us, wind-tossed trees. Beyond, light after light sparkles in the darkness. On the pretext of seeing further, I move out of range as I offer polite admiration.

'Horrendous in daylight. Darkness lends glamour,' he says.

'You prefer darkness then?'

'Naturally.' He laughs, his warm, familiar laugh. *'Men love darkness rather than light.'*

The English teacher in me notes the change from first- to third-person. I step away from the window, saying, 'Snow would have the same transforming effect, wouldn't it?'

'Probably,' he agrees. 'But how often does it settle in London? Darkness is dependable.' He draws curtains patterned with dark reds, blues and gold. 'I'll pour you some wine.'

On a low table between the two sofas it's already set out. Rioja. A deep red. 'Have you lived here long?' I ask. A measure of my self-consciousness. It's like a conversational gambit between strangers.

'Ever since I got the Thomas Paine job.'

I'm still standing up so I glance around as though I might be going to buy the place. 'Nice,' I say absentmindedly, busy formulating the question I'm determined to ask.

'It suits me. Are you starving?'

'No,' I say, as I abandon for the second time my plan to tackle him and get the subject out of the way. 'Not starving, but happy to eat.'

'Only pasta,' he says. 'I can't rival your wonderful food. It won't take long. Will you come and watch? Then you'll be able to put me right.'

I disclaim any intention of doing such a thing. I follow him into the kitchen. Nuts, celery, even M&S dips, set out on the table. I perch on a stool and help myself, glad to occupy my hands. He seems entirely competent. I toss salad, telling myself our activity prevents any proper conversation. There's plenty to chat about. The trivia of people who work together. It keeps us going while we eat the pasta, with the creamy mushroom and ham sauce he's made. He's got baguette and several different cheeses which he suggests we take into the living-room. I hope he'll sit down first, but he doesn't of course, so I settle into one corner of a sofa while he loads his plate.

'Pitch the cushions on the floor,' he says.

I'm more comfortable without them so I do as he suggests. He disconcerts me by drawing one towards him and sitting beside me, his back propped against the sofa.

He smiles up at me. 'My favourite position,' he says. He looks entirely at ease.

The consciousness of what I've left unsaid for so long dries my mouth, making it hard to swallow. It's getting ridiculous. 'Max.' It comes out abrupt as a command. 'I was in the library last Monday.' Last Monday. It makes it worse. Why didn't I say something before?

'Yes?' he says, on a note of innocent enquiry.

'You didn't notice me.' Implying he could have seen me if he'd wanted to. Not strictly true. 'You were talking to a student.'

There must be accusation in my voice because he says, 'Guilty, Isabel. I do it all the time.'

He's laughing but I think I see calculation in his eyes, as though he's trying to work out what I might have heard. 'I don't know her name but she said she'd watered your plants every day. Did she have to come here to do it?'

'No, no, I took the plants into school,' he says hastily. 'That must have been Helen you heard me talking to. Helen Pearce.' The familiar lazy drawl is back again, like a caress over her name. 'Sweet of her to take the trouble, wasn't it? I was away climbing for the half-term week. It's tricky when you live on your own. But thanks to Helen the plants are flourishing.' He turns to gaze across the room towards them. As though he expects my gaze to follow his. As though he thinks my interest is purely horticultural.

I squeeze a fragment of bread so hard it turns to pap between my fingers. I have to go on. 'Helen said she missed you.' I hear the words in her young, breathy voice. See her face turned towards him as they strolled out of the library side by side. Remember Max's laugh, cut off as the door swung shut behind them.

At once he looks at me again, his dark eyebrows drawn together. Then the smile is back, broader than ever. 'Yes,' he says. 'She was supposed to see me at break Monday morning. And she missed me. Which was why she caught up with me after school in the library. Because she'd missed me earlier. What did you think she meant?'

There's no way I can tell him. He knows that. 'I see,' I murmur vaguely, hoping he'll let it go.

'Do you think I've done anything wrong? Should I have rejected Helen's offer? She was coming in for rehearsals so I thought there was no harm in it.' He's all smiling innocence as his eyes meet mine. 'Was I stereotyping? Maybe I ought to have asked one of the boys to do it. I know you're sensitive to gender issues. I look to you to put me right.' And he laughs, a laugh of half-teasing affection.

I ought to have faith in him. I ought to believe that everything is exactly as it seems between us. That this is an open exchange between trusting colleagues. If there's one thing I'm good at, it's guilt. It rushes over me now, like a rip-tide across a level beach. Underneath, the doubts remain, shifting uneasily, as cold and hard as the stones the sea covers.

Max props his elbow beside me on the sofa seat. Casual. Close. Intimate. 'You'd be open with me, wouldn't you? You wouldn't think something and not say it? Everything you claim about the three of us working together implies that level of trust.'

The three of us. Jack, Max and me. I'm not sure how things stand between me and Jack. Only I can't think about that now. I'm too busy trying to convince Max that of course I'm open with him. Of course I trust him.

'I hope you do. It's delicate between us. Bound to be,' he says, shifting so I can't see his expression any more. 'I can't help knowing more about TPH and its ways than you do. It's a function of having spent five years longer in the place. I walked on eggshells last term because you were so touchy.'

For a second I think I must have misheard. He was walking on eggshells? Last term when I was so careful. I'm silent, struggling to adjust to this disconcerting shift of perspective.

Max locks his hands behind his head. 'Wouldn't it be easier for both of us if I had some independence? Some project I had sole responsibility for? So I could operate without referring decisions to you all the time?'

'Doesn't it feel like that now?'

'Not exactly, no.' I still can't see his expression but his dry tone makes it obvious it's a massive understatement.

'I'm sorry. Obviously I need more practice in the art of delegation.' An apology but a stiff one. I wonder how he hears it, with an uneasy sense that for each of us there is a different truth.

He looks at me again, his expression grave. 'Forget it. I'm asking more than you feel able to give.'

I came determined to challenge Max. He's explained and I've accepted his explanation. So I ought to make amends for my suspicions. No point in being grudging. 'Whatever you want,' I say. 'We can't sort the details now. Put some ideas on paper over the weekend. We'll talk on Monday.'

'Brilliant.' He smiles that winning smile of his. 'Thank you, Isabel.' He twists round further and I feel the weight of his arm across my thighs, the warmth of his hand enclosing mine. I press his hand and release it.

From my vantage point, I notice for the first time that his dark curly hair is threaded with grey and receding at the temples.

Chapter 6

December 1981

A scent compounded of spices, dried fruit and brandy fills the kitchen. I'm making my Christmas cake. Not before time – it's the second Sunday in December. There are plenty in the shops. I could afford M&S, if not Fortnum & Mason. But a bought cake is a cop-out. Running a school is not an adequate excuse. Not to the perfectionist in me. Besides, the process is soothing.

Underneath something niggles. My quarrel with Jack. Which it's absurd to call a quarrel. A professional disagreement. I know it was my idea to get tutors teaching Personal and Social Education but on Monday he seemed equally enthused. We were capping each other's ideas as though we were on exactly the same wavelength. When we met again on Wednesday, total mood-change. He set up one obstacle after another. I removed each one in turn. Not a wise move. It drove Jack into a massive sulk. I ended up apologising, for God's sake, though I can't imagine what for.

I beat butter and sugar together, using my largest wooden spoon with ferocious energy.

Jack continued to sulk for the rest of the day. Thursday all was revealed. Jack had talked to Max who pointed out PSE is Simon's baby and I'd be trampling on his toes. Trust Max to be much more sensitive to other people's feelings than I am. But why couldn't Jack explain the problem? How did it all get so fraught? I said I'd talk to Simon and sort it out. Hurt feelings couldn't be allowed to stand in the way of a positive change. Max agreed with me. Jack didn't. Though for some reason he seemed as angry with Max as he was with me.

I crack an egg on the rim of the basin, so hard the shell splinters into fragments which I fish out laboriously with the tip of a knife. I tap a second egg with such restraint that it has no effect and I have to have another go.

Things are back to normal now. Sort of. Distant politeness sums it up. I wish I understood my own feelings. Part of me would give anything to be on good terms again. To the extent we ever were. Maybe it's unfair to call it sulking. Maybe he was genuinely hurt by our disagreement. Maybe. Why did I appoint a Deputy who's all rough edges?

I tip flour into the sieve and begin to sift it gently into the cake mixture. The prospect of an imminent and fraught social encounter spooks me. Thomas Paine staff, I discovered too late, celebrate Christmas not with a single staff party but in a dozen different academic and social groupings. My innocent accept-ance of an invitation to the English Faculty 'do' has trapped me. Within hours my presence was requested at every other fes-tivity. More to do with my patronage than my popularity. No one's going to pass up a chance to influence the new Head. With my addiction to fairness I've felt bound to say yes to all of them. And at one of them I'm sure to come face to face with Jack. I live through the awkward encounter in my imagination, inventing what each of us will say and do. I give myself lines which convey detached friendliness. My hand jerks. Flour dusts the tabletop like a light snowfall. I prop the sieve across the bowl and fetch a cloth to wipe up the mess.

Adolescent to be so obsessed with our quarrel. Quarrel. That inappropriate word has crept in again.

I stand in front of my wardrobe in despondent mood. As I left this evening, Malcolm said he was looking forward to seeing me later, at the Jefferson House get-together. An unnecessary reminder. There's no way I can forget about it because all along I've assumed Jack will be going, as the Pastoral Deputy. An assumption only. Given the Siberian state of our relationship, asking him is an unthinkable intimacy. He might imagine I wanted him to go, for God's sake. Or that I was warning him to keep clear. I'm not sure why the second alternative matters. I slide hangers along the rail, hoping for inspiration. These last few days I've been avoiding him. I can't avoid him if he's there tonight. But then nor is it practical to avoid him for the whole of next term, since he happens to be one of my two Deputies. Which reminds me that Max might also turn up. Curiously, this doesn't bother me at all, although in theory it ought to add to my insecurity, since everyone's sure to buzz round him, like wasps around a pot of jam, making the isolation I fear even more obvious. He never brings a partner, so that will make two of us. I'm not sure about Jack. Not that it makes the slightest difference to me whether he comes on his own or with someone.

As I rattle more hangers I realise nothing's registering. I tell myself now, this moment, I have to decide what to wear. Nothing old and frumpish but nothing which looks like a desperate attempt to appear young and trendy. They'll be expecting something which matches their concept of 'Headteacher'. No, the truth is they won't be giving it a moment's thought. Or take the least notice of what I choose after all this agonising.

So why does it matter so much?

I seize my new black trousers. That's the easy bit. I scan my tops, finding something wrong with each in turn. I go back to the first one, a fine-knit white sweater. I fasten the silver necklace Laura gave me. Touching it like a talisman to reassure me, I face my reflection. I don't see anything to lift my despondency. Yet underneath I feel a surge of excitement like a mild electric shock.

Laura's downstairs, making herself a mug of coffee. We hug each other. She's tense too. She'll hear about her Oxford application in the next day or two. As we separate, she says the outfit's fine.

'All-purpose?' I ask. 'Simultaneously amazingly smart and totally casual?'

'Of course.'

'The necklace helps. I love it.' I give her another hug. 'Somerville is sure to want you. And if they're crazy enough not to, the loss will be entirely theirs.'

She smiles. 'Their loss and Warwick's gain.' Warwick is her second choice.

'Exactly.'

I pack the moussaka I've made into a box, before settling for a carrier bag as less obtrusive. Everyone's bringing food. Malcolm said it needn't apply to me. I've no wish to be an exception. I add a bottle of red wine to the bag.

'No need to wait up.' I register *weak joke*. God, I must be more uptight than I thought. 'Though an hour may be my limit. Or my colleagues' limit.'

'Have a good time.'

I pull a face at such an unlikely prospect.

My sole concern about Laura's Oxford application is that whatever happens is right for her. If I can be philosophical about something which really matters, why should I care about making an appearance in a world of couples? I'm not a freak just because I don't have a partner.

❑ ❑ ❑

I approach Malcolm's Muswell Hill house, a big Edwardian semi. Music. Chatter. Laughter. The sound of partying, more alarming than inviting. I can scarcely turn back now. A few paces takes me from the pavement to the front door. Why isn't the distance greater? Though to match my reluctance would require the beech-lined avenue of a stately home at the very least. Within seconds I'm inside. The house seems full of people. Malcolm introduces me to his partner Zara. She's wearing a caftan in shades of purple and pink. The Earth Mother look. A bit of a surprise as Malcolm, whippet-thin with sparse sandy hair, doesn't look especially nurtured. She relieves me of the moussaka, exclaiming that it looks delicious, and puts it into the Aga to heat. It's that sort of kitchen. My bottle joins the assortment on the dresser and Malcolm fills a glass for me.

The protective preliminaries are over. I'm on my own. The room throbs with the beat of music. I nerve myself to join Toby Grigor-Smith. We don't have much in common apart from governors meetings. Which is not a festive topic. His greeting is friendly. Another partner introduction. Ruth this time. I ask what they're doing for Christmas. Within moments it gets easier. I'm part of a group laughing about the disasters of Christmas past. I don't need to say much. Through the haze of other people's cigarette smoke I scan the room. If there's no sign of Jack, I can relax, can't I? I don't spot him. Yet I don't relax. I put it down to the fear that he'll appear at any moment. With a partner, presumably. Will that make it better or worse? I smile and laugh a bit more.

It takes me by surprise when Zara summons us to eat. The group melts away. I have to follow. I tell myself it brings closer the time when I can make a tactful departure. There's masses of food as there always is when everyone contributes. I accept a plate and help myself to a modest amount of curried chicken and rice. Jack must lack my sense of social obligation. Or his desire to avoid me was enough to override it. I find a quiet corner to eat. I'm flattered to see Stephanie, one of the English teachers, heading purposefully towards me. Without partner. She squats down beside me, spreading her long denim skirt around her.

'Love your top,' I say. It's thin Indian cotton, vivid green and red, perfect with her dark hair and striking colouring.

'Thanks. Are you enjoying it?'

I choose to apply the query to the food. 'Yes. I don't know who made it but it's delicious.'

She grins. 'Good. But I meant the occasion.'

'I wasn't at all sure about coming. I didn't want to spoil it for the rest of you.'

'Why would you?'

'You might not want me around when you're all unwinding after a long term.'

She nods. 'You don't impose. Not the way Will Fullwood did. He was that sort of person. Always the centre of attention wherever he was.'

I accept the judgement. More damning because Steph doesn't seem to mean to put me down. 'I wish I'd known him. He must have been an amazing person.'

'He was. But don't you think being amazing can be overdone?'

'Probably.' There's relief in my laughter. 'Like anything else.'

'I never knew what to say to him. Anything short of dazzling seemed inadequate.' Steph is laughing now. 'Fortunately, he preferred talking to listening.' She forks food from her plate before she says, 'You've got two children, haven't you? How old are they?'

I'm at ease talking about Laura and Daniel. Only at that

moment Jack puts in a belated appearance. He glances at the two of us before he retreats at speed. Nothing could make it clearer that my presence is unwelcome. But I'm not going to make a fool of myself by fleeing the scene. Touching the cool silver of my necklace, I pick up my conversation with Steph as well as I can. She suggests going into the kitchen to sample the puddings. Jack's there, drinking beer with Malcolm. I manage a casual hallo, to which he mutters some sort of response. I eat a little chocolate mousse, smooth enough to slide down despite my dry mouth. I set myself the task of saying a word or two to as many people as possible. Partners become increasingly jumbled in my head. Duty done, I seek out Malcolm and Zara, thanking them and saying how much I've enjoyed it.

I tell Zara no, there's no hurry for the moussaka dish. She walks with me to the door. As she opens it for me someone looms up behind her. Jack.

Out on the pavement, I say, 'Goodnight. I go left. I had to park miles away.'

He smiles down at me. 'Same here,' he says, falling into step beside me.

We can't walk in silence. 'Your partner couldn't make it then?' At once I worry that he's reading all sorts of nonsense into my question.

'I don't have a partner.'

Wincing at my own tactlessness I struggle for a better conversational gambit. 'I felt I had to come when Malcolm invited me.'

'So did I.'

'You weren't keen then?'

'No. I didn't want to meet you.'

The brutal frankness robs me of breath to answer, even if I could find a response. We're round the corner now where the street is poorly lit. He stops and turns to face me. I ought to walk on but I don't. It must be something to do with the way he's looking at me.

He says, 'I felt awkward. The way we'd quarrelled ...'

He's using the inappropriate word. Yet it makes me so happy I start laughing. 'That ridiculous argument. I still don't understand how it got so bitter, but don't you think it's time we forgave each other?'

He looks serious. Not making even a token attempt to share my amusement. 'I'm on your side. However it seems, it's your side I'm on. Do you believe that?'

Matching his gravity, I say, 'Yes, Jack.' Something's interfering with my breathing. I try again. 'Yes, I do.' My voice sounds small and tight.

He's smiling now. A different kind of smile. A smile which makes my lips curve in sympathy. 'Okay,' he says. 'Kiss and make up.'

He's joking of course. Only then he dips his head and kisses me lightly on the mouth.

With an effort at casual, I ask, 'Are we friends now?'

'Yes.' He draws me close and kisses me again.

My body responds in spite of me. I'm still trying to find an appropriate verbal response when he steps back. 'Sorry. I shouldn't have assumed ... Can you forget about it?'

'No,' I say. 'I don't think I can.'

'I know you and Max—'

I break in. 'What about me and Max?'

'That you're close.'

'Are we?'

'That's what I understood.'

'Then it was a misunderstanding.' Some spirit of mischief makes me add, 'You're the first Deputy Head I've kissed in my entire life.'

His face comes alive with joy. Then we're locked into a serious embrace. A crazy moment in which I'm caught up in the sheer delight of kissing. I'd almost forgotten how it could be. I choose not to listen to a disapproving inner voice, demanding what Isabel Lincoln, Headteacher, can be thinking about. How much more complicated does she want her life to be?

I'm lucky. I'm lucky. I'm lucky. I can walk under ladders. I'm so lucky ...

Joan Armatrading. The tune dances in my head. I thread my way through crowds of students. Laughter. Chatter. The whole place buzzes with excitement. What else would you expect from fifteen hundred adolescents nine days before Christmas? Thoughts dart through my mind, bright and elusive like tropical fish in an aquarium. Presents to buy. Decorations. My lesson – how does Shakespeare want us to feel about Shylock? Clare Henderson's comment: 'We're meant to be on Antonio's side. The trial scene doesn't work unless we are.' A bright student. And then the argument, with most of the class insisting what happened to Shylock was unfair. Real engagement with the text. The morning ahead weaves in and around the satisfying memory. Appointments. Phone calls. Home intrudes again. Laura's place at Somerville. Yippee. And Jack. What on earth am I doing?

I step out of the bustle into the cool silence of my room. My secretary Linda has left a pile of post for my attention. On top lies one of the bright pink slips we use for phone messages. The Hendersons. Clare's parents. Insisting on seeing me about her choice for Activities Week. Today. But Linda managed to postpone until 9.30 tomorrow, because I'm fully booked all day. I'm puzzled. Linda's brilliant at deflecting unnecessary calls. Lots of parents ask for the Head but are perfectly happy to speak to the relevant person. So why talk to me about Clare's choice? Or presumably her failure to get her choice? That's tutor business. In Clare's case, Trevor Bennett's business. Mystery solved. The parents will have tried Trevor. Being Trevor he's messed it up. Ten fifty-three. Seven minutes before I see Val and Toby to talk governors. Time to go and ask Max for the information I need to speak to the Hendersons. Activities Week has become his project. His alone without interference from me. Though I'm still slightly amazed he's taken on all the tedious business of slotting students into activities. Routine admin is not his thing at all.

Break's over and a hush has descended on the corridors. What shall I do if I see Jack walking towards me? I fantasise about the two of us drawing closer and closer. I don't want it to happen. Not in the least. It would be far too embarrassing. I reach my destination without incident. Max looks up with a warm smile of greeting. When I explain my errand, he does puzzled, raising astonished eyebrows.

'It'll be Trevor Bennett,' I explain. 'He's mishandled it in some way.'

He nods. 'I still can't understand it though. I'm pretty sure she got her first choice. I'll have to check the records and let you know.'

I'm impressed he has any recollection, after the hundreds of forms he's handled. 'That's fine. I'm not seeing them until tomorrow. The paperwork might offer a clue about what's bothering the parents.'

'Maybe.' He sounds uncertain. Frowns his bafflement. Then his face clears. 'Isabel, don't you think you ought to go to the Heads meeting about GCSE instead of me?'

It's my turn to be mystified. 'Why on earth? It's fine for you to go as my Deputy. The curriculum's your area of responsibility.'

'I was thinking about how it will look to staff. If you went, you could do the report back.'

'Why should I want to?'

'To make it clear where you stand. There's sure to be pressure to make this new system of examining elitist. The Tory government wants kids to fail. Everyone needs to know which side you're on.'

'I'll make that clear at the staff meeting.'

'It's not the same. If you went yourself tomorrow, it would demonstrate your commitment.'

He's got me worried now. 'Who's doubting my commitment?'

'You have to prove it so many times. After a while the doubts begin again. You know how it is.'

So much urging is making me obstinate. 'I can't go tomorrow. I'm seeing the Hendersons.'

'Wouldn't it be better if I saw them? Activities Week is my baby after all.' A look reminds me of the conversation in his flat. Of his plea for some independence.

I'm about to agree. Until I remember. 'No. I can't be out tomorrow. James Greville's coming to see me at eleven.' Max knows a Head can't mess the Chief Education Officer about.

'That settles it then,' he says.

It bothers me that he looks concerned again. I suspect some problem he's trying to protect me from. But I haven't time to go into it. Already I'm late for my meeting with Val and Toby. And yet as I speed along the corridor to my room at least half my thoughts revolve around Jack, in dizzy excitement.

'An afterthought.' David Graves, the Head of Music, sounds bitter. 'It must have been. No architect could design a Music Room this shape. At the last minute he must have said, "Bugger. There were supposed to be four Music Rooms. I know. We'll widen this corridor. That'll do."'

'It does look more like a corridor than a teaching space,' I say.

'Hopeless to teach in. Your class disappears into the distance. And as for the acoustics ...'

'Talk me through your solution.' I'm down here because I need to know exactly what I'm arguing for when I try to persuade James Greville to spend cash. We walk around looking and discussing until I'm confident.

'Thanks for taking the interest,' David says. 'I could never persuade Will there was a problem.'

I walk away thinking I have one person on my side. Max has infected me with his anxiety. For the last five hours, I've been pushing it out of my mind. It keeps finding its way back in again. It's so unlike Max I know it must be serious. I misread him this morning. I thought it was the Hendersons' phone call he was uneasy about. I see now it must have been serious negativity around me. Something specific must have triggered it. Something or someone. Simon and his precious PSE. Crazy to make an enemy of him. I can see it happening. Simon dominating his audience despite his small stature, his voice clear and confident. Some comment from him, to general agreement, about how Will Fullwood would have taken on the whole educational establishment over the new GCSE. And won. He never did though, did he? Never won. So far only a handful of us are convinced enough to put his brilliant ideas into practice.

Back in my room I settle down to sign letters, the final task of the day. Except I have to see Jack. Not here though. This is not school business. When the phone rings, my pulse-rate doubles. I'm convinced it's him postponing.

'Are you free to take a call from James Greville?' Linda asks.

'Yes. Put him on.'

'Isabel. Alas, I have to deny myself the pleasure of your company tomorrow. I hope you're as wretched about that as I am.'

'Devastated,' I reply. James is shrewd and sharp-witted, but he seems to think my gender obliges him to begin every conversation with this sort of teasing.

'I know you wanted to meet before the end of term.'

I treat it as a question, not an apology. 'Yes, please.'

'There's a panic on here.'

'What are you panicking about?'

'Money. Nothing induces panic like money.'

My hopes for the Music Department fade. They're hardly going to panic about too much money, are they? 'A familiar panic, then.'

'Yes. But yet again I have to argue the figures with Treasurers.'

'I'm sure you'll do it brilliantly. When can you squeeze an hour for me?'

'Friday. Could you bear Friday? I know it's the last day of term but twelve noon Friday is the best I can offer you.'

'Fine. I'll see you on Friday then.'

'Brilliant. The prospect will brighten my weary hours of toil.'

I laugh politely. 'As it will mine.' I put the phone down, wondering as usual about the pros and cons of participating in this banter. So now there's nothing to stop me going to tomorrow's meeting instead of Max. I ring through to him.

'Great.' He sounds delighted. 'I'm sure you've made the right decision. I'll bring the documentation across for you straightaway.'

'Thanks.' I glance at my watch. Plenty of time to find out what Max has heard to alarm him.

Chapter 7

Slumped in his chair, Jack flicks through the channels. A comedy show with canned laughter seems preferable to silence. He's sat through the news, though he can't now recall a single item. Then the weather forecast. Cold and wet tomorrow, the odds against snow for Christmas lengthening. Plenty of snow where he's going. Skiing. Ten days away with a crowd from school, Steph amongst them. It no longer seems such a bright idea. He'll need to be careful.

He still isn't sure how it's happened between him and Isabel. Thursday night it seemed to make sense. All the puzzling feelings, the contradictory impulses, were explained. Kissing her made everything simple. Simple? Christ, the complications stretch ahead in an infinite progression.

Isabel coming to his house tonight is just the beginning. She said they had to talk about it. When she drew away from their final embrace. A gentle withdrawal. Reluctant, he likes to think. As though she found parting as hard as he did. So he'd suggested she came here, confident it would be just as it was Thursday evening. Only he's not sure. Not now, four days later. Four days in which he's scarcely seen her and then only in meetings with other people. Supposing she's coming to say that's it, forget it? *His* suggestion after that first tentative kiss. He half-expected her to cancel, because if that was what she wanted she'd never come to see him here. But she hasn't. So the chances are he's starting a new relationship. A high-risk relationship, since it happens to be with his boss. There doesn't seem to be any choice about it. If they never saw each other again, maybe. Which would mean one of them leaving at once. People would read stuff into that. Sudden departure of Head or Deputy. They'd suspect the worst. It's the last thing the school needs when Isabel's worked so hard to change the public perception. A new relationship it is then. He just wishes he had more confidence in his ability to do it right. His past record isn't encouraging.

It's complicated by the need to warn her. He does have to warn her, doesn't he? He tries to fix the visual image. The way Max looked, triumph blended with resignation, as he declared that Isabel was crazy about him and he was doing his best to let her down lightly. Jack doesn't remember the exact words but the meaning was plain enough. Isabel's denial carried such instant conviction, he felt like rushing off to punch Max for lying about her. But he can't even bring it up. Why would he, unless he had a personal interest? It would be a waste of time in any case. He knows, because it's happened before. More than once. *I never said that,* Max objects. *It's not what I think, so I can't have done, can I?* A denial doesn't mean he won't say exactly the same to someone else.

Like the PSE business. Max dead against it. Warning what a dangerous enemy Simon Clarke would be. He'd never accept any interference. How could he, when Isabel was undermining the Thomas Paine ethos? And Max has to be the best judge of what's right for the school. He was Will Fullwood's closest ally. His confidant. So Jack was persuaded. Only when the three of them met, Max seemed all for it, his only caveat the need to square Simon. Jack found himself cast in the role of the awkward bugger. When all along he'd thought he was looking out for Isabel. Suddenly the truth became elusive, like trying to grasp one of the solid-looking objects in a trompe-l'oeil painting.

Maybe there's always a gap between the message intended and the message received. Which Max deals with in his own way. Jack's done it himself. Only not as skilfully. Maggie, quoting his words back at him while he protested that hadn't been what he meant.

But remembering that other failed relationship while he waits for Isabel seems like a bad omen.

If her Deputy talks that way about her it's not going to do her any good. No one says she's the wrong gender. Not at Thomas Paine High. They're all too right-on. It comes out sideways. Emotional. Not combative, the way Will was. No use looking to her to fight her corner to the bitter end. Jack's fist clenches, the comments already loud in his ears. *Wants to have it off with Max, does she? Can't keep her hands off him is what I've heard.* Switch the genders. A Head with a young female Deputy. The jeering's transformed into envy. *Lucky sod.* So it's urgent to warn her, because she's vulnerable. But when he tries to find the words he's defeated. Anything he comes up with sounds insulting.

An outburst of clapping breaks into his preoccupation. The comedy programme's ending. Seven o'clock. He could have a beer before Isabel arrives. No, not a beer. She'd notice. Another instant coffee. The kitchen is cold and cheerless. He never cooks in it. Looking around with her eyes the whole place seems bleak, scarcely lived in. The truth is he's there as little as possible. Running the Youth Club at school, teaching his evening class, playing rugby or squash. Afterwards always an hour or two in the pub. It's how he fills his time, now there's no longer Maggie and the kids. Though she moaned he spent too much time that way when they were together.

No, he won't think about how it all went wrong.

Startled by the buzz of his doorbell, he hesitates with the mug of coffee in his hand, slops a little of it down the sink, then dumps it on the draining-board while he hurries to the door.

It might be kids carol-singing, but no, it's her. Isabel. 'Hi,' he says. 'You found it.'

'No problem.' She slips off her coat.

He takes it and hangs it on one of the pegs in the narrow hall, feeling her warmth on the fabric. The space is so limited she'd have to brush past him to get into the living-room. Or he could turn his back on her and lead the way. Instead, he steps closer. He feels the chill of the outside air on her skin and lips. Already it's as though it's something expected, this drawing her against him and kissing her mouth. It leaves no room for doubt about the way either of them feels.

When he gives her a chance to speak, she says, 'I came to talk, Jack. Remember?' But teasingly, as though she's enjoying the delay.

With his arms around her his confidence has come flooding back. 'You came for this as well, didn't you? If it was just conversation you wanted, Mrs Lincoln, we could have talked at school.'

'Who gave you permission to read my mind?'

They're both laughing as he takes her hand and leads her into the living-room. 'Have a seat,' he says.

She ignores him, standing before his painting. 'Yours?' she asks.

He admits it is. A shed with the door half-open. Inside, glimpses of a spade, a broken chair, a dead plant, a sack with a shredded corner. She gazes so long he wonders what she's seeing in it. Though he was pleased with it when he did it. The way he'd captured the sunlit garden and the shadowy gloom of the shed. He's found time to paint again, since he split up with Maggie.

Isabel turns round to him at last. 'It makes me think of secrets. All those secrets about ourselves which we're desperate to keep hidden, even though we know we only draw close to another person by being open with them.'

'Do you have secrets?' he says. But he's thinking of his own secrets. Of the way he's messed up previous relationships. Of his failings as a parent. Of how her face would close down if she ever heard about them.

'Yes.' He hears her sigh. 'Lots of them.'

It's too much, too soon. He remembers his mug of coffee with relief. 'I'd just made myself a coffee. Would you like one?'

'Please.'

When they sit down with their mugs, she takes an armchair. He glances towards the settee and then takes the chair opposite her.

Isabel doesn't look at him. She says, 'I don't know where to begin,' and makes a small, helpless gesture with her hand.

He'd grasp it, if he was close enough. He doesn't offer to help her with words.

'I don't want to make assumptions.' She sips from her mug. 'Maybe this is just pre-Christmas madness. But now it's happened I can't carry on without mentioning it.'

'I'm glad it happened.' He says it without knowing whether it's true or not. 'Aren't you?'

'I'm not sure. Last Thursday it seemed to explain a lot.'

'About the way we'd been with each other?'

'Exactly.' At last she lets her gaze meet his.

The way they smile at each other makes words redundant in Jack's view, but he says, 'We'll go on meeting, won't we? Outside school?'

'Do you think that'll make it easier?'

'Nicer, anyway.' He's glad that makes her laugh. He likes the way it takes all the toughness out of her face, leaving her helpless and pretty.

'Be serious though. This isn't going to make working together any easier. The closer you get the more risk there is of hurting the other person. Professional relationships work at a much lower temperature.'

'We'll have to live with that. There's no way of undoing what's happened.'

'I guess I've acquired another secret,' she says. 'We can't afford to let anyone know about this, can we?'

He swallows his coffee, cold now, to avoid replying. He doubts it'll work. Those times in the past when he was sure Maggie would never know. She always found him out. Every time. He can hardly tell Isabel that. He tries to believe it's different. Maggie never needed people to tell her. There was something about him which gave it away, though he was always convinced he was behaving just the same. This time there are no suspicious partners.

'People at school mustn't know,' she urges, 'must they?'

'Better they don't.'

'It's so complicated,' she says. 'I wish you'd already met Laura and Daniel. Been to the house as a colleague.'

'I could still do that, couldn't I?'

She blushes a little, a faint flush over her perfect cheekbones. 'Don't you think we might give ourselves away?'

'Would that matter?'

'I don't want to keep anything from them. The trouble is, they've already met other people from school.' The briefest hesitation. 'Like Max.'

It's Jack's opportunity but he avoids. 'Your kids wouldn't gossip about us, would they?'

'I've been trying to imagine. I shouldn't think so. Daniel

might tease, but he can't stand Max.'

Another opportunity. It seems important to establish something else first. 'So they've met one of your Deputies. Can't they meet me the same way?'

'I guess that's best. I can't be lying to them all the time. If we're going to go on meeting like you suggest.'

'Which we are.' He adds clumsily, 'Has Max got hold of the wrong end of the stick? About you and him? I didn't just make it up. He mentioned it to me.'

'Mentioned what?'

Already she looks so outraged the truth's out of the question. 'Suggested you were ... close.' He wishes he'd never started on it.

'What did he say? Exactly?'

'Don't remember the words. You know the way people imply things.'

'He has no right to imply anything of the sort. We had some meals together last term. It seemed a good idea in such a potentially fraught situation. Me taking his job. He's been to the house a few times. I've been to his flat. Once.' As though Jack's spoken out of jealousy, she adds, 'We're no more than colleagues so it's uncomplicated. Nothing like coming here, to be with you.'

It's to reassure her that he gets up and walks towards her. She stands up into his embrace. His first kisses are light, holding himself back as you do when you don't want to come too soon, prolonging the seconds of pleasure. Then he's aware of nothing except Isabel, her scent, her skin, her mouth, her warmth against him.

A long time later when she says she can't believe Max suggested there was anything between them Jack pretends he must have been mistaken. A lie seems much safer than the truth.

❑ ❑ ❑

Jack's plan was to get to the meeting ahead of Max. Once they've parted, some Doppler effect distorts his clear sense of his relationship with Isabel. He needs to re-establish contact by the way he smiles at her, the way he greets her.

Only it doesn't work out that way. Determined to finish his lesson promptly, he's on the point of asking his class to clear away their work when Alice calls out a despairing, 'Jack'. An overloaded brush has deposited paint in the wrong place. 'My best piece,' she wails. 'You said it was the best thing I'd done and now it's ruined.'

Jack can't ignore her despair. He offers consolation as he applies prompt first-aid. Around him the rest of the group remain absorbed in their work. He doesn't react to the hum of students in the corridors until Gavin says he's supposed to see Malcolm this break and he'll be murdered if he fails to turn up. With sudden rueful awareness that his plan is in tatters, Jack carries on until Alice is reassured while the others clear up around them. The start of the next period overtakes them so he sends them off to science as Len appears to reclaim his Art Room. When he explains what's happened Len is sympathetic, but Jack still feels an obligation to put things straight before he leaves. And then to carry the more fragile pieces to the safety of his office for storage.

Isabel starts to laugh as he walks into her room. Max joins in, looking pleased with himself. Weird how shut out you feel when you can't share the joke.

'Hallo, Jack,' she says, giving him the briefest of glances. She switches straight back to Max. 'Why were they complaining then?'

'You were absolutely right. They'd spoken to Trevor Bennett.' Max spreads his hands, shrugging. 'Nuff said.'

Isabel seems unconvinced. 'Even so.'

'The guy has a gift for it. Doesn't he have the same effect on you? He sure as hell does on me. I can get on with most people but Trevor Bennett ...'

Jack asks, 'What's he done now?'

Isabel answers him. 'Annoyed Clare Henderson's parents. Max had to soothe their ruffled feathers yesterday, while I was out at the meeting.'

Jack looks to Max to explain but Max says it's all settled now anyway. He smiles at Isabel, saying her day was much more important. He wants to hear about the new GCSE.

'Not encouraging,' she says. 'It's going to be rigid. Our own syllabuses will be phased out.'

Jack's interested now. Interested and appalled. 'But that's what enables us to get some success for every student.'

'Exactly.' She passes them each a photocopied sheet, hand-written. 'I've summarised the most significant points.'

Jack's dismay grows as he scans it.

Isabel breaks into their reading. 'I'm getting Linda to type it up. A lot of staff are asking. Should I distribute this?'

Max looks up. 'Maybe not.'

'Why not?' Jack asks. 'People want to know.'

Isabel seems to agree. 'Why be secretive?'

'So it's out tomorrow and we break up the next day. It's the wrong note to end the term on.'

'I'll add a paragraph. The boards will accept a syllabus from a group of schools. That's what we'll have to work at. I spoke to a few like-minded Heads yesterday and I've agreed to convene a meeting in January.'

'Brilliant,' Max says. 'You're being pro-active in the fight-back.'

Jack's 'Good idea' sounds lukewarm in comparison.

Isabel begins to roll the edge of her sheet, saying half to herself, 'I'm not sure how high our chances of success are but I'll put it as strongly as I can. So no one can imagine I'm letting it go by default.' She looks up and turns her gaze on Max. 'I'm still bothered by what you said on Monday.'

What did Max say on Monday? Jack seems to be left out of the conversation again.

Max leans back in his chair, smiling and shaking his head. 'Isabel, I told you not to worry about it.'

Meant to be soothing, presumably. To Jack it sounds bloody patronising.

Isabel seems to think so too. 'Please, Max,' she says sharply. 'I don't need that. You can't tell me there are teachers questioning my commitment and then refuse point-blank to name them.'

So that's it. Jack's heard nothing but then he's outside the magic circle.

'Why does it matter who they are?' Max asks.

Isabel's chin goes up. She looks stubborn. 'I like to know who's on my side.'

'Isn't it easier to stay on good terms if you don't know?'

'I'm perfectly capable of staying on good terms with people who disagree with me. But the conversation is bound to be different if I know they're still to be persuaded.' She's fidgeting with the piece of paper again. 'Simon Clarke is at the root of it, isn't he? Controlling PSE gave him power. He can't forgive me for robbing him of that. Any consideration of what's good for the school or the students seems quite beyond him.'

'Simon has been making waves,' Max admits.

Jack hears what he says. Only he doesn't take it at face value like he would have done a week ago. If Simon got to hear of it, would Max wriggle at once into denial mode?

'You can't blame Simon,' Max is saying.

'Not blame him? PSE is a disaster. Heaven knows why Will

allowed him to get away with murder for ten years. He surely didn't expect the same indulgence from a new Head?'

Max makes no attempt to answer her criticism. 'We ought to try to think of some way of compensating him.'

'Compensating him? You must be joking. I'd like to challenge him directly.'

'No, no.' Max sounds alarmed at the possibility. 'That wouldn't be wise.'

'No. Satisfying. But not wise,' Isabel admits. 'Jack.' She turns towards him and it's like they're in contact again for the first time since Monday evening. The electricity flows between them. He has to fight a powerful urge to reach out and touch her. 'What do you think?'

He'd like to come up with the perfect answer. He can do no better than mutter it will take time. Whatever happens he's on her side. Sometimes that seems to be the only certainty.

Chapter 8

January 1982

'Yes, it's fine to go to the Resource Centre,' I say, 'providing you've got a permission slip from Michael.' I've said it five times in as many minutes. I'm forcing my smile and there's an edge to my voice.

'I can't get on with my project then.' The boy produces this as a triumphant fact, which convicts me, his Headteacher, of sentencing him to an hour of idleness.

'Go back and get a slip and then you can go.'

The boy heaves a sigh, loaded with his adolescent impatience of this impenetrable adult bureaucracy. 'If you say so, Isabel.'

'I do say so.' I make each word distinct and separate, jokey.

He grins, dawdles back towards the classroom, fails to re-emerge. I have the small satisfaction of one escape prevented.

Private Study. Another of Simon Clarke's responsibilities. Another disaster. Until next September and a new timetable, Max and Jack agreed the three of us would support the teachers who have to struggle with it. How has it happened that I'm the only one who takes the supporting seriously? I grudge the time it wastes. I loathe the petty interventions it requires. Why

don't I let myself off the way my Deputies do? A gender thing.
Yet which gender has the right of it? It does little enough for my
image and even less for my temper. But it's as though I have
some synapses missing, the ones which connect the logic area
of my brain with wherever my conscience is located. Knowing
myself, I'll carry on until the end of the year when I can imple-
ment my personal resolution to put Private Study and me out
of our collective misery.

So when the sixth student of the afternoon emerges from
the classroom, I prepare the familiar question. Against the dark
bricks and concrete floor of the corridor, she looks exotic. As
she passes a window, the January sunlight turns her blonde bob
to gold. She wears the obligatory jeans and sweatshirt but the
fit is perfect. 'Dana,' I say, glad to have a name, which makes it
more friendly. 'Have you got permission from Michael?'

'Yes, Isabel.' She is eagerly compliant, extracting her folded
green permission slip from the little pocket in the front of her
jeans.

I scan it. Name, date, time, all correctly filled in. And the
reason. 'To see Max. (Pastoral matter.)' I hand it back with a
smile. 'Thanks.'

Dana's trainers squeak faintly as she heads off to Max's room.
I glance at my watch. If no one emerges in the next five minutes,
I can assume the group is settled for the afternoon and make a
start on my list of urgent phone calls. I reach for the Education
Authority's information bulletin, propped temporarily behind a
fire extinguisher, and continue scanning it for anything relevant
to us.

Forty minutes later, I've managed no more than two out of ten
phone calls. The second, protracted one, with the Educational
Psychologist, has left me in despair. It doesn't need a psycholo-

gist to work out that Kevin needs help urgently. How can she say she'll 'try' to talk to him again on her routine visit in four weeks and then 'perhaps' the long procedure to give him support 'might' be set in motion? In several minutes of self-blame, I convince myself I mishandled it. Safer not to move straight on to something equally delicate. Remembering new instructions in the bulletin about how the Authority requires us to present our curriculum analysis, I decide to point them out to Max, before he wastes time doing it the old way. Since none of the minor changes ever seems to make any significant improvement, I suspect our education officers of inventing them for no better reason than to catch us out. With Max they'd probably succeed. He gets his own copy of the bulletin, but he takes a lofty view of the avalanche of paper which descends on us with every post, dismissing it as bumf. I groan and read it. The gender thing again. I could write him a note, but a friendly word seems preferable.

I set off along the corridor, flapping over the pages of the bulletin as I walk, to locate the relevant section. I'm still raw from my fruitless encounter with the Educational Psychologist, inventing too late the responses I should have given. Why am I beating myself up like this? Max never indulges in self-flagellation. His soothing take on life is exactly what I need this afternoon. I'm already smiling as I tap on his door. Without waiting for a response, I open it. And stand silent in the doorway, resisting an urge to back out with a murmured apology.

It looks like the cover of one of those cheap romances. Old-fashioned artwork, pastel colours, an instant turn-off to serious readers. Max, dark and handsome, though not tall, is perched on the corner of his desk. He's smiling down at blonde and beautiful Dana, seated close beside him in a chair. She's gazing up at him, her mouth curved in an answering smile, her hands clasped like those of a saint in ecstasy. Max and Dana. Even the names fit the genre. As the eye reads the scene, the brain clicks forward to the kiss which is bound to follow.

They are too absorbed in each other to notice my entrance. 'Sweet of you, Dana,' Max says in a sexy drawl. (No. A loaded description. Unfair since he talks like that all the time.)

'When can I see you again, Max?'

He puts his hand on her shoulder.

At which point I snap out of my trance and say, 'Dana, you need to go back to your classroom.' I step aside, holding the door open for her.

Max draws back his hand. Dana jumps up, saying, 'Yes, Isabel.' She throws one appealing glance towards Max before fleeing the scene.

Turning on my heel I march off to my own room. And sit, trying to collect my thoughts.

When the phone rings, it affects me like the knocking on the door in *Macbeth*. I tell myself I've done nothing wrong. Why should I feel guilty? It's still an effort to lift the receiver. I'm relieved to hear my secretary, telling me she has Mr Stewart from Queen Elizabeth's on the line. Taking a deep breath to steady my voice, I say yes, I'll talk to him.

'Isabel. Just to remind you of our date tomorrow. See you here about 8.30?'

It's a relief to hear this friendly voice from another world. 'Yes, I'm looking forward to it.'

'Splendid. I know you're far too efficient to need a reminder. I rang you to cheer myself up.'

'Are you in need of cheering?'

'I've just had a blazing argument with James Greville, part of an ongoing row about staffing. I can't stand the man.'

I can't agree about James so I avoid answering and offer

general sympathy. When I tell him about my catastrophe with the psychologist, he says it's all about saving money. They're under such strict orders to drag their feet that even my amazing powers of persuasion can have no effect. I feel a bit better about my failure. I'm tempted to ask his advice about Max and Dana, but a telephone line seems too insecure. I can always bring it up tomorrow. Although I don't see how I can avoid talking to Max before then. I finish the call with a few more polite generalities.

Like a repetitive bass-line beneath the treble of what I say and think, one question keeps repeating itself. Why didn't I stay and challenge Max? In the silence after the phone call, I can't avoid any longer. I was startled. Yet not surprised. How can that be? The answer is obvious. I saw him with Helen in the library. And I didn't believe his explanation. Not for one moment.

I have to take the initiative. It's too feeble to leave it to Max to react. I must summon him. Or go and see him. But what on earth am I to say?

Safest to write down exactly what I saw. So I can't be wrong-footed. So I can't be persuaded it wasn't the way I know it was. The way Max sees things is always different. Even when his reputation isn't on the line. Writing it down is necessary, not my excuse to postpone.

I reach for an A4 pad. I alter words until I get the exact shade of meaning. Yet when I read it back, the incident slides out of focus. What does it amount to after all? It was the sense of what was going to happen which was unsettling. How can I capture that? I shouldn't have intervened. I should have waited for something there could be no argument about. But maybe that would count as entrapment. They didn't even notice me come into the room. Isn't that evidence enough? No way I can ignore it. I worry a bit about just walking in. But it's normal practice. Max does it to me all the time. When I think about it,

I hardly ever go to see him. There's a subliminal sense that I'm intruding. Why did I go this afternoon? I scan my account again, to convince myself I haven't got enough to act on. Or at least not yet. I'm inventing a drama.

Only I know I'm not.

I can't face Max's room again. I ring his extension.

'Max here.' He doesn't sound any different.

My mouth is dry. I can feel my heart racing. I announce myself. 'Isabel.' I'm surprised when it comes out quite cool and collected. 'Max, we need to talk. Can you come to my room? Now.'

'Yes, we certainly need to talk. I'm on my way.'

I hear a threat in that *certainly*. I get up to open my door. Avoiding the knock and enter ritual.

As he walks in, I'm taken aback by his smile.

He closes the door and chooses a chair close to mine. 'You're upset, aren't you? I can tell you are.'

I won't let him seize the initiative. 'Not upset. Puzzled. I need an explanation.'

He nods. 'I could see you'd misread the situation when you popped in just now.'

His casual language infuriates me. Which makes it easier to go on the attack. 'Possibly. If you had any judgement, you wouldn't put yourself in a situation where such a misreading was likely.'

'Isabel, that's old-style thinking. Remember where you are.'

'I know very well where I am. In a school. You're the one who seems to have forgotten that. Forgotten you're a male teacher and Dana is a female student.'

'Not any old school. Thomas Paine High. Where relation-ships are different. You say you understand that. Value it. Yet you're talking as though you're still at Moorlands.'

I can't allow this. I have to get back to what I saw. 'I came into your room,' I begin.

'Yes,' he says. 'Let's talk about what happened. Not what you may have imagined.'

On safer ground, I glance at what I've written. 'I saw you perched on the corner of your desk.'

'Is that a hanging offence? Come on, Isabel.' He sounds playful, not aggressive. 'I've looked in when you're teaching and you do just that.'

I can't deny it. But it's not the point. Before I can say what the point is, Max goes on.

'You heard me say something like "Sweet of you to say so", didn't you?'

He's going to admit it then. 'Yes.'

'Dana's having a miserable time at the moment. Split family. The usual thing. She's in turmoil because her mother's talking about marrying again. Step-parents are always tricky. Imagine how Dan and Laura would react.'

He's pushing all my buttons. Reminding me of my *angst* about possible reactions to Jack. Of my compassion for all the kids trapped in homes which no longer feel like home. Of my bitter condemnation of Richard for putting his tawdry romances before the happiness of our children. But I won't be deflected. 'So where do you come in?'

'She had some crazy idea about running away. An attractive, middle-class girl like that, imagine the moral danger she'd be in. When she said she wanted to talk to me about it, I wasn't going to turn her away, was I?'

'Why you?'

Max looks puzzled. He does puzzled as charmingly as he does everything else. 'Why not me? We always say students have a right to choose. It doesn't mean anything. It's not a snub because the obvious person is left out of the loop. Why might you choose to talk to Jack, instead of me? Or vice versa? It's just one of those things.'

I concede the point. 'Accepted.'

'It's the third or fourth time we've talked. I thought Dana was coping. But she was in a real state again this afternoon.'

I don't believe it. Not after that encounter in the corridor. 'Was she?'

'A question of trust, as it happens.' A quick, quizzical lift of his eyebrows. 'Dana's always had a brilliant relationship with her mother. Until this bloke interferes. Wanting to know exactly where she's going. Laying down the law about when she has to be home. Just before you came in, she was telling me how much it helped talking to me. Which, as you heard me say, was sweet of her. Because it was nothing special. It's what we're here for, isn't it?'

I'm not convinced. How could I be? Yet doubt begins to wriggle uneasily in my mind. I try a different approach. 'So as far as you're concerned it's a straightforward transaction?'

'Of course.'

I wish I could hear Dana's take on that. But I can't question her without putting his career on the line. I can't do that. Not yet. 'Don't you think you're taking a risk?'

'We take risks all the time here. I'd never let a risk stop me helping a student.'

The trouble is, I agree with him. If we were always watching our backs, we'd never do anything. Was that all it was? Max too concerned with a student's distress to bother how it might look? 'Dana might not understand.' I hear irresolution in my voice. 'She might get the wrong idea.'

'Yes, she might. If I was an irresponsible probationer, getting my kicks from adoring kids, I might be doing more harm than good.' He presses his palms against his chest. 'I'm your Deputy, Isabel. If we can't trust each other, who the bloody hell can we trust? I trust you. I have from the beginning. Think of the games I might have played. I could have fucked up your chances of success, with one hand tied behind my back. But I haven't. Because I trusted you. Trusted you when you claimed to understand. Trusted you to carry on where Will left off.'

'I know that. And I'm grateful to you. You've been astonishingly generous.' I hesitate, wondering why I can't apologise. 'So I misinterpreted what I saw?'

He looks at me. 'Yes, you did.' He sounds angry. Not surprisingly.

There's an awkward silence, because although I accept what he says, I still can't get my tongue round that apology.

And then he astonishes me. He apologises. He says he's been too defensive. If I could misinterpret, so could other people. Perhaps it's not enough to be innocent. Perhaps it matters just as much to appear above suspicion. It's all part of gender awareness. A different dimension. Something he knows I'm sensitive to. It's what he came in to say. Only somehow we got off on the wrong foot.

'Bizarre, isn't it?' he says. 'The way you have something you mean to say and end up saying something quite different?'

It's not until Friday evening that I'm able to talk to Jack about it. I think I've been blocking. As though speaking about it might make it different. Or more definite.

I do my best to make my account objective but I end up asking, 'It was unwise of Max, wasn't it?'

Jack's answer is another question. 'What would you have thought if it was me? If you'd walked into my room and found me with a girl? Doing the same. Saying the same.'

I don't like the question. Or any of my possible answers. I force myself to relive the scene, with Jack replacing Max. I'd be jealous of the intimacy I sensed. I wouldn't want to believe he was doing anything wrong. So I'd assume the best. More than I did with Max. He had to convince me. It's unsettling to find it's all so relative. That who's doing it matters more than what's done.

I'm quiet for so long that Jack strokes my hand, telling me I don't have to answer. Perhaps it hasn't helped to ask.

'Max is right. It is a matter of trust. I trust you and that makes it different.'

'But in the end you decided to trust Max?'

'Yes.'

'It's a good job you did.'

Does that mean he trusts Max? 'Why do you say that?'

'Christ, Isabel, think of all the complications if you decided you couldn't.'

I try to think about it. I really do. To think about what's right and what's expedient. About how to tell the difference between what you believe and what you want to believe. About whether you can ever know how close your perception is to reality. Only it's like trying to understand eternity. It teases the brain out of thought. So I kiss Jack. To forget. And as usual it's the perfect shortcut to oblivion.

Chapter 9

Max is already on his feet. 'Have a whisky chaser,' he urges.

'No. Just another pint, thanks.'

'Go on,' Max says. He grins at Jack. Almost like he's flirting with him. 'It's what I'm having. Join me.'

'No, honestly. Thanks.'

With a shrug he's off to the bar for their drinks. Jack watches his progress past dark wainscoting, across deep-pile carpet. As though fixing the visual image will help to get his bearings. The pub is unexpected. Like everything else about the evening. As unlike the Sutton Arms as it could be. Hushed, where the other is raucous. More olives than pork scratchings. Why did Max suggest meeting here? There's a straightforward answer. Because it's just round the corner from where he lives. Why meet at all? Again, a straightforward answer. A friendly overture from one Deputy to another. The straightforward answers no longer satisfy Jack. He seems to have a compulsion to complicate everything. Which must be why he can't lose the suspicion that Max wants to pump him. To find out what? Something about Isabel. Only that can't be right since no one knows about their relationship.

Max sets down two glasses and slips onto the bench seat alongside Jack. He sips from the smaller glass. 'It's a good one. Sure you won't change your mind, Jack?'

'Sure, thanks.' He gulps beer. He feels under scrutiny as Max shifts into the corner.

'Christ, what a week! But they're all the same, aren't they? I go in every Monday thinking this week I'll be bloody organised, instead of running to catch myself up the whole time. Ten minutes and ten unexpected things have been thrown at me. So there I am. Back to square one.'

'I'm glad it happens to you too.' And he is. If it happens to someone with six years in the job, it's no wonder it's happening to him after less than six months. 'Depressing though. I thought it was my inexperience. I imagined you had everything taped.'

'Sorry to disappoint you. The longer you're there, the more convinced the staff are you can solve all their problems. And the kids as well. Bet you find more and more of them seek you out.'

Jack nods agreement, thinking back to the first few easy days. And then there's all the times he and Isabel need to consult each other. He grins at the memory and speaks to banish it. 'I guess we wouldn't be doing our job, if that didn't happen.'

'That's the good news. The bad news is there never seems to be time for us to have a decent conversation. You've got your feet under the table now. We ought to talk about how it's going.'

So there it is. A straightforward reason to meet out of school on a Sunday evening. Yet Jack is still wary. 'You're a better judge than I am. Am I doing the job you hoped I would?'

Silly question. Max goes to town praising Jack's performance. He's got a gift for it, bringing up stuff you think no one else notices. It's way over the top. It's embarrassing, but it gives Jack a glow as well. He needs affirmation, like every other teacher. Their achievements are intangible. A breakthrough with a disaffected student. A lesson which takes off. Nothing permanent left behind. He makes a token effort to reciprocate but it's not natural to him. He has a lot to learn from his fellow Deputy. He gets up to fetch another round.

Waiting at the bar, his suspicions stir again. He suspects Max of some motive for charming him. But that's balls. To Max, charming is like breathing. He can't help himself. All the same, Jack decides to take the seat opposite, as though the width of the table provides a safety zone.

'Thanks, Jack,' Max says. He takes a thoughtful sip or two. 'It makes all the difference, having someone I respect as a colleague. After the Val Stephens experience.'

Jack's stuck for an answer. He rates Val but he accepts she must have done something unforgivable to Max, knowing how generous he is towards everyone. He mutters something about how good it is to work with Max.

'And Isabel? How are you getting on with her?'

God, what a question. Unbidden, he gets a picture of her soft thighs. There's something obscene about his arousal when it's their Headteacher they're talking about. 'Okay.' It comes out gruff.

'She does her best,' Max says, apparently interpreting the grunt as criticism. 'And I like her, I really like her.' Elbows on the table, he leans towards Jack, studying him intently. 'Don't you?'

Not a question Jack has any wish to answer. And he's restless under the scrutiny. He looks down at his glass, saying, 'Liking her's not the point, though, is it? It's the job she does that matters.'

Max leans back. 'Fair comment. But everything runs more smoothly when you like your colleagues, doesn't it?'

'Guess so.'

'It's something we need to talk about though. Does she really understand where we're coming from? It's bloody hard, following in Will's footsteps but does she have his total commitment to the ethos? Does she really understand it?'

'She's not stupid.'

'No. That's what worries me in my more paranoid moments. If she'd come out against the ethos from day one, there'd have been a revolution. So it made sense to sound positive about it.'

'Is that what you think? That she's conning us?'

'No, I don't believe it. Only you know how it is sometimes. You don't want to suspect people but you have these dark moments of thinking the worst.'

'I know what you mean.' And indeed Jack does. 'Has she done something to make you suspicious?' He feels he has to find out for Isabel's sake, though it may be a risky question.

'Yes.' It comes out slow and thoughtful. 'There was an incident.' Max twists his glass. Clockwise. Anti-clockwise. Clockwise again. 'Don't want to make too much of it. Has she mentioned anything to you?'

He's bound to be referring to something quite different. But Jack wishes Isabel had never mentioned Dana to him. The knowledge seems to defy concealment. He feels like a kid at school again, denying he's eating while the gob-stopper bulges in his cheek. 'Like what?'

'She interrupted me when I was counselling a student. I was pissed off about it at the time. You know how it is, Jack. Kids don't open up the moment you snap your fingers. I'd been as tactful as I knew how. And it was serious stuff. Things going badly wrong at home. Kid threatening to run away. Which does happen. Plenty of statistics to show that. And the number who end up on the streets.'

Jack tries to look non-committal. He hopes it's convincing. 'Isabel understands that, surely. I don't see what it has to do with TPH ethos.'

'Isabel was hung up about me being on my own with a

female student. I mean, for Christ's sake! Do you refuse to talk to students because they're the wrong gender?'

'No,' Jack says, though he feels a bit of a traitor as he says it. 'When they start talking, you have to let it run.'

'Exactly.'

'Isabel understood that, didn't she?'

'Yes, but grudgingly. My informality seemed to alarm her. She complained that I was perched on the corner of my desk, would you believe? So how far adrift is she from the way we do things at Thomas Paine?'

Jack has no answer. They drink in silence and he wonders about the two different versions of the same incident. Is either the truth? Does it matter? Maggie was insistent she wanted the truth about Jill but what good did it do her? His truth was he'd fancied Jill. He'd fucked her a few times. And enjoyed it. Compared to his feelings for Maggie, Betsy and Matt, it was trivial. Not significant enough to require major self-denial on his part. Though maybe it's the beer, giving him an easy-going take on it. He's felt bad enough about it at times. He still denies it was what Maggie called it. A betrayal. Sufficient reason to throw him out. Though the way things are he can't be sorry. What would he have done if he'd still been involved with Maggie when he felt the chemistry between him and Isabel? He doesn't kid himself he'd have resisted. So it's just as well he was free again. Because he suspects Isabel shares Maggie's views. Neither seems to understand there are feelings no one can resist. Then he realises Max is talking to him.

'We have to educate her,' he's saying. 'Get her to see the closeness between teachers and students is one of the strengths of Thomas Paine. Most schools try to alter kids' behaviour through confrontation so the last thing students want to do is please teachers. At TPH we do it through caring relationships.

The kids do it for me, for my sake. Don't you find that, Jack?'

He does. Of course he does. Getting on with kids. It's how he's always worked. 'All the time. What makes you think Isabel would disagree?'

'The way she reacted last Monday. Christ, she behaved as though she'd caught me out in some hideous wrong-doing.' Max is shaking his head in disbelief.

Jack shifts uncomfortably on his chair. There's no way he means to be on the opposite side to Isabel. But that's how he's ended up. He struggles to turn things round. 'She's right in a way though, isn't she? We have to be careful nowadays. If a girl misunderstood, you could find yourself in trouble.'

'Agreed. But Isabel was the one who misunderstood. You should have heard her ...' He empties his glass and gets up to fetch another round.

Jack wonders about Max. About the curious blank of his private life. He's never had a partner, to Jack's knowledge. No known lovers, male or female. Is – has always been – unattached. But there's nothing cold or bloodless about him. On the contrary. Sensuous warmth is more like it. Jack's never analysed it before, and as Max heads back towards him he wishes he hadn't done so now. It's yet another reason to feel uncomfortable.

Settled on the bench again, Max asks, 'Does Isabel talk to you?'

'She has to, doesn't she? When there's school business to discuss.'

'Business-like and professional then? No friendly chat?'

'Sometimes,' Jack mutters. 'She's said a few things about her kids.'

'Of course.' Max beams. 'Something you've got in common.'

It doesn't feel like that. Not when Isabel's such a hands-on parent and he's an absent father. He's put it on Maggie. Her wish to exclude him and start a new life with a new partner. Drawing undeserved sympathy and admiration for his self-denial from Isabel. 'Sort of,' he says.

'Maybe her daughter's had a bad experience with some guy and it's made her hypersensitive. She's never mentioned anything like that to you?'

'No.' Keen to suggest a distance between them, Jack adds, 'I doubt she would though.' He wants to change the subject but the harder he tries to think of a new topic, the more his mind goes blank.

'Pity. I was hoping you had more insight into her thinking than I have. Because we need to work together on this.'

Jack drinks beer to avoid replying.

'It's no good ignoring sex as an issue, is it? I'm not stupid. I know why female students hang on my words. Having a crush on someone my age is part of growing up, isn't it?'

Jack's often thought he ought to say something about Max's fan club. And Tim's. And Simon's. About the risks and the need to act responsibly. He's never spoken because he's never been sure enough of his ground. Maybe he just envies all that fascinated attention. Now it seems too late. He has a try anyway. 'Isn't there a risk someone will get hurt?'

'There's always a risk. The only way to avoid pain is not to care about anyone ever. Love has been hurting from Romeo and Juliet onwards.'

Jack wants this conversation like he wants a hole in the head. But whisky seems to have loosened his companion's tongue. He carries on without waiting for a response.

'Every secondary school is a sexual hothouse. Look at what happens in single-sex schools. Boys hung up on boys, girls on girls. Adolescents are hormone-driven. They've got to experiment. So no one ought to be surprised when girls fancy their teachers.'

'As long as the teachers don't fancy the girls.'

'They do. Of course they do. Come on, Jack. You can't pretend it's never happened to you. Pert young breasts. A bum in tight jeans. You're not claiming it's never a turn-on?'

He'd be lying if he claimed that. But he never thinks about it. He doesn't want to face it. It happens and he ignores it. For him the real turn-on has always been someone more mature. Like Isabel. Luck, not virtue. He's never been any good at saying no when the urge is strong. He struggles to find a way out of the moral maze. 'It's not right though. A teacher and a student could never be right.' He couldn't explain why it's not right but he's safe because there's no way Max can disagree. There are some things no one can admit to, even if they're happening.

'What makes it wrong? The age difference? What about Jill? You were what? Ten years older? Did that make it wrong? It's all relative, isn't it?'

'That's different. She wasn't a student.' Though Jack would be glad to forget the episode.

'The students we're talking about aren't children. They're nubile young women. They're lucky if they fall for me. Much better me than some clumsy, spotty fifteen-year-old.'

'What are you saying?'

Max shrugs. 'That it happens. That it will go on happening, however many rules Isabel makes.'

'But you wouldn't—'

Curled into the corner of the bench, relaxed and elegant, Max laughs his familiar easy laugh. 'I'm not confessing to criminal activity, if that's what's worrying you. I'm pointing out that girls are going to have that first experience. They're safer with me than with some testosterone-fuelled lad who can't wait to get their knickers down.'

Jack's struggling to think straight. He hopes Max is saying it's all in the mind. Nothing physical. Which is okay, isn't it? Only it means there is something going on between him and Dana. Something Isabel would never approve. Guilty knowledge. You'd think Max would want to keep it dark. *It*. Whatever it is he's up to. He should be worried. But the knowing seems to put Jack at a disadvantage. In his mind he sorts back for the moment when he could have made it clear where he stands. He can't find one. *It's all relative*. And that's how it seems. If he'd always been a saint himself, he could tell Max his risky games stink. But part of him understands too well. 'You'll never persuade Isabel to see it that way.' Not good, but the best he can manage.

'Probably not. But if we both work on her we can persuade her to loosen up. Get her to accept it's the way things are at TPH.' Max leans forward. He looks mischievous, the smile crinkling the skin around his eyes. 'Tell you what. Couldn't you flirt with her a bit? Get her into bed? Some casual sex would do wonders for her inhibitions. I can't risk it myself. She'd never let go.'

Max knows. Jack's convinced of it. Rage pumps in his chest and his breath comes hot and fast. He mustn't give way to it. If he lands a punch on Max, it'll give the game away completely. Through gritted teeth he manages, 'No, thanks.'

Max laughs a lot at that. 'I'm joking, Jack. I've got a lot of time for Isabel. I just think the sooner she gets used to our ways the better.'

Joking. That must be it. He gets up to go to the bar again. Max says he'll have a pint this time. On the way Jack diverts to the Gents. There's the familiar chill, the familiar whiff of ammonia, the familiar gush of running water. Normality. He's been muddling everything. The beer must be stronger than he thought. Max is a good mate of his. All that crap about students. The whisky talking. Fantasy, most of it. Everyone has fantasies. It's happening to him now. All he has to do is tell himself the story a bit differently and nothing's changed. He doesn't have to report the conversation to Isabel. Put the worst interpretation on it. Make wild accusations. Who'd believe them, if it came to the crunch? Max would start a grievance procedure, claiming he was the victim of character assassination. All hell let loose. No, it's unthinkable.

So he isn't going to think it.

Chapter 10

February 1982

'Move it.'

'Seconded.'

A minimal lifting of hands and the governors meeting proceeds at the pace of a slow bicycle race. I can't afford to give way to impatience. There are too many people to keep happy. Separately, it's achievable. Like particles they zoom around, following their own eccentric paths. Together, they collide, which sends them shooting off in unpredictable and alarming directions. Governors meetings act like some particle accelerator. The risk of accidents multiplies. The teacher-governors are friendly but quirky. Both enrage Gordon Lindsay, Toby Grigor-Smith with his membership of the Socialist Workers Party, Val Stephens with her feminism.

I remain alert through routine Item Six and potentially tricky Item Seven. Approval of the final Activities Week programme. Tricky because it's far too late to change it. Students have been allocated, bookings made, deposits paid. Max insisted I should take it through the governors. Odd, because normally he derides their function. I puzzle over this as I draw their attention to the activities likely to win their approval. Not

Jack's Graffiti and Murals, though he's enthused some of the most disaffected boys. This lot would never see the point. The Vice-Chair, Colin Blaine, singles out Field Archaeology for admiration, causing me private amusement. Nothing to link it to Max, which would have provoked instant denunciation. I'm praised for putting a stop to the nonsense of the First Year Residential Experience. I avoid Toby Grigor-Smith's eye and we're on to Item Eight: September Entry, 1982. Good news. The numbers are up, pleasing everyone. Two hundred and eighty, fitting tidily into ten classes. The satisfied murmurs are converted into a formal motion, congratulating me on the steps I've put in place to boost parental confidence. I allow myself to feel the relief of being on the final, downhill run.

Item Nine. The School Day. Gordon Lindsay's suggestion. I'd agreed promptly. Even eagerly. Resisting the Chair of Governors would look suspect and anyway I'm confident I can handle it. From the governors' perspective, the point of the discussion is how to extend the day. From my perspective, the point is to prove any extension is unnecessary. I'd explained to Toby that I was as opposed as he was to making teachers work longer hours, but maybe it wouldn't help our case to say that. He'd grinned and agreed.

I take a quick peek at my watch. Almost ten o'clock. The position on the agenda is deliberate. A gamble they'll all be too keen to get in a few drinks at the Conservative Club, or whatever, to keep it up for very long. Gordon is asking Colin to introduce it.

He starts with a tribute to me. 'I'd like to add my personal congratulations to the Headmistress.'

How many times have I asked to be called Headteacher? A waste of breath. Obviously.

'Already she has made a significant difference to the ghastly regime she inherited.'

I fix my gaze on the papers in front of me.

'But she'd be the first to admit there's more to do. I'm sure the governing body is with me when I say we want to back her all the way.'

Murmurs of 'Hear, Hear' from the governors, while I grit my teeth to endure.

The link between hours taught and academic achievement is, he declares, self-evident. But he can't leave it there. He attempts to prove the connection in a number of convoluted ways. It takes forever.

And then they all join in. They each want a turn. Like children queuing up for a helter-skelter. Which may well be a more educational experience. Their comments are inconsequential. They don't move on from the previous speaker. Or care that their precious point has been made many times before.

Gaynor Jones holds the floor for several minutes. She's a Parent Governor. In my innocence, I assumed as a breed they'd have the interests of the school at heart. Not at all. They seem to think they've been elected to get exactly what they want for their own children and the devil take the rest. Gaynor has a grievance. She looks aggrieved. Even the sharp outline of her geometric haircut seems to signal resentment. Her daughter Josie wanted to take both Art and Textiles at O-level. The timetable doesn't permit that. It is already too late, since she is in Year 5. The connection between this and the topic under discussion is tenuous. But Gaynor is in full flood. I switch off, thinking about tomorrow evening and Jack. A brief, vivid daydream. Self-indulgence. When Gordon steps in to thank her for her contribution, it takes me by surprise. Luckily, he has to do it three times before she splutters to an indignant conclusion, giving me time to focus again.

Gerald Findlater is next. Navy suit with a heavy chalk stripe. The public school he claims to have attended must have existed in some alternative universe. Where it was possible to study for more than twenty-four hours in any one day. And probably for more than seven days in a week. On top of which they played rugby and cricket. No wonder logic was squeezed out of the curriculum.

At last I have a chance to make my points. 'I'd like to focus on optimal use of time. Making every second count when our students are in school. For example, by having only four periods, instead of the usual eight, we reduce to a minimum the time spent in movement.' I do not allow myself to imply there is something morally degenerate about schools which offer opportunities to lurk in corridors. Though I'm tempted. Why shouldn't I be as irrational as everyone else at this meeting? It's getting late and I hurry on. 'Our extra-curricular programme provides an additional hour of learning four days out of five.'

Fitzroy Buchanan sneers. 'Extra-curricular activities.' He mouths the words as though he dislikes the taste of them. 'Hardly a byword for academic rigour.'

Gordon hates interruptions. He prides himself on being a forceful Chair. Not that he's ever been known to keep a discussion on track. A steely glare accompanies his sharp, 'One meeting, thank you.'

I respond to Fitzroy's sneer by lauding the flexibility extra-curricular activities offer, meeting individual needs. As opposed to one-size-fits-all. Then I play my trump card. Transport. The London rush-hour. In order to keep clear of it we can neither start earlier nor finish later. Resigned nods ripple round the table. Gordon is actually drawing breath to move on when Fitzroy Buchanan, having learnt his lesson, raises his hand.

Determined not to be overlooked, he leans forward in his chair. I glimpse the blue handkerchief in his top pocket which matches his true-blue tie. 'Mr Chairman,' he says. (He despises

Chair which he categorises as Women's Lib nonsense. He insisted on having that minuted at my very first governors meeting.) 'Mr Chairman. With your permission.'

To my disappointment, Gordon accepts the intervention. Maybe he limits himself to one snub per evening. Fitzroy lets rip. He's an aspiring Tory politician, so dedicated to making his mark that he's prepared to sit on any committee which will have him. Within seconds I realise it's a cause close to his heart. He launches into a vitriolic attack on the power of the unions and their destructive influence on every aspect of our lives. Assuming he's warming up to bash the teacher unions I glance at Toby, wondering if our agreement will hold. But it's the transport workers Fitzroy has in his sights. (I never realised they engineered the surge of commuters in and out of the metropolis. A cunning ploy to keep themselves in work, I assume.) Are we prepared, he demands, to allow these wreckers to dictate the length of the school day, on which higher standards depend? We owe it to the country to take them on.

There's another ripple of nodding, a good deal less welcome to me this time. Gordon, who's more of a pragmatist, is looking nonplussed. He's happy to let me respond.

'However much the governors agreed with Mr Buchanan's arguments, such a change is bound to take time. Don't we need to focus on what we can do meanwhile?' *Meanwhile.* Which tactfully implies that Fitzroy will prevail in the long run.

I can see most of them are realistic enough to let it go. A very little would tip the balance. So I tell them what's on my mind. The change I'm planning. No more Private Study taking up two lessons per week in Years Four and Five. Making ten percent extra teaching time.

It does the trick. To the governors the equation is simple. More teaching equals more learning.

Except Fitzroy is scowling. I've taken the shine off his campaign. Robbed him of the chance to make his mark in local politics. He can still pursue it, but the governors have lost interest. I allow myself to feel smug. It takes me a few moments longer to notice Val's looking thoughtful and Toby pugnacious. Maybe I'm not at my brightest after fourteen hours plus at work. Because even then I can't understand why.

Jack takes over my mind again. I drive home with that Elvis Presley song on the brain. *I can't help falling in love with you.* Just as well no one's watching me. They'd wonder what I have to smile about.

Coffee scorches on the hotplate. To offer it would trivialise the occasion. Max is not in the mood for social gestures. But I still can't grasp why he's so vehement in his opposition. I gaze at him, alarm rippling through my disbelief. 'I don't see the problem.'

This morning his usually mobile features look set. As though some bitter wind has frozen them. 'You announced it to the governors without any consultation,' he says, all friendliness drained out of his voice.

I'd gone home thinking that even for a governors meeting it was well up the tedium scale. Both in quantity and quality enough was said to try the patience of a saint. But I'd survived without mishap. Misplaced confidence. I got to school this morning to find myself in the middle of an almighty row. I managed a quick word with Val but before she could say more than 'You know what this is about?' (which of course I didn't), we were interrupted. I couldn't wait to meet with my Deputies. Okay, because I'd see Jack. But also in confident expectation of reassurance. Wrong. Jack remains silent while Max is talking as though I've started World War Three. It's irrational. 'Since when did we consult over every timetable change?' I ask.

'You seem intent on dismantling Will's legacy.'

Guilt stifles my response. I thought I was putting Private Study out of its misery. Max makes my act of mercy sound like cold-blooded murder.

'I've tried to support you, Isabel, Christ knows, but over this ...' His sentence hangs in the air.

I attempt clarification. 'So the point at issue is my failure to consult?'

'*One* of the points at issue,' he corrects. 'Not even a mention to me as your Deputy.' Jack shifts in his chair. Sufficient, it seems, to remind Max he is not the only Deputy. 'Had you heard about it, Jack?'

How will Jack respond? Both of us damned either way, I guess.

'Not until this morning,' Jack answers, opting for the truth.

'No consultation with either of us, giving us no opportunity to put the academic case or the pastoral one.'

What about Will's attitude to consultation? Undertaken to hear staff agree with him, not to have his time wasted by absurd objections, Max often jokes. So how is this so different? 'It was invented to fill a hole in the timetable,' I protest. 'There's no principle involved. I thought everyone would be glad to see the end of it.'

'There certainly is an issue of principle. The governors were against it from the word go. That speaks for itself.'

'So it doesn't matter what it is. If the governors are against it, we have to be for it.' Not a tactful response, I realise, as his expression grows more thunderous. Max, to whom a conciliatory stance appears as natural as breathing.

'Of course not. But it shows their ignorance.'

Mine too, by implication?

'They see education as force-feeding. The more you cram in the better. I thought you understood, Isabel.'

I intercept a glance between my two Deputies. It does me no good since I can't interpret it.

Max goes on, 'It's what students learn that matters.'

'And what do they learn in Private Study?' I resist saying, *Apart from how not to timetable.*

'To manage their own learning.'

I look at Jack, trying to fathom his silence. Maybe he agrees with Max and is keeping quiet out of loyalty to me. Or maybe he's on my side but afraid of giving some hint of our relationship. Or maybe it's connected with their meeting in the pub last Sunday. He said they had a few drinks, that was it, but he's seemed more wary around Max this week. More likely Jack's just being himself, never rushing into speech as I do.

Max meanwhile is busy expounding the virtues of Private Study. 'Look at the opportunities it provides for pastoral work. It's a time when I can take students out to talk to them individually. Why do you want to deny me that opportunity?'

I think of Dana, and the discomfort I felt when I burst in on them floods back as vividly as ever. 'I can see that's useful.' It's a struggle to get the words out. 'Is it sufficient justification for the curriculum time it takes up?'

'Depends how much value you place on pastoral care,' he replies.

I want to protest but he gives me no chance.

'A lot of these kids don't have a place to work at home.' He leans forward, spreading his hands. 'They're desperate for a space where the telly's not a constant background. Private Study offers them that.'

So now I'm insensitive to social issues as well as pastoral ones. I draw a deep breath. I do my best to sound conciliatory. And at the same time more casual. 'I accept the value of that, but I've got myself in a fix. The governors are enthused with the idea of getting rid of it. Where do you suggest we go from here?'

'Where do you go from here?' The second person sets a chilly distance between us. 'That's up to you.'

I struggle with anger. I can't believe it's come to this. And over something so entirely trivial.

Max sits back. He picks up his copy of the agenda – a waste of time that's proved to be – and folds it. He sharpens the crease by running his thumb and forefinger down it. 'Consult with staff,' he says. 'You're bound to do that, belated as it is. I think you'll find they're solidly against you on this one.' Perhaps the prospect pleases him. The tension around his mouth relaxes. 'If so, you'll have to go back to the governors and tell them Private Study is staying.'

'I'd have to explain why.'

Max is smiling now, his face alight with enthusiasm. 'Yes. It's a great opportunity for you. Tell Gordon and his pals your colleagues have vetoed it and you have no intention of over-ruling them.'

'I can't say that.' I glance at Jack who gives no indication he's listening to the pair of us. He's absorbed in covering his agenda with an elaborate doodle, bank after bank of clouds.

'But it's a great opportunity. You taking on the governors, the way Will used to all the time. Your chance to prove you're not their puppet.'

Can Max be serious? 'There is a difference,' I tell him. 'I assume Will stood his ground because he believed he was right and they were wrong. I'd do the same, on an issue of principle.'

His face shuts down. 'So you don't understand,' he murmurs.

Ignoring this, I turn to Jack. He doesn't meet my gaze. And I'm afraid. Afraid of what it may mean for the two of us, as well as for Head and Deputy. No choice but to go ahead and ask, 'What do you suggest?'

'Tricky,' he says. 'Max is right.'

I struggle with my disappointment.

'You have to consult. Doing it after the event puts you at a disadvantage. You'll have to spell it out. Do you just want to know what they think? Or will you stick with their decision? Either's honest.'

'Balls, Jack. Consultation's a farce if Isabel's going to say thanks very much and take not a blind bit of notice.'

Jack grins. 'The way Will used to, you mean?'

'It was different for him. He was an inspirational thinker.'

I bite my lip, determined to keep out of it.

Jack says, 'I agree it would go down better to tell staff it's up to them. If Isabel thinks she could live with that.' He gives me a quick glance. 'In my book it's not an issue of principle.'

Common sense at last. How have I managed to paint myself into a corner over it? 'I'll need to think about that,' I say, still not sure it's the molehill Jack's suggesting. If that's all it is, why is Max arguing as if it's a mountain?

Jack nods. 'No reason why you shouldn't make the case for getting rid of it. Talk to the students. They think it's crap – a total waste of time.'

I listen in wonder as the rest of my management meeting is consumed in the fierce heat of the row between my Deputies.

Friday evening. In a few minutes, when the children finally go out, I can be alone with Jack. I feel bound to observe the proprieties while they're around. Why does everything in their world start so late? I'm getting impatient. I enjoy being with him in the ordinary circumstances of our working day. Any meeting is brighter for his presence. Even a glimpse of him along a corridor makes my heart lift. But to have him here in the house and to have to wait is fuelling my libido. I give his hand a quick squeeze and force myself to step away, feeling like a teenager in the Sixties. Though even twenty years ago only old-fashioned parents would have imposed this level of constraint.

To distract myself I go back to the topic that's still bothering me. 'I don't understand why. How can it be so important to Max? Is it because it's become an issue between the two of us? Does he just want to win? That's normal enough. I like to win myself.'

Jack's grinning. 'Do you? I'd never noticed.'

I hit him. He grabs my hand and snatches a quick kiss. The door flies open. Laura on her way out. Seconds too late, thank goodness, to witness this extraordinary behaviour. Daniel is close behind her, off to spend what's left of the evening with Holly. I want them to like Jack. I try to read some reaction into their casual farewells but I can't.

As the front door slams, he settles himself on the sofa, stretching out his long legs. He urges me to join him.

'Be serious,' I order, tantalising myself as well as him. 'We need to finish the discussion before—' I break off, lacking the nerve to articulate what I'm happy to do. 'You said it from the beginning. There's no principle involved. Although Val Stephens seems to think there is.' I pause, puzzling over the fervour with which she urged me to stand firm.

'Max has it in for her. Maybe she's against it because he's all for it.'

'Maybe.' I try to come up with a more high-minded motive and fail. 'Max insists it's a good use of student time. I think it's a waste of student time and if we keep it I may look a fool with governors. So I have more to lose. Yet he's the one who's turned it into a massive row.'

'Maybe he's getting restless. He was running the place before you came. Before that, when Will was in charge, there was always some feud going on. Mainly between Will and the governors. Max tried to convince you to start that up again. Why?'

I relent and join him on the sofa. 'You tell me.'

Jack settles his arm around my shoulders. 'He likes it that way.'

'That's bizarre. You get on with him, don't you?' His eyes narrow. Reminded of their bitter argument I add, 'Or you did.'

'Still do.'

'After this morning?'

'That was nothing. It'll all be forgotten after a few drinks together.'

Which takes me back to last Sunday. I can't help being curious about their conversation in the pub. Did they talk about me? Did Jack give anything away? And the worst nightmare, did they joke about me? I can't lose the fear that our relationship matters less to Jack than it does to me. 'What's going on?' I ask. 'Hasn't he given you any clue?'

Jack's taken advantage of my abstraction to slide his hand between my thighs. 'You take the rows seriously. My guess is, Max doesn't. It's a game. He's getting bored with the harmony you've created. Like being in heaven. All that sitting around on clouds twanging a harp. Hell's more exciting.'

'So you don't think Max is on the side of the angels?'

Jack releases me abruptly and gets to his feet. 'Interesting question. But since you ask me, no, I don't.'

He sounds solemn. Solemn enough to send prickles of alarm down my spine. I ought to pursue it. Except he's standing in front of me, taking both my hands to draw me out of my seat and into his arms. And like a teenager with her first boyfriend, I'm incapable of resisting the invitation.

Chapter 11

I take a tentative sip from the glass of red wine on my desk. Australian Shiraz. Left over from Sunday and already it's Thursday. But it tastes okay. I poured it to celebrate. This afternoon staff voted to abolish Private Study. Problem solved. Except already I'm grappling with the next one.

When James Greville phoned to tell me we could have the improvements to the music area, providing they could start next week, I agreed at once.

'Bless you, Isabel,' he said. 'If I don't spend this cash by the end of the financial year, I lose it. You are the most flexible woman I know.'

'I hope you regard flexibility as a virtue,' I retorted.

'You have given me no opportunity to test your virtue, more's the pity.' His familiar nonsense.

The work will take three classrooms out of use. I'm juggling classes and spaces. A job for Max but as things are I couldn't ask him. Since the argument, it's delicate between us.

The doorbell. Faint up here in my attic study but unmistakeable. Jack. It can't be anyone else. It's as though the strength of my longing has conjured him here. Pushing back my chair I rush downstairs, pausing on the first floor to tell the children I'll get it.

I'm smiling my welcome as I open the door.

'Max,' I say. A single wintry syllable. But maybe it only sounds that way to me because I know how different my greeting would have been. The vote solved only half the problem. The other half is here, on my doorstep.

'Hi, can I come in?'

I've already stepped back. Which he could interpret as an invitation. And in any case I'm too much of a captive to convention to tell him to go away. He crosses the threshold, confident though more solemn than usual.

I ask, 'Would you like a coffee or a beer?' Convention again.

'I could murder a beer.' He follows me into the kitchen.

What makes him think he can drop in when he feels like it? Resenting it as I fetch him a beer. Bought for Jack, but he can't know that. I take one for myself. I need to have something to do with my hands.

'Have a seat,' I say.

He sits down at one end of our big kitchen table. I can't take the opposite end. It would look confrontational. And ridiculous. So I take a chair at right angles to him.

'I'm not interrupting anything, am I?'

Maybe there's more chill emanating from me than I thought. I say, 'I was wrestling with the timetable.' I pour beer into my glass. Max ignores the one I handed him and drinks straight from the can. 'Sorting out how we can cope when the work begins in the music area on Monday.' There's an edge of criticism in my voice.

'I'd have done that.' The tone is soothing. The tone of the Max I thought I knew. 'Why didn't you ask me?'

'I created the problem by agreeing the timing with James Greville.' I take a mouthful of beer. It tastes malty and bitter on my tongue. 'And it seemed awkward the way things are.'

Instantly he's grave again. 'It's what I came to talk about.'

But he doesn't talk about it. Only gazes down the length of the table.

I wait for him to start, studying his profile. Noticing his hair, cut neatly around his left ear. More grey than dark in it there. And noticing for the first time the definite line of his lips. Michelangelo might have chiselled them. His nose is delicate for a man. Though perhaps that's because Jack's stronger features have become the norm for me.

Even when he speaks, he doesn't turn to look at me. 'I don't want to be at odds with you.'

My turn to be silent. I won't be wrong-footed into apologising.

'The school's much more important than either of us.'

It's unfair to come here to talk school. Then I remember I invited him the first time to do just that. I offer a neutral 'No question.'

'It's divisive.' In profile it's hard to tell, but I think he's frowning. 'People have been coming up to me and saying they're on my side. I say, "What side? There are no sides." I doubt it fools anyone.'

'There are two sides,' I remind him. 'Yours and mine.' I wish he'd look at me. I hear what he says without having the least idea what he's thinking. 'We had a vote four hours ago.'

He shakes his head, a slow, regretful shake. 'The vote didn't help. A divided staff. When we ought to be united against all the external threats.'

Wasn't it ever thus? Will thrived on dissension. Manipulated it to his advantage, according to Val Stephens, who has a different take on the school's past. Only I neither like nor want it that way. So I admit Max is right. But I'm determined to challenge him too. 'I still don't understand why you made such a big issue of it.'

He turns to stare at me. 'How can you ask that?' Disbelief in every syllable. 'Staff are judging you all the time. Appearances matter as much as actions. More, probably, when we're in the business of winning hearts and minds.'

'So it doesn't matter whether I'm doing the right thing or not? Only that it should look that way?'

'That's right.'

I can't believe what I'm hearing.

'Because the High School depends upon what all of us do. The sum of those actions is much greater than anything you can do on your own. Lose staff loyalty and you can wave good-bye to achieving anything.'

The trouble is, I see the logic of what he's saying. But if I surrender the point, what next? 'Loyalty? You're my Deputy and yet you became the leader of the opposition.'

He looks hurt. 'I'm always on the same side. Will's side. You were the one that crossed over to the enemy, dismantling what he'd created. I accept you said it off the top of your head. Hoping to placate the governors.' His fingers spread, flat against the table. 'You couldn't admit you'd made a mistake.'

I swallow some more beer, to give myself time. It doesn't taste any better. 'It wasn't a mistake. I still think it's right for Private Study to go. But as for dismantling Will's legacy, it's the last thing I want to do. I want Thomas Paine High to be the school he meant it to be.'

'Whereas I don't?'

'Of course you do, Max. It's still a dream though. Before I came, I thought it would be perfect. The school I'd read about in his books. Stupid of me. You can only ever work towards per-fection.'

He's looking straight ahead again as he says, 'You reckon you're improving it then?'

I nod. A small nod. I don't want to claim too much.

'Is there another school anywhere to touch it? Anywhere else where kids' learning is enabled by the way the whole place is organised? Where competition and aggression having been taken out of the equation? Where students and teachers feel part of one close-knit community? That's what Will had the genius to conceive and that's what he created.'

Max is right, of course. I'm miles out of my league. Yet some obstinate devotion to the truth as I see it compels me to say, 'Will believed in continuous improvement, didn't he? You said it at the staff meeting. He wouldn't want what he did to be set in stone.'

'Not every change is an improvement. I'm a good enough historian to know that.'

I twist my glass round and round, waiting for him to develop his criticism. I'm astonished when he turns towards me, arm along the back of his chair, smiling the smile it's so hard to resist. The skin creases around his eyes as he holds my gaze for the extra moment that makes me feel I matter to him.

'Isabel,' he's saying, 'you meant it for the best. We've let the disagreement get out of hand. I argued too fiercely. Forgive me.'

For a few seconds I try to hang on to my annoyance. Then I smile back at him. I'm not quite sure how it's happened. Except that to do anything else would be churlish. Besides, I need Max on my side. If only because he has the gift of enchanting every-one, me included.

'I guess we both care too much,' he says. 'And that makes it harder.'

'It must be tough for you, after working with Will the way you did.'

His face abruptly sad, he murmurs agreement.

'I said I'd abide by the vote. Private Study will have to go.'

'Yes.' He draws the word out, as though he's thinking. Then he smiles again. 'We'll work it out together. We'll get over it somehow.'

I feel an immense relief. I can't afford to lose my faith. The faith which drives my professional life. Faith in other people. Now it's all back in proportion. 'Thanks for coming round, Max,' I say. 'How about another beer?'

'Why not?'

I pass him a can. I don't help myself to another. I've drunk less than a third of the first one.

There's a faint hiss as he opens the can. 'I've been meaning to update you on the Dana situation,' he says. 'I knew you'd be wondering.'

My hands close around my glass. 'Why should I wonder?' I ask quickly.

'You were concerned, weren't you? When I explained the problem. Her difficulties at home.'

'That?' I say. 'Yes. Naturally, I was concerned.'

'She's been coming to see me twice a week. Sometimes more. Perhaps you've noticed?'

It feels like he's taunting me. But why would he do that when he's come round to apologise? My teeth are clenched. With an effort I relax my jaw muscles to tell him no, I hadn't noticed.

'She came yesterday with good news. Romance over. Her mother's realised the guy's a freak.'

'Very good news,' I say. I look at him directly. 'It means you won't need to see her any more, doesn't it?'

'I don't know about that. I wouldn't want to withdraw my support prematurely. Though I've been very sensitive to the gender issue. Since you gave me that hint.' He sighs. 'Adolescents are so vulnerable.'

'And impressionable,' I say. 'Teachers have a heavy responsibility.'

As warnings go, it's feeble enough. But I can't accuse him again. I've got no more evidence. He'd claim his frankness proved his innocence. I raise my glass and swallow more of the bitter draught.

Mildly flustered, my clothes disarranged, I kiss Jack and draw apart from him, admitting I'm embarrassed.

'What's embarrassing you?'

'The extent to which you arouse me. Which I can't hide from you.'

'Don't you think I mean to arouse you?'

I glance away. 'Yes, I suppose so.'

'If it didn't work, how would I feel?'

I bury my face in the soft twill of his shirt, laughing. Sitting up, I button my blouse. 'I came to talk as well,' I say.

'As well? So you came for some lovemaking too?'

I'm laughing again as I tell him certainly not. After a bit more teasing he goes to fetch the bottle of wine I brought.

While he's opening it, I say, 'What did you think about our management meeting yesterday?'

'Fine.' The cork comes out with a faint plop.

'Harmony restored,' I say. 'I always have this need to prove myself to Max. Because he'll be thinking all the time how he would do it.'

Jack fills our glasses. 'Not if he has any sense. What good does that do him?'

'How can he help it?'

'By moving on,' he says, taking my hand. 'If he can't do it in his head, he needs to do it literally. Get another job. It would be much better if he left. For you. For everyone.'

I glance at him in surprise. He's never suggested it before. 'You'd miss him, wouldn't you?'

'Not particularly. He's a bit of a loose cannon these days.'

I'm distracted by the way Jack's stroking the back of my hand with his thumb. I draw it away as I say, 'I don't expect him to agree with me all the time. We should be more like critical friends.'

'Will demanded total allegiance. That's how he achieved so much. Because we were all committed to the same goals.'

'Fine as long as you're quite sure you're always right. I'm not. Isn't it possible to have total allegiance to working together to get it right?' As I say it, it sounds unlikely. Too cautious to inspire enthusiastic loyalty.

Jack strokes my cheek. Perhaps he's trying to console me. 'It's more honest and more interesting your way. But harder, I'd say.'

'You trusted Will? Totally?'

He frowns as though he's trying to understand himself. 'I needed to. I wouldn't let myself see anything wrong. Not about him. Not about Thomas Paine High. In Will's presence, it was easy to believe.'

How am I expected to follow that? 'So it was more than admiring his ideas. Or believing what he said. You believed *in* him.'

'Sounds crazy when you say it like that. I guess he had charisma.'

Total trust. That was how Will did it. In a way I never can. I put down my wine and slip my hand into Jack's. I need its warmth, curved around mine. 'How about Max?' I ask. 'The anointed successor?'

'He's not creative, the way Will was. You have more ideas than Max does.'

'Max has charisma too,' I insist.

'It's when it's needed, isn't it? Thomas Paine High needed

Will when everyone was against the school. We needed Max when Will was dying. Not now. Not now you're here.'

'*Cometh the hour, cometh the man*,' I murmur. I hope Jack's right. Though the hour might come when Max is needed again. Through some disastrous failure on my part.

Jack has a drink of wine, looking thoughtful. 'Trust isn't the same as belief, is it? You either believe, or you don't. You can trust people in some ways. Not in others.'

I jump to a conclusion. 'That's how you are with Max?'

'Yes. Working with him, seeing him in close-up, he's a mixture. Like most of us.' He sets down his glass and gazes into it. 'I trust what he does more than what he says.'

My turn to study my glass, while I digest this. 'But you get on well with him? You're friends?'

'Friends? I wouldn't say so. We play squash together. Or against each other. Meet for a drink. That sort of thing.'

Men with men. Relationships which are more hearty than heartfelt. 'So you wouldn't be open with each other?'

'Christ, no. I don't go in for that much.'

Sitting beside him on the sofa, I gaze across at the painting which dominates the room. At the shed door. Half-open. And half-closed. Revealing and not revealing what lies within. I want Jack to be open with me. Why won't he tell me what happened between him and his partner? I need to know. Because even as I'm caressing him I can see Max. He stayed for ages the other evening, drinking beer in my kitchen. I hear his warm drawl as he said, 'Poor old Jack, one relationship after another. He just can't help himself. Endless entanglements. I keep clear of all that.' Malice, I told myself. He had an agenda. To get under my skin. Jack doesn't trust what Max says, so why should I? Yet I crave reassurance. 'You keep in touch with your partner?' A clumsy question.

'Ex-partner. Spasmodically. About the kids. She doesn't want to know.'

I have to come right out with it then. 'There isn't anyone else?'

'Anyone else?' He's frowning. 'You mean, do I do this with you on Fridays and Sundays and with A.N. Other on Mondays and Thursdays? Can't you tell how important you are to me?' He kisses me on the mouth, very gently and very tenderly.

I look into his eyes. Flecks of colour making an indeterminate hazel, the lashes unexpectedly long. I think I can tell. So I believe him. Even though he hasn't answered the question. It's Jack I trust. More than I trust Max.

Chapter 12

April 1982

The woman is already in the room, unannounced. In the doorway Linda is attempting explanation and apology. Fingers
spread, I gesture acceptance to her. Protocol can't stand in the
way of parental concern. My secretary backs out, closing the
door softly behind her.

'Have a seat. I'm sorry, I don't know your name.'

'Peterson. Deborah Peterson.' She sounds breathless.
Outside it's pouring. April shower doesn't begin to describe it.
Rivulets of water are still trickling off her mac, her bags, her
umbrella. Her dark hair is wind-blown. She sinks into a chair.

'How can I help you?'

'It's my daughter Rachel. I'm sure it's serious. I couldn't
rest until I'd seen you.'

Serious. Illness? Accident? 'What's happened to your daughter,
Mrs Peterson?'

She moves from agitation to alarm. 'Happened? I do hope
nothing's happened. You don't think it has, do you?'

'I don't understand. Could you explain from the beginning?'

'I'm sorry. It was such a shock. I can't think straight.' She closes her eyes and clasps her hands, as though she's struggling for composure. Then she reaches for the tapestry bag beside her. She draws out something wrapped in a plastic carrier. She leans forward to hand me an exercise book. One of the hard-covered kind. A5 size. Stuck all over with labels, some handwritten, some printed in different colours and fonts: 'RACHEL PETERSON', 'PRIVATE', 'KEEP OUT', 'STRICTLY PRIVATE'.

For a moment I hold it in my hands, looking at it. Then I look at Mrs Peterson. I'm frowning a bit. Enquiring. Puzzled. Not wanting to commit myself by what I say or do.

'I wasn't prying,' she says defensively, though I've made no accusation. 'That's not the way things are between me and Rachel. I was changing the sheets and it was under the pillow. Monday's the day I do it. It fell open as I picked it up.'

The book remains in my hands. Closed. 'You haven't spoken to Rachel about it?'

'No, no. She's here. In school.'

'How old is Rachel?'

'Fifteen. Just fifteen. She's sensible. Mature for her age. That's why it was such a shock. Though fifteen is still very young, isn't it?'

I nod. I glance from her to the exercise book. 'What she's written makes you anxious?'

'Anyone would be, reading that. Once I'd read it I couldn't just forget about it.' She shifts her chair a little nearer mine. 'You'll see when you read it. You can't defend it.'

'You want me to read it? Now?'

'Look at it at least.'

I have no basis for making a judgement. I don't know Deborah Peterson. I can't place her daughter. I don't know about the morality of reading something not intended for my eyes. I may regret it, but by this time I'm far too curious to hand the book back unread. I start at the beginning. It's a journal. Events, thoughts, feelings. Feelings mostly. Written, for the first few pages at least, in a very careful hand, with circles instead of dots over the i's and a great many plumply-shaped exclamation marks. Is there any teenage girl who hasn't done something similar? A year or two ago I used to be careful to avoid coming across anything Laura might have written.

I close the exercise book. I don't want to seem dismissive so I don't hand it straight back. I hold it in my left hand as I say, 'Your daughter's diary. If there are things in it which worry you, don't you think you should talk to Rachel about it?' Because not knowing them how can I tell whether it's a proportionate re-action? But Deborah Peterson's face expresses angry dismay. I try another tack. 'Would you like to make an appointment to talk to Rachel's tutor? We're always happy to do what we can to help, even if it's not strictly school business.'

She snatches the exercise book out of my hand and turns over the pages, saying, 'You don't understand, Mrs Lincoln. It is school business. You ought to be as worried as I am.' Her voice is shrill with accusation. 'Here. Read this.' And she thrusts the open book back to me.

From long habit I read at speed. I think it takes me only sec-onds to scan three or four pages. So it's not unconvincing when I stare at the page without speaking. I might still be reading. My heart's thumping and my brain's racing. I must have time. Time to get my thoughts straight. Time to talk to Jack. Time to think through all the consequences. But what will Deborah Peterson do meanwhile? Who will she consult? How much will she gossip? What will she say to Rachel?

I take a deep breath. I want to sound calm. In control. 'You're right. It is school business. I need to read all of it. May I keep it until tomorrow?'

She nods. A brief look of satisfaction – that she's right and I'm wrong – crosses her face. Then alarm washes over it again. 'Yes. Read it all and then see what you think of him. It's not right.'

'I understand why it's upset you so much, but I need to have all the facts before I make any decisions. Or take any action. I suggested you should talk to Rachel but I see now that wouldn't be a good idea.' Would I keep silent, if it were my daughter? Unlikely. 'Could you come and see me tomorrow morning? We need to discuss what action you want me to take. And afterwards we can talk to Rachel.'

'Yes,' she says, but she sounds uncertain. 'What time tomorrow?'

I don't bother to check my appointments. This has to take precedence. 'Eight-thirty.'

'Yes, I can manage that. But what will you do?'

I've no idea. I need to avoid the question yet I want to sound reassuring. 'We have to establish the facts. There are legal issues, so we both need to be careful. Neither of us can do anything until we've talked it through tomorrow.' Deborah Peterson's face remains creased with anxiety. 'Thank you for coming straight to me with this. It was very wise of you.' I stand up.

She gets to her feet as well, but reluctantly. She's dissatisfied. I don't know what else I can offer her.

Finally, after more vague murmurs from me, she takes her departure.

God knows it's not good news. I wish it had never happened. But somewhere a small exultant voice is repeating *Got him. Got him. Got him.*

When I realise I have to teach I feel incapable of it. I'll never be able to switch my thoughts away from that exercise book. But as soon as we start on 'My Last Duchess' the poem and the students' response to it absorb me. Except as we talk about the Duke's motive, I find myself questioning my own. Promising myself I'll read with an open mind, I focus on the class again.

Lesson over, I can't wait to get back to my room. Lunch hour. The corridors too crowded for rapid progress. Windows fogged with condensation as outside the torrential rain continues. Fifteen hundred students penned indoors. Tension in the air. It's the weather. Or I'm generating it. My room at last.

I'd thrust the journal into the top drawer of my desk, though I'm not sure who I was concealing it from. Or why. I close my door – a signal I'm not to be interrupted – before I take it out. I'll read every word. From the beginning. Within seconds I'm impatient. I flick on to find something more significant.

History!!! The best lesson yet. Alice away (thank you,
Alice!) so M sat down beside me to talk about my essay!!
He said it was brilliant! Stayed for ages going through it with me.
Everyone else dead jealous. From Ruth wanting to know every word
he said, to Sharon being mean about my new shoes. M so close, even
sleeves touching sometimes! Wish it had been summer. Bare arms –
imagine! I could smell his aftershave. Saturday I'll go into Boots. I'm
sure I'll know which it is. Don't care how much ...

Okay, I'm convinced. Rachel has a major crush. I'm looking for evidence. Against Max. Against my own Deputy Head. I want proof of sexual misconduct with students.

Want it?

Yes.

I know it's happening but until I can prove it I have to pretend it isn't. Act as though I trust him. As though I believe his denials. God knows how many girls he's exploiting and damaging. So the need to have the truth out in the open is urgent.

I am meticulous. I tear a sheet of file paper into strips. I put in markers tracing the development of the relationship, until the journal bristles with them. I try to establish dates. Tricky because Rachel often uses only days of the week. I resist putting any interpretation on her breathless accounts of lessons and encounters around school. I withhold suspicion about the so-called pastoral appointments with him during Private Study. All of it easy to explain away as her stuff. Until he invites her to his flat. The same excuse: his precious potted plants. But he's being careful the first time. He asks Alice as well. Students do go to teachers' homes. It's that sort of school. Rachel considers claiming Alice has been struck by sudden illness. The journal doesn't make it clear whether Alice refuses to play ball or whether it's a failure of nerve on Rachel's part. Anyway, they go together. Rachel's ecstatic about the intimacy of seeing Max on home ground. She records every detail. That way she can make sure she gets it right when she imagines him there.

I pause in my reading and watch the rain splashing up from the window-sill. Plenty of evidence that Max is encouraging an adolescent in a way which is grossly irresponsible. Rachel is at risk of serious hurt, even permanent psychological damage. I ought to be worrying about her more than about trapping Max. Except trapping him is the only way to protect others.

A nicely-brought-up girl, who prefers euphemism. I re-read ambiguous passages. The first kiss is clear enough. Max takes it slowly all through March. More and more caressing. Rachel's attempts to put her arousal into words. Then a darker note:

> ... crazy when I've wanted it more than anything else in the world forever and when he asked what the matter was I couldn't tell him. But being Max he understood anyway. He explained it all to me. Our society with all the hang-ups about sex, making us feel bad about something wonderful. The killjoys, he called them, who try to convince us anything we enjoy is wicked. They grudge other people

*what they haven't got. It has to be a secret not because we're doing
anything wrong but because they'd try to stop us if they could.
Something which makes two people so happy couldn't possibly be
wrong. The way he put it I knew he was right and I had to let go
of the weird feelings I had about it.*

I slap the journal closed and press my palms hard against its
covers. Max and his sly, persuasive tongue. I want to rush out
and challenge him. But I have to get it right. I have to read on
and find out as much as I can so that this time there's not the
tiniest gap for him to wriggle out of it.

Being wicked becomes their code. For heavy petting, I think.
Then a week ago, as far as I can work out, they had sex. Lots of
disbelief.

*Did it really happen? After all my dreams and daydreams? I can
hardly believe IT happened for real!!!*

But I believe it. It makes sense of Rachel's carelessness.
Leaving her strictly private journal under the pillow on the day
her mother always changes the sheets. It's become too much for
her. She wanted to be found out. It adds to my anxiety for her.
It helps my case, though. Makes it more likely she'll be ready to
talk to me.

How carefully has Deborah Peterson read it? A lot depends
on what she made of it. I don't fancy going through it word by
word, trying to agree exactly what it means.

And then I remember.

What's happened to your daughter?

Happened? I do hope nothing's happened.

Happened. Sex. Isn't that what she was talking about? She
doesn't think it's gone that far. So tomorrow morning am I
going to pick out key phrases and try to convince her she's mistaken? It's cruel to try to convince her it's even worse than she

imagines. What will that do to the mother-daughter relationship? Deborah Peterson already thinks Max's behaviour is unforgivable. Or maybe I shouldn't hesitate, because Rachel wanted her mother to find the diary and learn the truth. And from my point of view worse is better.

Alternatives chase one another through my thoughts. I can't decide which one to hang on to. My only certainty is that this time I have to win the single argument that matters. The argument with Max.

Each time I've accused Max he's side-stepped out of it. It makes me furious to remember how easily he did it. What was he thinking as he invented his easy lies? He knows how wrong it is. Any teacher does. He must feel some guilt. And to take such a risk ... For such brief satisfaction. I shiver, imagining the fierce longing which drives him to act as he does. But this time a parent is accusing him. This is my opportunity to make sure it will never happen again. To hang Max Truman out to dry. Already I have it all worked out in my mind. Faced with the written evidence, he'll see this is as serious as it could be. Sex with an under-age student. He'll realise I know the truth, even if Deborah Peterson doesn't. So he'll admit it. It's the least he can do. He'll resign at once. I don't stop to think beyond that. My need to share it all with Jack is overwhelming. I'm out of my chair and on my way in a single urgent movement.

Standing in Jack's empty office I come to a full stop. The usual clutter. Papers overflowing his in-tray. A rucksack hunched in the corner beside his squash racket. Artwork covering every available surface. Including a pile of drawings on his desk chair. On top I recognise his handwriting on a sheet of file-paper. Instructions for the teacher who was covering his lesson. How could I forget? Jack's away on a course for three days. I urged him to go though I knew I'd miss him. But not like this.

Not with this blend of alarm and desolation. Because there's no one else I can talk to about it. While he's still my Deputy Head there's no way I can discuss it with anyone else in school. It would be dynamite if it got out.

Will be dynamite. *When* it gets out.

How will his colleagues react? They're bound to rally to his support. Except by the time it's common knowledge he'll have admitted his guilt and resigned.

So there won't be a cause to rally to.

Not my problem any longer. The legal system will take over. A prosecution for having sex with a minor. A prison sentence, bullied as a sex offender by the other inmates. I don't want that. How likely is it? Deborah Peterson won't want to put Rachel through the ordeal of giving evidence. Rachel will resist doing anything which might harm Max. So nothing too serious will happen to him. Apart from losing his job. Why should I feel guilty? He'll bounce back, the way he always does. It's not my problem.

Down the deserted corridors I walk slowly back to my own room. As I walk I start to imagine what I'll say to Max. Stupid because no conversation ever happens the way you plan it. I can't help myself. He'll be smiling at me as he comes into the room not knowing what I'm going to say.

Then all smiles stopped together.

Do I share the Duke's problem? His chilly resentment of 'A heart – how shall I say? – too soon made glad'?

That's nonsense. Whatever my personal feelings, I have to act. Yet I can't help seeing Max as a fallen angel. Brightness turned to darkness. So many good qualities. His skills with students. The warm readiness of his approval. His unique way of seeing the world, making light of apparent disaster.

None of that outweighs the terrible harm he's doing. On the contrary. It makes him uniquely dangerous.

❑ ❑ ❑

'I couldn't believe it when I got the phone call from Deborah Peterson to say she wasn't coming.' I hold both Jack's hands as I pour it all out to him.

'What reason did she give?'

'She'd talked to Rachel about it. She was sorry, she knew I'd asked her not to. But her daughter saw her walking out of school and insisted on knowing why she'd come.'

'How did that change her mind?'

What I'm telling Jack seems to be troubling him even more than I expected. I lean forward to kiss him. 'Rachel convinced her it was pure fantasy. Not what had happened. Just what she'd imagined.'

'Maybe it was.' There's a note of hope in Jack's voice. 'Isn't that the most likely explanation?'

I draw back from him. 'How can you say that? She's been to his flat. As I have. She couldn't have invented what she described.'

'Did you argue that with the mother?'

'It was awkward, over the phone. I tried to persuade her to come in and talk to me anyway.' I sigh. 'She was adamant. She'd wasted enough of my time.'

'I guess she wanted to forget the whole business.'

'Exactly, that's the problem. My clinching argument, we have to stop him because he's having sex with your daughter, that wouldn't work. She'd still insist it was all invention. What was I going to do? Read out extracts over the phone in an attempt to convince her? She was embarrassed enough as it was.'

'So you gave up?'

'I gave up with her. When I said I'd still need to speak to Rachel, she tried to talk me out of that.'

'But you saw Rachel?'

'I had to, didn't I? Even taking it all on face value, I still couldn't ignore what she'd done. Her fantasies, so-called, were putting a teacher's career at risk. Besides, I saw her coming out of Max's room.'

'What! When was that?'

'After school Monday. At the time I logged it as yet more damning evidence. Helping my case.'

'Come on. You can't be suspicious just because you spot a student leaving someone's office.'

'Can't I? You'd be surprised.'

'I mean, it's not evidence of any wrongdoing. Why did you think Rachel was there?'

'She went to warn him.'

Jack shakes his head, objecting. 'But that was before she'd spoken to her mother.'

'She guessed her mother had found her journal. It's more than possible she deliberately left it under her pillow for her mother to find.'

'Why would she do that, for Christ's sake?'

'She was bothered about it but undecided. She couldn't decide whether she wanted her mother to know or not. She must have discussed it with Max. He persuaded her it had to be a secret.'

'How can you know that?'

'I couldn't shake her. Students usually let something slip. She was completely unshakeable. Insisting she'd invented the whole thing. That was all it was. Pure invention. A silly child-ish fantasy. Everybody had them, didn't they? Only she'd been crazy enough to write hers down and start all this trouble.'

Jack draws me close. He's playing with the hair at the back of my neck. 'You don't believe her.' Statement, not question.

'No. She wasn't appalled enough.'

'How do you mean?'

'When I suggested bringing Max in. She said it would be very embarrassing. But she wasn't appalled.'

'I know Rachel. She's tough. Intelligent.'

'I believe you. She asked me to return the diary.'

'So you don't have it any more?'

'She was very insistent. You can guess who put her up to that. But I refused to give it back. I pointed out her "fantasy" was dynamite. She could cause serious trouble for herself and for my Deputy Head if it fell into the wrong hands. I wasn't prepared to take that risk.'

'Why did you want to hang on to it?'

'For the reason I gave Rachel.' Which is only a partial truth, but I'm not bound to share everything.

'So you got to keep the diary, only it's no use as evidence because Rachel denies it all.'

'Yes, she won. Apparently. And I lost. Apparently. There was nothing I could do if she wouldn't play ball.'

'Maybe it's for the best.'

'Are you serious?'

'Yes. It's better in every way to accept that Max is innocent.'

Happiness. I relax into it like a warm bath. But it's draining away from me as I wake. A dream only. I try to hang on to it but there's nothing to grasp. No events. If I lie still maybe I can drift back into it. Instead, as memory returns the questions start to pound in my head again. I twist onto my side. Jack. A solid presence in my bed. Fast asleep. Why is he untroubled by the doubts that vex me into wakefulness? The resentment of the sleepless towards the sleeper swells within me.

Yet I urged him to stay, after weeks of refusing to allow him to share my bed when the children were in the house. It was all my stuff anyway. Hannah and Daniel aren't stupid. They'll have drawn their own conclusions long since.

After three sleepless nights I needed Jack to guarantee me one night of oblivion. Even more than the urgent lovemaking which preceded it, I wanted untroubled sleep. I sense without checking the clock that it's lasted no more than a few minutes. I'm caught up again in dreadful uncertainty. Since I've lost all hope of proving the contrary, I want to convince myself that Max is innocent. Jack argues it may all be Rachel's fantasy. It would be easier if I could believe that. Believe it was all her fevered adolescent imagination. Then I could stop tormenting myself.

Max talks a lot about trust. Is that the problem? A failure of trust on my part? But I can't stop the doubts. I doubt everything. I don't even know what's right and what's wrong any more.

Jack's deep breathing is driving me crazy. I shift with an impatient desire to rouse him. He sleeps on.

Could it be the suspicion is all in my mind? I was sure I had hard evidence. But it's slipped out of my grasp. Has Max crossed the line between caring teacher and gross exploitation? Even the line wavers. Jack doesn't see it my way. That's what worries me most of all. He wants me to forget the whole business. Because I'm being unfair to Max? Or because it's dangerous to make an enemy of him? Or because of the harm it might do the school? Relationships are different at Thomas Paine High. There are no rigid barriers between teachers and students. We're all learners together, engaged in a common enterprise. Maybe there's nothing suspect about that level of closeness. Maybe it's not sinister, except in my eyes.

Or maybe it's as dangerous as the governors think it is.

But that would mean abandoning my whole approach to education. So perhaps Jack's right. Safer to stifle my suspicions. Press the pillow down on them until they stop wriggling.

I turn my own pillow over for the umpteenth time.

How can I carry on with Max as though nothing has happened? Is he worried I might still challenge him? Or laughing up his sleeve because he knows he's got away with it? Will it make him more cautious? Or does risk excite him? He's the kind of person who likes to live on the edge of danger. Being a Head is hard enough without this. I want to succeed so much. Not just because I can't bear failing but because Thomas Paine High needs me to. Even after a year, I remain the interloper. Isn't there some resentment lurking underneath, colouring my judgement? I never worked with Will, never even met him. He didn't choose me as his heir apparent. I'm not even the right gender. And there are so many things Max does so well, with an effortlessness I could never equal. His judgements are always generous, making my honesty seems harsh in comparison. No wonder he has the support of so many of our colleagues. Beside such a role model I shall always be found wanting. I'd have to be a saint not to wish sometimes there was a flaw in the perfection.

So much charm. But doesn't he overdo it? Misuse it for his own dark purposes? It makes me feel uncomfortable to see him with female students and that can't be right. Shouldn't it worry him? Shouldn't he feel it's wrong?

'That's Max,' Jack said.

'That's Max?' I echoed, voice shrilling with indignation.

Yet I know exactly what Jack means. The flattery of total focus. As though at that moment there's no one else in the universe for Max Truman. He does it all the time. With everyone. No wonder fifteen-year-olds flutter round him, like moths around a lamp. That same bemused blundering. It's not his fault, if that's the way he is. And since he beguiles me too, doesn't that prove innocence? It would be pure lunacy to start imagining I'm the target of his seduction.

Why should I see believing the best about my Deputy Head as a temptation? If I had any sense I'd forget all about my suspicions.

Until something else happens. Something there can be no argument about.

Until, not *unless*. Which means I believe he's guilty, doesn't it?

Chapter 13

May 1982

Isabel doesn't have hang-ups about nakedness. Hands behind her back she unhooks her black bra, glossy dark against the creamy paleness of her skin. She stands smiling slightly, within arm's reach of Jack. There's no problem about him staying the night and appearing at breakfast. Since last week she's given up the not-in-front-of-the-children crap. His erection hardens. He wants her. But as she steps towards him he flinches away. She notices. Maybe that's what he intends. Why has he been such a fucking coward? Why didn't he tell her as soon as he realised? He can't start on it now.

Isabel's taken a step back and a frown's replaced the smile. 'What's the matter?'

He's caught. If he dodges the question she'll be imagining all sorts of things. 'School stuff. We can talk about it tomorrow.'

'Jack, something going on at school that's serious enough to put you off sex and you tell me we can talk about it tomorrow! You must be joking.'

She's grinning. Teasing. But there's a glint in her eye. 'It's just the training session,' he mutters, offhand. 'For Personal and Social Education. It can wait until tomorrow.'

'What about it?'

'Just some people saying it's their own time and they're not coming.'

'Some? How many?'

'A few. Quite a few.'

'How many? Six? Ten?'

Jack curses his clumsiness. He's been meaning to tell her for several days. He meant to do it yesterday morning. And he absolutely meant to do it four hours ago. As soon as he saw her. Instead, he's chosen the worst possible moment. Plus he's doing it in the worst possible way. 'Thirty or forty.'

She repeats the numbers in disbelief. 'That's half the staff. Why? It's a Thomas Paine tradition, giving up an Occasional Day to meet together. They always did it for Will. They did it for me last summer term when I was new. How can we make the change unless tutors do the training?'

'That's what's bothering me.'

Isabel sits down on the bed, draws up her knees and hugs them. 'Let me get this straight. Thirty or forty teachers told you today they won't be coming?'

'It wasn't quite like that. The first two or three, a couple of weeks ago, I thought I'd be able to change their minds. Tell them everyone else was coming. They were the odd ones out.'

'So it's been happening over weeks?'

'A week. Ten days.'

'You've tried to persuade them to come but you haven't succeeded. And now it's a majority who refuse to attend.'

'Yes.'

'Are they giving a reason? Or reasons?'

'They all give the same reason. You're messing with the Thomas Paine ethos. They're not giving up their own time for that.' He expects her to blame him. He feels he's to blame. He's in charge of pastoral. He ought to be able to sell the change to tutors. But she only nods and is silent.

At last she says, 'Simon Clarke. Fighting a rearguard action.' She sounds calm. Analytical. 'It's the first significant change I've made. It has to happen or I'll have lost all authority. Only I don't see how we can make tutors responsible for Personal and Social Education without any preparation. It'll be a disaster. Which will prove to everyone that Simon's right. It ought to be left to his specialist team.' She hugs her knees a little closer. 'Clever.'

It's been bothering him for days. It doesn't make it any better, hearing her spell out what he sees as his cock-up. And somehow Isabel's on the receiving end of his anger. 'D'you think I haven't worked that out?'

'Shouting at me doesn't help.'

She speaks calmly. Which makes it worse. It would have been easier if she'd shouted back. He looks at her, baffled rage melding with urgent desire, one stoking the other, choking off speech.

'I have to win this one.' It sounds as though she's talking to herself. 'And the only way to win is to persuade everyone to come after all. To come willingly.' In a single lithe movement, she uncurls and settles herself on her back, hands clasped behind her head. 'It doesn't sound very likely, does it?'

Juggling. The way it is in school. Always too many demands and too little time. But not this morning. This Monday morning, when Jack would welcome delay, there are no phone calls from frantic parents, no teachers with problems that demand instant solution. So he's in plenty of time for his meeting with Isabel and Max. Supposedly to sort the PSE problem which screwed up their weekend.

Dust dances in the bands of sunlight falling across the empty corridor. A faint scent of cut grass drifts in. Outdoors, inviting escape. The meeting could be over in minutes if he offers an instant solution. Pure fantasy. He has no solution. He doesn't think there is one. Friday night, when he'd lapsed into hurt silence on the grounds that anything he said seemed to be making matters worse, Isabel accused him of sulking. What was he supposed to say to that, for Christ's sake? He tried taking her in his arms. *You think sex solves everything.* Though that was how they patched it up in the end. He didn't say I told you so. Saturday morning they talked it out. Agreed being open with each other was what mattered most. Promised each other they'd never let anything which happened at school come between them. Peace or truce? To Jack it still feels fragile. A discussion – edgy and fruitless as it's bound to be – could smash it into bits again.

Then he's standing in Isabel's doorway and she's smiling her welcome. The smile a bit more lingering and special, because Max hasn't arrived yet.

Jack watches Max. Watches the shifting triangle of the frown between his dark brows. He'd give a lot to know what's going on inside Max's head.

The frown lines deepen as Max says, 'You can't back down on this one. The timetable won't work unless tutors take over from September. Besides, you'd lose all credibility if you had to give way.'

Saying it makes it worse, Jack thinks. More real.

'Exactly,' Isabel says. 'Simon Clarke's behind it, isn't he?'

Max sighs. 'It's what I was afraid of.'

'Which is why you advised me to compensate him. I still think it's ridiculous. I should be able to make a change for students' benefit without having to bribe piqued colleagues.'

Max shakes his head, looking rueful. 'That's the way it should be but not how it is. And we have to live with how it is.'

'I don't want an almighty row but I can't just ignore the mass revolt at this evening's staff meeting. I'll remind everyone all tutors will be teaching PSE next term and point out it's their opportunity to change students' hearts and minds. To be pro-active, instead of waiting until there's a problem. But I doubt they'll let me leave it at that. There'll be protests. Will Simon keep his mouth shut or come out in public as a saboteur?'

Jack feels his anger rising. Bloody Simon Clarke, dropping him in the shit. Words boil in his brain, more abuse than argument. 'I'll take Simon on,' he says.

'I know you would, Jack. But it might not help.' Isabel meets his gaze, a loving look which interrupts his anger.

He glances at Max, wondering if he's noticed.

Max leans back, smiling. A smile as hard to interpret as La Gioconda's. 'Leave it to me. I'll make the case.' Their doubts must show in their faces because he adds, 'It's the best way. No one's going to question my commitment to the Thomas Paine ethos, now are they?'

'I can't see that working.' Isabel sounds impatient. 'Simon and his allies are bound to try to provoke me into answering them so they can draw me into an argument.'

'Refuse to be drawn. It's important to leave it open. It would be disastrous for you to be isolated publicly, with the staff lining up against you. We haven't a hope in hell of convincing all the doubters this evening. We need space to work on it before the training day.'

How come Max is so confident he can manage the situation? Jack's been working on it for days. 'What do you think I've been doing?' he asks.

Max turns to him. 'Jack, you've done wonders. From what I hear, there'd be much more opposition if it weren't for your efforts. But Isabel didn't realise what was happening. From now on, it'll be the three of us, working together.'

Which begs two questions. Did Max know what was happening? And if so, what was he doing about it? But Jack doesn't ask. Maybe because it's better not to know. Or maybe because the magic's working. The glance, the smile, the reassuring words, which make it crazy to doubt Max is an ally.

A soft mauve shadow is spreading across the patio. Isabel reaches for her glass and takes another sip of Chardonnay. 'You did it brilliantly, Jack.'

Relief is like a gloss over her face, smoothing out the fine lines of anxiety. He shares the relief. If her credibility was on the line, so was his. The detail of the day was down to him. 'It worked,' he says. He'd sweated in the small hours, imagining failure. Token attendance. The prevailing mood cynical disengagement. Everything he'd planned falling flat. Lying awake, with his brain in overdrive, he'd tried to invent an effective response. And failed. He can forget all that now. He reaches for his glass.

'Record attendance.' Isabel is half-gloating, half-admiring. 'Giving up a precious Occasional Day. And such a perfect summer day too.' She starts to laugh. 'Simon Clarke's fleeting appearance as Banquo's ghost was almost my favourite moment.'

Jack chuckles too, remembering Simon's lurching entry, his face the colour of Isabel's York stone paving. 'He must have had a heavy drinking session yesterday.'

'Jack!' She's reproachful but grinning too. 'He had a migraine. You know he's a martyr to them.'

'Migraine, hangover, same difference. Whichever, I owe him. I didn't want the guru there, judging my amateur effort—'

Isabel interrupts. 'It wasn't amateur at all. I told you, it was brilliant.'

He reaches out to squeeze her hand. 'You're biased. From my

point of view it was ideal. Turning up and seeing everyone else there was a public admission that he'd lost and you'd won. You acting the considerate boss and insisting he must go home—'

She interrupts again. 'Acting? I am a considerate boss. Look how well I treat you.'

'I hope you're not as good to everyone as you are to me. That would be overdoing it.'

Isabel springs up, looking threatening. Then, unexpectedly, she resumes her seat and sips her wine. Daniel and Laura are coming out to join them. 'Hi, how was your day?' she asks.

Boring, Daniel groans. Laura has had an unsatisfactory General Studies lesson. An exam it's impossible to revise for, she complains. Why is Oxford demanding an 'A' grade in that as well as everything else? And why does it have to be her first exam, instead of something straightforward like Maths or Physics?

Jack joins Isabel in offering practical advice. And reassurance. Of course she'll be fine.

Laura doesn't look convinced but she wants to know how the training day has gone.

It surprised Jack at first, the way Isabel's children follow her progress at Thomas Paine High. Almost as though they're parenting her. But perhaps that's the way to be if you want a good relationship with adolescent kids. On equal terms. As a father, he never got to that stage.

'It worked like a dream,' Isabel is saying. 'Jack got everyone involved. You could feel the buzz.'

'And they all turned up?'

'Yes. The great boycott never happened. Thanks to Max and his powers of persuasion.'

Daniel rolls his eyes. 'Max.'

'You really think they'd have stayed away but for him?' Laura asks.

'I bet,' Dan says. 'He invented the whole thing. He's a con-man.'

Isabel objects that she can't see how he could have done, while Laura wants to know what Dan's got against Max.

'He flashes his smile around and we're all meant to succumb to his charm. Yuk!'

'You're envious,' Laura says. 'You'd like to be able to charm people the way he does.'

Jack's envious too. He used to accept that Max was out of his league. Someone to look up to, almost the way he looked up to Will. Isabel changed all that. Now he can't help competing. It irks him to accept he failed where Max succeeded. So for Jack today became a performance. One in which he had to shine. In front of his colleagues. In front of Isabel. But most of all in front of Max.

After the kids have left them, Isabel says, 'It's puzzling though, isn't it?'

Wondering what he's missed, Jack asks her what's puzzling.

'The way Max managed to change everyone's mind like that. How strong was the opposition?'

'Strong enough. There was plenty of negativity at the staff meeting.'

'Max announces he's all for tutors delivering PSE. And that convinced everyone. Which proves how much we need him. Because his influence is much stronger than ours.'

Max playing the hero, galloping to the rescue. Jack would like to see it differently. But that was how it happened. 'Yes. It's more than a year since he was Acting Head but people still look to him to give a lead. And where he leads, they follow.'

'It was my idea.' She smiles at Jack. 'Our idea. Max wasn't altogether convinced. So he did it for my sake. Out of loyalty to me.'

'Must have done.'

'Max and Simon are close. Simon was dead against the change. He wanted his precious PSE team to go on peddling the bright ideas he had ten years ago. Even though the teachers find them a yawn, let alone the students.'

'Simon didn't want to let go.'

'But he did, didn't he? When he'd got me trapped if the training didn't go ahead, he swung open the cage door and let me out.'

Jack can't see the point of going back over it. There are better things to do. Like going up to her bedroom and undressing her. But he humours Isabel. 'You're right. We'd have been a mess, if the training hadn't happened.'

'I bet you can't be sure there were thirty or forty refuseniks. You didn't keep a list, did you?'

Jack admits he didn't. 'A list seemed too final. I kept hoping they'd change their minds.'

'So you probably exaggerated the number. A dozen vocal ones, egged on by Simon Clarke, would be enough to make it seem dire to you. Call Simon off and the rebellion collapses. I wonder how Max persuaded him.' It's growing dark now and Jack can't see her expression clearly. 'It could have been smoke and mirrors. They could have cooked it up between them. An apparent disaster, from which Max has saved me.'

'Why would he go to so much trouble?'

'To impress me with his loyalty. To give me good reason to be grateful.'

'You are grateful, aren't you?' Jack says. Some perverse part of him wants her not to be grateful to Max but common sense tells him she must be.

Isabel twirls her empty wine glass. Her *yes* is too drawn out to carry conviction.

He finds that encouraging. 'And it's good that he's loyal.' He states it as a fact.

'I don't want him to be disloyal. But loyalty's dodgy, isn't it? I mean, loyalty to Hitler wasn't good news.'

Jack laughs. 'You're no Hitler, are you?'

Isabel doesn't laugh. She's put down her glass and her fingers are fidgeting with the silver necklace she's wearing. It glints in what's left of the light. 'Max has demonstrated his loyalty to me, which puts me under an obligation to be loyal to him. I won't be, though. Not if I'm sure Max is doing something wrong. I'll pursue it. No loyalty, no debt of gratitude, could be allowed to stand in the way of that. Only I can't be sure.'

'Why complicate everything? Isn't it sometimes better to take things at face value?'

'I guess you're right.' She draws breath as though to say more but no words come.

In the silence Jack hears a police siren, urgent but distant.

Then she says, 'Max demonstrating effortless superiority. Is that what's bothering me? Out of resentment I'm inventing plots where none exists? Do you think that's what I'm doing, Jack?'

It puts him on the spot. He can't explain why he feels suspicion may be too dangerous, even where it's justified. He mutters, 'Sort of.' He waits for her response.

At last, she murmurs, 'So the simple truth is, my loyal Deputy Max Truman has saved the day and I have to be deeply grateful.'

As she says it, Jack sees Isabel shiver. Maybe she's feeling the chill of the gathering darkness.

Chapter 14

I reverse, manoeuvring the Saab closer to the kerb. A bit closer, anyway. That will have to do. Grabbing my briefcase from the passenger seat, I lock the car and hurry along the pavement. It's not all that late. It's not even dark yet. Though in May that luminous deep blue sky lasts a long time. I have my keys in my hand, ready to unlock the front door.

As the door swings open, I hear Laura laughing. There's another laugh, a laugh I recognise. Max. The words of apology die on my lips. I don't stop to analyse the intense discomfort I feel. I head for the kitchen, the source of the laughter.

My daughter and my Deputy Head are sitting side by side at the table with their backs to me. They're studying something together. A reason for their closeness? Or an excuse? They both look round at me. Max half-rises in his chair and when he sits down again his chair has moved a little further away from Laura's. Making space enough to turn and look at me.

'Isabel,' he says. 'You're back.' He turns to Laura. 'There you are. I told you there was nothing to worry about.'

Cue for me to explain where I've been. Instead I say, 'Why were you worried, Laura? I told you I might be late.'

As she stands up to face me her chair rasps on the floor. 'You did not. You knew I wanted you to help me with General

Studies. You promised you'd talk to me about it this evening.'

The memory I have been suppressing surfaces to appal me. I know how tense she is about Oxford wanting an 'A' in General Studies. An exam for which it's impossible to prepare with her normal meticulous revision programme. 'That's all right.' Why do I say this, knowing it is not all right? 'We can do it now.'

She glares at me. 'No we can't. It's too late. Anyway, as you weren't here, Max has been talking to me about it.' Her smile is for him alone.

I can't identify all the feelings churning within me. But for sure gratitude is not amongst them. So it's the need to keep up appearances only which prompts me to thank him and offer coffee.

'We've had coffee,' Laura snaps. And indeed the mugs are there on the table for anyone to see.

I want to ask him what he thinks he's doing in my house, with my daughter. Only that falls outside the range of conventional politeness to which I must remain in thrall. Because I can't prove anything, can I? So instead of accusing him I say, 'Did you need to see me about something, Max?'

He gets to his feet. 'Nothing urgent. Nothing that can't wait until tomorrow.'

Why did he come then? And why, now I'm back, is he ready to leave? Some Iago voice whispers *I like not that*. Common sense tells me he's leaving to keep clear of a family argument. He wouldn't make a pass at Laura. He's not that stupid. Unless the urge is so strong he can't help himself. The arguments buzzing in my brain as I say, 'Are you sure?'

'No problem,' he says. He turns to my daughter, smiling reassurance. 'You'll be fine, Laura, absolutely fine.' He rests his hand on her shoulder, as any uncle might. 'Promise me you won't worry about it any more.' His gaze holds hers.

Did she flinch from his touch? No, I imagined that. I think I flinched myself. She's smiling back at him. 'I'll try not to. And thanks for all your help.'

'My pleasure.' His gaze lingering on her for a moment before he turns to me. 'See you tomorrow, Isabel.'

I follow him down the hall. As much to postpone my encounter with Laura as to see him off the premises. I'm feeling as defiant as a guilty teenager.

I march back into the kitchen. 'What was Max doing here?'

'He came looking for you.'

My urge to distribute blame is all-consuming. 'Where's Dan?'

'Gone round to Holly's.'

'Hadn't he got homework to do?'

'God, how am I supposed to know? I suppose that's my fault too.' She glares at me and then drops her gaze. 'No need to ask where you've been all this time.'

'What do you mean?'

'You were with Jack, weren't you?'

I feel as though Jack's handprints are visible all over me. A dozen silly teenage answers offer themselves. I manage the simple truth. 'Yes.' Only I can't leave it there. 'If you were so sure where I was, why did you pretend to Max you were worried?'

'What lie was I supposed to tell him then? It's meant to be a big secret, isn't it, your affair with Jack?' Sneer turns to plea as she says, 'And you did promise you'd be home.'

I ought to be sorry. I am sorry, very, very sorry. Only I can't find any way to say that. 'It was bound to make Max curious. Make him wonder what on earth was going on.'

'Whose fault is that? Aren't you being a teeny-weeny bit unreasonable, Mother?'

Between Dan and me the formal title is a joke. From Laura

I hear it as an accusation. What sort of a mother is it who lies in her lover's arms and neglects her child? I've justified almost half my life by claiming my children matter more to me than myself. Yet I've allowed my passion for Jack to distract me when my daughter needs me. Shame swells in me, a physical sickness. I have to swallow against the nausea before I can speak. 'Why was Max still here?' Not a defence. Not an apology. A counter-accusation. 'Why didn't he go once you told him I wasn't here?' Suspicion sharpens my voice.

An angry jerk of her head sets her long dark hair swirling. 'Don't give me that shit. You said you'd be back around seven. I hung around waiting for you. Wasting my evening. I finally grabbed something to eat just before Max turned up. It was after eight by then. I told him I was sure you wouldn't be long. I told him that because I trusted you.' A torrent of words. 'You didn't come and you didn't come. What the fuck was I meant to say? I gave him all that crap about being worried because I was trying to cover for you.' Every pronoun is loaded with rage.

Beneath the fury I hear the fear of a child waking in the night to find her mother isn't there for her. Even that might not have been enough. Only then the tears that have been glinting in her eyes overflow onto her cheeks. Laura, strong, stoical Laura, who as a four-year-old bore the disappointments of Richard's deser-tions with a stiff upper lip. Laura is weeping. I dare to put my arms around her. She is too forgiving to push me away. I mutter over and over again that I am so very sorry. It is all my fault. She says she's sorry too, sorry about the shouting and the language. I don't know how long it takes us to comfort each other enough to grab handfuls of tissues and settle ourselves at the table. What is my obsession with Jack in comparison to the love for my children? Flesh of my flesh as no man can ever be. I have to try to explain the madness to her and hope she will understand.

'I can't believe I forgot,' I tell her, 'when I knew you were worrying about it.' How can I go on? I'll have to acknowledge sex happens to parents too. But how can I stay silent after what I've done? 'Here with you, the way I feel about Jack seems a kind of insanity. Something which transforms my world into a strange and different place.' Unlike Daniel, Laura doesn't go in for serial romances. I'm not sure she's a fellow-sufferer. 'No one can understand unless they've experienced the same kind of craziness.'

'I have. You know I have. Vincent,' she says.

Vincent. The sixth-former she went out with for three ecstatic months when she was fourteen. Before he dumped her. I've buried the memory. Knowing the answer, I ask anyway. 'That's how it was with him?'

She twists a tissue between her fingers. 'I'd have done anything to please him. Anything.'

I'm twisting my own tissue now. Remembering her un-prompted confession she'd had sex with him. Remembering my own inadequate response. Though I can't excuse my failure, I understand it. With our own children, as with our own parents, sexuality is too fraught to acknowledge.

'I didn't realise it was possible to be so happy,' Laura says. 'Or so utterly miserable. I thought about it a lot after he'd fin-ished with me. Thought as well as felt, I mean.' For a moment there's the ghost of a smile. 'For the first time I understood you and Dad. Before, I couldn't believe you let him do that to you. Let him bully you and exploit you the way he did. It made me so mad to watch. Only then I saw that's how it would have been with me and Vince if we'd carried on. I made up my mind I'd never let it happen to me. Some man making my life a misery. Friendships, yes, but not what you call insanity.'

Hearing her wary distrust, I feel like I'm the lovesick

adolescent. Maybe wary is the safest way to be with predators like Max around. Maybe the feminists are right. Maybe there really is that 'casual continuing war against women' they talk about. Yet I feel bound to disagree. 'Not all relationships are disastrous.'

'No?' The word lilts upwards, full of disbelief. 'Isn't there always more love on one side than the other?' The way she says 'love' casts doubt on its authenticity. 'Which is why it all goes wrong. That's how it was with me and Vince. He fancied me. I adored him.'

I try again. 'It could be equal on both sides.'

'Is it equal with you and Jack?'

I owe her an honest answer. It feels equal but how can I be sure? And how can I expect it to last that way with a lover ten years my junior? 'It's too soon. The scales are still settling.'

'Did you stay with him tonight because it was what he wanted or because it was what you wanted?'

I offer the quick, obvious answer. 'We both wanted it.' It's as true as any other. And as untrue.

She gives a sort of laugh. Disbelieving, as though she doubts I'm even trying to be honest.

'It doesn't feel like there's a choice,' I tell her.

'Do you think that's how it is with everyone? They don't have a choice?' Her steady gaze challenges me. 'Even when it's an adult abusing a kid?'

What has Max done? Helen. Dana. Rebecca. And now my own daughter. No. My overheated imagination. Not Laura. She'd never have kept quiet if he'd ... 'That's different. If it's wrong the moral choice has to override desire.' Who am I kidding? When I am drawn towards Jack by a force as powerful as the gravity which binds moon to earth. If it ever happens to her again, Laura won't be able to resist it either.

'It doesn't though, does it? Doesn't override desire, however wrong it is.'

'Not always,' I admit.

For weeks off and on I've had that old Elvis song on the brain. I've caught myself humming it with a dreamy smile. Because it's the way I feel about Jack. *I can't help falling in love with you.* Only now it sounds like a jeering echo. Mocking my failure of will. So I change the subject, falling back on the feeble parental line, 'It's late and you've got an exam tomorrow.'

I watch Laura switch back to the immediate concern, her forehead puckering as she re-connects with her insecurity. 'Why does my first exam have to be crappy General Studies, instead of something I can do, like Maths?'

'You can do General Studies. It's just that you don't trust yourself. You're learning useful stuff all the time, only it doesn't seem like learning because it's not a lesson.'

'Max said I was absolutely fine when we were looking at that practice paper together.'

I stifle the unhelpful response his name stirs in me. 'There you are then.'

'Would you just go over one of the French passages with me?'

I agree at once. Her request is generous. A balm to the wounds of the evening.

I turn my pillow over in the forlorn hope of making myself comfortable. It seems unlikely, since it hasn't worked the last dozen times. There isn't the smallest chance of sleeping while my brain is recycling the events of the past few hours.

How did this evening happen? I'd agreed to meet Jack after school. Tutor groups for the new first years. Our last opportunity to settle them if we were to keep to the schedule I'd published. He appeared in my room around five o'clock saying I'd kill him.

He'd left the paperwork at home. I was angry and said so. Head-teacher to Deputy. But underneath, a frisson. Lover to lover. A quarrel, followed by the pleasure of making up. When he said we could go back to his place and sort it, I made him wait a bit before I agreed. I wondered if he'd forgotten on purpose, because we both knew what would happen. I didn't mind. Mildly flattered to think he couldn't keep his hands off me, I guess. Back in his house, I made it businesslike. Kept the hugging and kissing brief. We had coffee. The real thing, because I'd moaned so much about his disgusting instant stuff. Then we started work. It took us a couple of hours, with only the occasional caress we couldn't resist. Alone together like that, postponing the moment builds the excitement. We'd hardly allocated the final student when he slid his hand inside my blouse. He complained about the telling off I'd given him. Was I still cross? I told him yes, he'd deserved the telling off. There was a lot of teasing about how I'd punish him. I was so aroused it was obvious I'd never carry out my threat to walk out. Somehow I started apologising to him. Joking, yet until he'd forgiven me it didn't seem possible to go. Though at the back of my mind I had this uneasy feeling about how long it was all taking. Then the perfect reconciliation. The lovemaking I wanted to last forever. In conflict with the fierce urge to reach the pinnacle of excitement which ends it. The cuddling afterwards to forget the isolation. And the back-to-earth moment of struggling into my clothes and hurrying out to the car. The evening slipping deeper and deeper into disaster.

Laura may have forgiven me. I can't forgive myself. Or accept the moral relativism. If I can't resist, how can I condemn Richard's endless betrayals? He always claimed he couldn't help it. And Max with his procession of susceptible adolescents? That suspicion I can neither prove nor give up. Can't he help it either?

I can't help falling in love with you.

It's the last thing I ever intended to happen, this crazy passion when I ought to be focused on succeeding as Head of Thomas Paine High. It's a distraction. It muddles relationships. Do I treat Jack like every other colleague? No, of course I don't. So what's happened to the scrupulous fairness I claim to subscribe to? And if we're both caught up in a *casual continuing war* hasn't he found the perfect way to disarm me? I've surrendered without a struggle. I've allowed myself to believe that Jack, an attractive man in his thirties with a reputation as a womaniser, finds me irresistible. It's pathetic. I've made myself vulnerable where I can't afford vulnerability. They're laughing behind my back, because they all know my big secret. People always do. Max is bound to have noticed, even if Jack doesn't share the joke with him. Which puts me at risk.

No, that's ridiculous. What do I think Max will do? Blackmail me? It's not a crime for a divorced woman and an unattached man to have an affair. Not even mildly shocking in 1982.

But it's not wise. Not in my position. Only I can't help it. When Jack walks into the room, my body responds in spite of me. I'm like a drug addict. Hooked. I have to have more of him. And I have an addict's mood swings. Being at odds with him plunges me into misery. When all's well between us, I'm euphoric.

But not tonight. Tonight has shown me I have to break my habit. I won't put myself on a level with Richard and Max. I'm as weak-willed as the next person when it comes to another slice of cake. But I've always believed I could trust myself when it really matters. As this does. No half measures. Only a total break with Jack will do. A cold shiver of dismay runs through me, strong as an orgasm.

The worst of it is, it can't be total. Not unless I find another job. I'll see him day after day. Close enough to observe all the mannerisms I've learnt to love. I'll hear his voice, the way he says *Isabel*, not quite like anyone else. Our hands touching by accident, hands which have discovered all the secret pleasures which stoke and satisfy desire. Which would be worse? Never to see him again? Or to suffer this tantalising proximity?

Open-eyed, I gaze into the semi-darkness of the bedroom I used to share with Richard. If I could bear my life with him, I can bear anything. I have only to make up my mind. I won't postpone. I'll do it tomorrow. Or rather today, for it's already Thursday. Thursday Jack has his evening class. I can't do it at school. Not today then. Friday evening. Definitely Friday evening.

Decision made, perhaps I may even sleep.

Except these days I only ever sleep lulled by memories and fantasies of Jack.

'More pudding?' I ask.

Across the table Jack grins at me. 'Don't tempt me. Your chocolate pudding is so addictive it ought to be a banned substance.' His gaze holds mine, lover to lover.

I stand up to clear plates, glad of the excuse to move away.

The air is heavy with my awareness of what I have to do, of a thunderstorm about to break.

It was already arranged, Jack coming for a meal. Almost a Friday routine. After we've eaten, the children go out and we make love. I correct myself. *Have sex*. Taking the romance out of it. I can't finish with him without seeing him. Well, I suppose it would be possible to do it over the phone or by letter. Neither is a serious alternative, the way things are. Almost as bad as a memo in his pigeonhole. One of the printed slips we use. From:

Isabel. To: *Jack*. Dated, because that's important for official business. *Our relationship is over*. Folded and stapled the way we do when it's something confidential. In case it flutters out onto the floor and the wrong person reads it. No, he had to come here. Changing the arrangement would have brought it all out into the open. Carrying on as though nothing had happened seemed the only choice left. So I gave myself the tiniest portions and hoped no one would notice I was pushing them around my plate because my mouth is too dry to eat. I scrape the mess into the bin. Jack glances at me as I let several forks clatter to the floor. I gather them up and add them to the rest of the cutlery, taking unnecessary care. Once the dishwasher is loaded, my excuse will be gone. I'll have to face Jack again. Have to appear normal while all the time my head is full of what I have to say and how I'm going to say it. Worse, I find myself observing every moment with aching intensity. Because none of it will ever happen again.

The children have been too busy joking with Jack to offer to help. I want it that way, yet at the same time I'm a bit aggrieved. It's like being behind an invisible barrier. Isolated from the mood which prevails all around me, though I smile and even laugh occasionally, so as not to draw attention to myself. Friday evenings are always a time to unwind. Tonight especially, because it's the start of the bank holiday weekend. And Laura is on a high because the dreaded General Studies papers are safely behind her. If she blamed Jack for last Wednesday there's no sign of it in her manner towards him.

When Daniel announces it's time for coffee and stands up to make it, I accept with a mixture of relief and dread, knowing that I can't postpone much longer. In my head, I phrase and re-phrase ways to begin. As though I hadn't been mentally rehearsing through two wakeful nights. In minutes, Laura and Daniel will disappear upstairs. I tell myself we can't be interrupted, I need to wait until they've gone out. Only what can I say to Jack meanwhile?

The children fill their mugs and retreat up the stairs, chatting and laughing. In the kitchen the silence seems to thicken into something too tough for words to penetrate. Without speaking, I put milk, coffee, mugs, on a tray which I carry into the sitting-room. I set it down.

We are both still standing when Jack says, 'Isabel, what is it? What's worrying you?' His expression is all concern.

I get as far as, 'Jack,' and then my throat closes, stifling further speech. Which is disastrous.

He takes me in his arms, murmuring over and over into my hair, 'It's all right. We'll sort it out, whatever it is.'

For a moment I cling to him. There's no tactful way to move from our embrace to what I have to say. But delay is making it worse by the second. So I blurt out that it's over, it can't go on, saying the same thing in several different ways. I'm only half-coherent. It's no wonder he wants to know what's upset me like this.

'Nothing's upset me. I want to end our relationship, that's all.' *That's all.* Everything about me gives the lie to my words. The worst of it is, Jack looks as though he's received a physical hurt, face drained of colour, in clinical shock. More than anything I want to unsay what I've just said.

Where does pain end and rage begin? I know he's furious as he says, 'Sure about that? It's all over?'

I look away, nodding confirmation.

'Right. I'll leave you in peace then.'

He turns on his heel. And goes.

Chapter 15

As he drives away from Isabel's Jack doesn't try to make sense of what's happened. He's not going to put himself through that. What he needs is a drink. But not at the Sutton Arms. Not where he's bound to meet someone he knows. Parking the car near his front door he walks a few yards down the road to the Red Lion. His local, though he's never set foot in it before. It's as dismal as his mood. Looking as though it hasn't had an update since the fifties. Paint darkened to an indeterminate yellowish beige. Dusty curtains and carpets, reeking of tobacco, stirring his dormant habit. He gets a pint of bitter from the unsmiling barman. Settles in a darkish corner. Swallows beer steadily, hoping for the anaesthetic effect.

Out on the pavement in the mild May darkness, he's more aware of how much he's drunk. But he's okay. And in any case he's close to home. The pain hasn't gone away. Sod Isabel, what does she think she's playing at? He stokes his fury against her. Anger is better than pain. The holiday week stretches blankly ahead. That trip to the country they'd planned for Tuesday, that's out of the window. He'll get more sketching done if he goes on his own. But the prospect's too bleakly different from what he's been imagining. As uninviting as his empty house.

He can see the dark windows now, reflecting the orange

lamplight which glints on his Golf and on the Saab, parked behind it. Deep blue, like Isabel's.

'Jack?'

Christ, it is Isabel, getting out of her car and saying his name as if she's not quite sure it's him. As he walks towards her, she stands with the open door like a shield in front of her. Ready to slip back into the car and drive off. Why doesn't she? What can they have to say to each other? 'What are you doing here?' More challenge than greeting.

She steps away from the protection of the car and faces him. 'I have to talk to you. To explain.'

They're standing a yard apart. It might as well be a mile. 'What is there to say?' But he can't help being curious.

She gives a little shrug. 'I thought you'd never come.'

Caught off guard he asks, 'How long have you been waiting?'

'I drove over as soon as Laura and Daniel went out.'

More than an hour then. Not that it makes any difference. 'Why? Why did you come?'

'To talk to you. Please.'

There's nothing left to say. But he can't argue the point out here on the pavement. So he mutters, 'You'd better come in.'

While she locks her car, he unlocks his front door, with only marginal clumsiness. He leads the way into his living-room. He says he'll make coffee. Not hospitality. The need to counteract the beer. Yesterday she would have followed him into the kitchen. Not tonight, though. So there's nothing to stop him dowsing his head under the cold tap. How can everything be so different in so short a time? He reaches for the instant coffee, telling himself he's in a hurry. Anyway he doesn't need to bother about her likes and dislikes any more. Except he must reek of the dingy bar he's spent the evening in. The smell of ground coffee will drown it. Not that there's any chance they'll get close enough for it to matter.

He finds her still standing. Without inviting her to sit, he takes a seat himself. On the settee. She takes the nearest arm-chair. He never expected her to sit beside him. He pours coffee, pushes a mug in her direction. She clasps both hands around the mug. He doesn't care how long they sit there he's not going to break the silence. Only he has the three-quarter view, the curve of her cheekbone, the small, straight nose, all so familiar. Traced with his finger dozens of times. In her absence, he's often tried to sketch her, without ever producing a drawing which satisfies him. Which catches the essential Isabel. He'll never waste time doing that again. What he's feeling is justified fury, not pain.

'I want to explain why our relationship has to end.'

She's said it again. And almost calmly this time. But he wonders about the *has to*. Has Max found out? Is there some risk to them both which has decided her? No. He's not going to comfort himself with that sort of pretence. He says curtly, 'What's the point in explaining?'

She looks hurt. But she lifts her chin and says, 'Because ending it is bad enough. It makes it worse if you think it's just that I've changed my mind. Something happened on Wednesday evening which made me realise it had to stop.'

Wednesday evening? Wednesday, when she seemed like she couldn't get enough of him? 'What did I do wrong?' Sarcasm, not a straightforward request for information.

She goes on as though she hasn't heard him, in a steady monotone. 'Yesterday was the start of Laura's A-levels. General Studies. I knew she was bothered about it. I promised to help her. Wednesday evening. I came here. I forgot my promise. Forgot all about it. Or that's what I say. The truth is my failure to remember was deliberate.'

He protests she can't know that. Again she ignores him.

'I have total recall of my diary. Everything I'm doing. Every minute of every day. So I blanked it out. Because I wanted to stay here. With you.'

'And that's what this is all about?'

'I told Laura it seemed as though someone else was doing it. Not me at all. I'd lost control of my own actions. That's how it is, isn't it, when you fall in love?'

Love. It's not a word they ever use. They're not teenagers. So he hears it from her now for the first time. And it makes him furious. Because it's already too late. She doesn't care what she's doing to him. She's too wrapped up in her own guilt-trip. He's the last person she's thinking about. If she imagines he's going to try to persuade her to change her mind, she couldn't be more wrong.

'Laura asked me if I believed everyone could claim they couldn't help it, however wrong their actions. I produced some glib answer about using will-power to resist desire. When all the time I lack the will-power to say no to you.'

What's she suggesting? He's forcing her or something? 'And you want to say no?'

'I don't want to, Jack. But I can see all the problems our relationship causes. It undermines my credibility at school.'

'I never talk to anyone about it. Do you?'

'Of course I don't. But that doesn't mean people haven't noticed.'

'So they've noticed.' He can't seem to break out of this pointless angry argument. 'The Headteacher turns out to be human.' One of the reasons he felt at home at TPH from the outset. The acceptance that teachers are human too. With the normal human weaknesses. 'Does that bother you?'

'Yes. It's hard enough for them to accept me as Will's

successor without the close-up view of our relationship. At best
it's a distraction.'

'I don't see that.' More stubborn opposition, though he
knows it's not the way to change anyone's mind. 'Relationships
drive behaviour. You accept that with students. You and I work
so well together because of our relationship.' Though maybe
the present tense is already out of date, their precious relationship falling in tattered fragments around them.

Her face softens. The yearning's back in her eyes as her gaze
meets his. 'If only I could believe that.' Then her jaw tightens
and her mouth settles into a determined line. 'Not that it would
change anything. Unless I have the will to say no, how can I
condemn Richard, for wanting to leave me when I was pregnant? And all the paedophiles who claim they can't help themselves, are they guiltless too?'

Is that what she thinks of their relationship? It's on a par
with some sick perversion? Jack can't believe what he's hearing.
It would serve her right if he let her get on with it.

A memory stirs, making his breath catch in his throat.
Exactly what he'd thought with Maggie. If she wanted to
believe Jill meant more to him than their partnership and their
kids, so be it. He'd apologised, done his best to explain and then
shut up. So they'd parted. And he'd lost all three of them. Is he
going to do it again? Keep up his angry sulk and lose Isabel?

She's gazing at him, a little frown of anxiety drawing the
arch of her brows together. 'If I loved you less, it might be all
right. But the way things are, it can't go on. You understand
that, don't you?'

Like fuck he understands. He doesn't say the words aloud
but they seem to carry away some of his anger. He asks, 'Where
do I fit in?'

'How do you mean?'

'You may be able to do it. See me all the time at school. Meet with me alone in your room. Look to me for support. And behave as though you're entirely indifferent to me. Even though you're in love with me.' He speaks the words with a kind of wondering pain. 'I don't reckon I can.'

She catches her lip beneath her teeth, shaking her head. 'Oh, Jack.'

'Don't my feelings matter?'

'Of course they do. You're the last person I want to hurt. Only there isn't any other way.'

It's not working. She's going to stick to it.

Then Isabel adds, 'Is there?'

'No,' he says, 'if that's how you feel. It's tough on both of us but there's no alternative. Only you don't want us to part on bad terms, do you?'

'No, I couldn't bear that.'

'So we won't. We'll part like two people in love. In a very loving way.' He gets up and stands in front of her, holding out his hands to her. He hopes the stink of the pub isn't too lingering.

'No, Jack. I can't. If I kiss you, I shan't be able to go through with it.'

Does she think he doesn't know that? It's what he's banking on. But he nods acceptance and sits again, leaving plenty of room for her beside him. 'Okay. We need to talk it through, though. Work out how to make it as easy as possible for each other. You came to do that, didn't you?'

She nods. 'It'll be really hard for me. I've been imagining how hard, ever since I decided.' She smiles, a rueful sort of smile. 'Realising how much time I spend thinking about you.'

'It'd be easier if we didn't want to stay friends.'

'We do, though. We must.'

Hearing the note of panic, Jack knows he's going to win. It's for her own good. Guilt is a rotten reason for doing anything. Besides, what he wants is what Isabel really wants. But trying to kiss her, that was rushing things.

She stays for an hour, discussing how they're going to manage their new relationship, as she calls it. She doesn't join him on the settee. They part without a kiss. Though she lets him take her hand in both of his.

And she agrees there's still so much to talk about that they'd better spend Tuesday together as they'd planned.

'I believe in free will, believe I make choices,' Isabel says. She sits on the rug, clasping her knees, their picnic postponed while she tries to explain it all to Jack. 'But choosing is never simple the way it's supposed to be. You know, I could do this, or this or this.' Her hand separates alternatives. 'But on balance I'll do the other. Life's not like that.'

Jack's in no hurry to answer. He doesn't want to show the impatience he feels with Isabel's hair-splitting. He offers a neutral, 'You've made your choice though.'

He sees uncertainty in the little nod she gives. 'I spent so many years trying to please Richard. It's like—'

He interrupts her. 'It's not the same with us. You don't have to try to please me. You do please me, Isabel.'

She smiles then. Puts out her hand and skims his bare arm, stirring the hairs on it. And stirring his desire for her. 'I like to hear you say that. I can't help liking it. It's not you at all. It's me. Wanting to be whatever you want me to be. Surrendering the freedom I have to be the Isabel I want to be.' She plucks a blade of grass and begins to split it. 'Laura asked me if ours was a relationship of equals.'

'That's how it feels to me.'

'It's better with us because of our professional relationship.'

She grins. 'That stops me being too subservient. Last Wednesday, while we were at school, even back at your house while we were working, I was in charge. But afterwards ... I know you were only teasing.'

Teasing? Or had he been proving something? She might be the boss at work but not in their relationship. Safer not to think about it. 'It was a tease,' he tells her. 'You didn't mind, did you?'

'Not at all. I was enjoying it. That's the worst thing about it. Even today, with this decision hanging over me, you make me so happy. I love being with you. It seems worth giving up anything to make it last. Becoming a doormat, the way I did with Richard.'

'I can't believe I'm hearing this. At school you're so in charge. Doing something which would scare most women stiff. You're tough. Much tougher than Will ever was. You refuse to turn a blind eye to what's actually going on the way he used to all the time.'

'That's the problem. Something in me wants to prove I'm not really tough Isabel Lincoln, Headteacher. Underneath, I'm the sweet little womanly woman my mother wanted me to be.'

'Then what we need to do is work at it. Work at having that relationship of equals. We can, now you've explained all this to me.'

She glances at the grass she's destroyed and shakes it off her fingers. She clasps her hands round her knees again, like she's protecting herself. 'That's the dream, Jack. I'm not convinced it could ever be the reality.'

'Why can't it be? If you're right about free will.'

'I can imagine that's the choice I'm making. But it's not a once-forever choice. It's choosing every second I'm with you. And I have no confidence I can do that.'

'No? That's what you'll be doing if we end our relationship. Unless you're planning on resigning. I'm not. So we'll be together. All the time you'll have to choose not to care that I've come into the room. Not to let our hands touch by accident. Not to smile at me because we know we're both thinking the same thought. When we're apart, not to miss me.'

'How do you know that's how it is with me?'

He unhooks her right hand from her left. She doesn't try to stop him. He grips her hand, which is cold in spite of the sunshine. 'I know because that's how it is for me.'

She looks at him for a moment before she leans towards him. Then she cuddles against him. Kissing arouses him even more than usual, because all morning he's been tantalised by her, close yet untouchable. He slides his hand beneath the cotton skirt she's wearing and up the hot smooth skin of her thigh. It's lucky there's no one about, because neither of them can wait.

Chapter 16

Max is grasping the crook of my arm to guide me. I am conscious of the warmth of his hand against my skin. I wish I'd worn long sleeves. It's extraordinarily alarming to have to rely on him for guidance. There is an upward pressure on my elbow. My foot gropes, if a foot can, and I am mounting stairs. I can't recall ever going upstairs in this building. Having no visual memory of my whereabouts is a new uncertainty. I think of David Balfour in *Kidnapped*, saved by the flash of summer lightning from stepping off into space in the ruined House of Shaws. Though of course that's ridiculous. Max will protect me even from the humiliation of a stumble. The alternative would be too blatant.

How shall I know when I reach the top? I fear both one step more and one step less. A jolt despite my caution. I've arrived on the level.

No, we're on our way up again. Maybe the pause came exactly halfway. I wish I'd counted the steps. Max is laughing a little. It's not a jeering laugh exactly but without sight it's hard to tell. I have a desperate desire to see his expression. We've reached the top yet my paces grow more and more tentative. I advance in the absolute conviction that I'm about to walk into a brick wall. Thus far I've kept my eyes closed. Partly to prove I can be trusted. And partly to make it my choice not to see. Within my power. I can see if I want to. And as a door creaks open I do want to see. Very much. But when I open my eyes I discover the blindfold prevents me from seeing. I press my lips together to prevent myself from crying out. If I ever doubted it before I know beyond all contradiction that I do not trust Max Truman.

Only that's nonsense. It's just a game. One of those silly games it's fashionable to use in management training. A game which proves nothing at all.

It re-plays in my mind like a nightmare that waking has failed to dispel. Except it's not a dream which haunts me. It happened.

Max set the whole thing up. 'It's the perfect opportunity,' he said.

I remember the leaflet he handed me. Heavy black type on orange paper. A one-day management course. Trust and the Process of Management. 'You want to go?' I said. Across the room Jack caught my eye and smiled. I was doubtful about returning the smile. Too late. My mouth curved in spite of me. I didn't want to look at his lips. It reminded me of kissing him. Of my joking question, 'How did you learn to kiss so well?' And his response, light, yet wary, 'Is kissing learnt behaviour?' It wasn't the moment to have such thoughts about one of my Deputies. Not at the start of our management meeting.

'All three of us should go. We've been working together for less than a year and, let's be honest, we're still cagey around one another. For all sorts of understandable reasons.' Max smiled at Jack and me. As though he was absolving us of any blame. 'But the more we trust each other the more effective we'll be as a team.'

I agreed we should go. The irony of it robbed me of arguments. And I think I hoped for a miraculous breakthrough. Me
suddenly starting to trust Max. Or Max proving himself trust-
worthy. Neither happened. We played the Trust Game together.
But nothing changed.

This Thursday evening I feel as helpless as I did three weeks
ago in that blindfold. A week today Max goes off to camp with
seventeen students. When the Education Authority decreed
that this year the summer term should end on a Wednesday I'd
commented that it was awkward, splitting our Activities Week
into two segments.

'Brilliant,' Max countered, eyes sparkling. 'A chance to have
a full week, instead of the usual five days.

Not that it's significant. Five days is five days too long. How
much difference can two more make? Absurd to be so bothered
about a detail of timing.

I can't fault Max. Every regulation is being scrupulously
observed. Ten girls. Seven boys. A female member of staff to go
with him. So that's all right then. No, it isn't. Suzy, in her first
year of teaching, sweet innocent Suzy, standing up to Max
Truman? Pigs might fly. She'll be so dazzled by him she won't
notice a thing. Which is exactly why he chose her. His independent project. Managing Activities Week. All that tedious
admin. Giving him carte blanche to set up Field Archaeology
just the way he wants it. And I can't do a thing about it.

You're taking it too personally. I'm accusing myself. Which is
worse than hearing someone else accuse me, because who knows
my weaknesses as well as I do? There never was anything
between me and Max, as Jack suggested after that first kiss.
Except ... Was I as immune as I like to believe? Right at the start,
finding empathetic support where I'd anticipated grudging
rivalry, wasn't I drawn to him? And didn't I indulge myself,

listening half-soothed, half-unsettled, as he cast a retrospective rosy glow over events, softening the harsh outlines of my blunders? So maybe I'm jealous, watching him offer others the attention I crave.

A tidy theory. But it can't be true when I'm in love with Jack. It's Max who's the problem. Not me.

I've taken advice. Discreetly. I've no wish to reinforce the widely-held view that Thomas Paine High is an anarchic place where anything could – almost certainly does – happen. So I've asked other Heads whether they ever have a problem with teachers becoming too friendly with students. Not hinting at any feminist objection to the exploitation of young women by men in positions of power. Not mentioning Deputy Heads or unlawful sex. Nine times out of ten the reaction is dismissive. *It happens all the time.* What do they do about it? Which prompts a shrug. *What can they do about it? Except give the bloke a good reference and hope he moves on.* Maybe a disciplinary hearing? *I must be joking.* At which point the responses divide between those who assure me the governors aren't going to accept a pupil's unsupported testimony against a teacher so the charge would never be upheld. And those who warn of the dire consequences if the governors, in a fit of collective madness, took a pupil at her word. It would create open season for every disaffected female to invent accusations.

Forget the disciplinary hearing. I don't have even the beginnings of a credible case. Only a load of suspicions. And my gut feeling, which seems like a physical cramp whenever my thoughts circle back to Max.

Jack's tongue teases my lips. His right hand slides beneath my t-shirt while his left hand curves around my bum.

With an effort I draw away. I have to talk to him. I'm clinging to the conviction that talking to him will make a difference. Though my mind is blank about what either of us could do at this stage. I get as far as telling Jack we have to talk.

'Why?' he asks. 'When kissing is so much nicer?'

'Because Activities Week starts on Wednesday and Max is taking his Field Archaeology lot camping.'

'Bully for him.'

'Jack, for God's sake.' Manufacturing indignation so the softness of his lips, a handbreadth away, won't beguile me. 'We both know he's not to be trusted around young women. Why are we letting it happen?'

Responding at last to my fierceness, Jack frowns. He straightens up, stretching his arm along the back of the sofa. 'Because we have no way of stopping him.' My face must make it clear this isn't helping because he has another go. 'He's not going to try anything with so many witnesses. He wouldn't risk it.'

'That's how he gets away with it. He's not furtive. He's blatant. We see it but we can't believe what we've seen. We invent a different explanation.'

Jack's frown's become established now, lines scored deeply around his eyes and mouth. 'We haven't seen it though, have we? It's still only what you suspect.'

'What *I* suspect?' Heavy stress on the personal pronoun. 'You mean, you think he's entirely innocent?'

'Christ, Isabel, which of us can claim that? I meant there's no proof.'

'No, there's no proof. And I need proof to act.' I start to play with his fingers, lifting each in turn. 'So I can't stop Field Archaeology going ahead. I've done what I can.' I hesitate. I hope I'll feel more comfortable about it if I confess to Jack. 'I spoke to Suzy.' Saying it brings back her embarrassed astonishment.

'And said what?'

I hear alarm in his question. 'I made it general. Asked her if she'd thought about why the regulations insisted on a woman teacher with a mixed group. She said it must be to look after girls' welfare. When I pressed her she seemed fixated on menstruation. So I told her Max could be vulnerable. He must never be left in a situation where anyone could allege improper conduct.' I stop short. When I said it, it seemed like a brainwave, but the doubts have been growing since.

'How did she take that?'

'She went on about how lucky she was to be going with Max. All his experience meant there couldn't possibly be any problem.'

Jack laughs. 'She's like a student herself. Maybe Max will go for her.'

Intended to be comforting, I guess, but it misfires. I feel more uneasy than ever. 'I didn't do any good.'

'It doesn't sound as though you did any harm. You haven't made Suzy suspicious.'

'But that's exactly what I'd like her to be. Suspicious.'

'Think about it, Isabel,' he says. As though it hasn't been obsessing my every waking moment. 'A probationary teacher suspecting the Deputy Head of having it off with schoolgirls. Dynamite. We don't want that becoming staffroom gossip.'

'When the truth emerges, what then?'

'If it's the truth,' he qualifies, 'we'll have one massive problem. There'll be a lot of people who back Max. Bound to be.'

I don't want to ask. I shouldn't need to ask. But I have to. 'Will you back him?'

'No,' he says. It comes out wavering. Uncertain. 'If people take sides, I'll be on your side.' He draws me close and kisses me. 'How can you doubt that?' He starts to play with the hair at the back of my neck. 'Only ...'

'Only what?'

'It's complicated. Teachers have a lot to answer for. They can damage students in all sorts of ways. Pick on them all the time. Destroy their confidence. Kill their enthusiasm. Turn them off the whole idea of school. I'm not sure I can judge what Max is doing.'

I feel a hot wave of outrage. 'Are you saying it's okay?'

'It's not okay, no. But the accusation could destroy him. It doesn't have to be proved. Who'd appoint a Head with that in his background? Even though what you suspect him of isn't a crime, is it?'

I think it's fear that makes me silent. The fear of opening up a rift between us. I keep very still, as though I'm in physical danger.

'A guy in his thirties, flirting with fifteen-year-olds who've got crushes on him. It gives them a thrill. Probably makes him feel good about himself, which is a bit pathetic. Is there any real harm in it?'

I don't rush into indignant speech. I'm careful. Measured. 'Aren't you making quite a lot of assumptions? It may not give them a thrill. They may feel threatened by it. And you know how kids hate favouritism. If Max fancies you, you're in favour. What about the girls he doesn't fancy? Not to mention the way it looks to the boys. How far does the flirtation go? Sex with a minor. How about that?' Finally my control snaps. 'No real harm in it?' My voice shrills. 'What are you saying?'

He stands up. Moves away from me. Stands with his back to me, looking out into the shadows of the garden. It's so warm I've left the patio doors wide open to the July dark. 'I'm saying you don't have any proof. You admit that. So there's nothing you can do. You'd be better off forgetting the whole thing.'

The space between us bothers me. I walk across to him and

put my hand on his shoulder. He turns towards me. I can see his face again but I can't read the expression on it as he asks, 'What's the point of keeping on about it?'

I know there's truth in what Jack says. I ought to shut up and stop wasting nervous energy. Men never understand women's need to go on talking about a problem even when there's nothing to be done. But I can't quite give it up. 'It's wrong though, isn't it?'

'The three of us have to work together. Max has done a hell of a lot for Thomas Paine High. Still does. Isn't it better to focus on that?'

I could argue the point. Often I enjoy sparring with him, disagree for the fun of disagreeing. Not tonight. I ache to have my fears soothed and words aren't working. I step in front of him and press close against him. 'You're right,' I say, between kisses. 'I'll shut up about Max.'

He holds me hard against him and it's a kind of reassurance.

Chapter 17

I hump a comfortable chair down the stairs from my bedroom and into the sitting-room, already crowded with furniture. Counting, I decide that will have to do. I spent the afternoon welcoming back the groups who went away for Activities Week. Only not the one around which my thoughts circle. Field Archaeology isn't due back before six at the earliest. Yet I wish I'd waited. To do what? Confront Max? Interrogate the students? Subject Suzy to the third degree? When I've already decided any enquiry would be futile. Lacking evidence, I'm stuck with the pretence that nothing's amiss.

Yesterday's phone call from Max remains like an answer-phone message I forgot to wipe, heard over and over.

'So much going on here. Not a hope of getting away before two or three. Which means we'll hit the rush hour. Don't wait for us. No telling when we'll be back ... Yes, the kids have let their parents know.'

Forty words or so. Into which I've read endless layers of meaning. And found an excuse for avoiding an encounter which could only reinforce my helplessness.

I wish I hadn't quarrelled with Jack. My plans for the summer – a summer of freedom from parental responsibility, with Laura working as a Camp Counsellor in Maine and Daniel away for three weeks with Holly and her parents – start to unravel like a child's knitting ... There was no problem when I walked along to admire his mural. And I did admire it. The magic which had transformed the blank wall of the car park into a road curving between hills, with the powerful Harley-Davidson bike seeming to roar towards me. And the even more potent magic which had so enthused that unlikely gang of lads that they turned up every single day to work on it. It wasn't that I didn't want to spend the evening with him. As he very well knows. I told him ages ago about the Women's Group. But as we strolled back to school together he asked did it have to be this Wednesday? I said yes it did. He said fine, he'd go to the Sutton Arms. I expected him to call in before he left. Until I saw his red Golf driving away. What about tomorrow? We haven't made a definite arrangement. It's just a friendship. No promises. No ties. No reason ever to meet again. Except professionally. Management meetings, Max and Jack and me, with Jack no longer my ally. My heart shrivels at the prospect.

A car stopping outside. Jack's thought better of it. Convinced I recognise the sound of the Golf engine, I dash to the window.

Not the Golf. An MG sports car. Max. My heart lurches. A confusion of disappointment, dismay and something close to alarm. I check the time. Less than an hour to get him out of the house before the Women's Group arrive. Val among them.

I let him in, faking interest, to hide the calculations going on in my head.

'Amazing. An amazing week. The best ever,' he declares.

'So. Did you discover a second Sutton Hoo treasure hoard?'

'Not quite.' He sounds as though he's heard sarcastic. 'You'd have thought the kids were part of the professional team. They were amazing.'

Amazing. For the third time. Resisting the temptation to

parrot the adjective back to him, I say, 'Great.' There's an awkward little silence. Four bottles chilling in the fridge. Four reds on the work surface in plain view. Not intended for his consumption. But I ask, 'How about a glass of wine?'

I'm moving to fetch a bottle when he says, 'I thought we might go out and eat together. Celebrate the end of another good term.'

Unable to accuse him, I'm locked into the friendship game. Fumbling for an excuse, I say, 'You can only have been back an hour or so. You must want to unpack, sort yourself out.'

'All done.'

'That was quick. You can't have been held up in traffic then.'

He grins at me. Mildly flirtatious. 'I'm a very speedy operator when I want to be. But no, the journey was fine. Much better than I expected. I've been home, showered, changed. And now, Ma'am, I'm looking forward to the pleasure of your company.' He does a little mocking bow.

'What time did you get back to school?' I don't know why I'm asking except to give myself time to frame a polite refusal.

He shrugs. 'Just after five, I think. Does it matter?'

'No, no. I missed you by minutes then.' Why did he mislead me on the phone? *Mislead* is wrong. Time doesn't matter to him the way it does to me. He thinks it's okay to be late. I don't. Except now I'm blaming him for being early.

'Where shall we go? Venezia again? Or somewhere different?'

My avoidance has made it worse. 'Sorry. Not tonight. I'm tied up. Another time.'

He looks seriously disappointed. 'Shame. I was looking forward to it.'

Asking me out and to Venezia – like a parody of the relationship I once aspired to – Max and me the best of friends, a stunning demonstration of my talent for being on good terms with

everyone. It was never real. I know that now. But I haven't
found a way to abandon the pretence. I apologise again. 'Sorry.
It's been arranged a long time.'

'Something nice?'

'Yes.' I stretch the word to sound vague, yet positive. I reach
for a bottle of red wine and open it. Twenty past seven. What's
the earliest anyone might arrive? While I'm filling two glasses,
from the fifteen set out on the worktop, I ask him what the
weather was like. A bit desperate, that. I invite him to join me
at the kitchen table, keeping him away from the cluttered
sitting-room. I'm censoring madly. Everything I might say
seems to carry some unwanted implication. Yet I can't help
probing. I ask, 'Did Suzy emerge from her shell?'

He assures me it did wonders for her.

The conversation stutters. 'No mishaps this year?' I say.

He's quick to assure me nothing went wrong. He goes into
detail about the discovery of a coin, of some broken pottery. I
know this is the reality of digs, slow painstaking stuff. But not of
Max. Not that I'm listening properly. The soothing drawl grates.
The winning smile jars. The lips seem too red, the flash of teeth
too white. The distorting mirror of my suspicion? Or the true
Max revealed?

I won't refill our glasses. Ten more minutes and I must get
rid of him. But how?

I'm trapped in the fine-spun threads of my deceit. I've kept
quiet about my friendship with Val, about the Women's Group
where we meet. Suspect activities at Thomas Paine High where
a laddish culture prevails. Which I mean to challenge. Only not
yet. Not until my own position is more secure.

He holds my gaze for those extra moments, as though I'm
special, the focus of his total attention. But it must be a con
because he's failing to react to my inattention.

With the minutes ticking away I'm forced to choose. Max and Val despise each other. Better admit to the Women's Group than allow those two to meet. Why on earth didn't I come right out with it when he turned up and save myself all this awkwardness? Delaying the announcement has drawn attention to it. I swallow the last of my wine in a final sort of way and set my glass down on the table. 'I'm going to have to throw you out, Max.' It comes out high-pitched. My vocal cords are tight with tension. I take a deep breath. 'I'm expecting fifteen women to arrive any minute. The Women's Group I belong to. My turn to have them here.'

His eyes narrow. Only because he's smiling that irresistible smile of his. 'I didn't know you belonged to a Women's Group. Very sly of you, Isabel. You're more radical than you let on.'

Deceit is my ally. He has to fake approval. Because demanding the same rights for everyone is all part of the progressive agenda. Feminist. Anti-racist. Pro-gay. In favour of everything the reactionaries deplore. Which prompts a thought. 'Better not tell the governors.' I say it lightly.

'No way. It's our secret. Well, yours, mine and the fifteen members of your cell.' He drains his glass and stands up. 'I'd love to be a fly on the wall.'

I close the door on him with a relief I recognise as disproportionate. Why do I collude in the sham that we're friends and he's welcome to drop in whenever he feels like it? I wash our two glasses with meticulous care. Without evidence it's as if Max's visit never happened. But the open bottle of wine betrays the truth.

I raid my cupboards for coffee mugs, lining them up on my largest tray. For the next three hours I can be entirely myself. The urge to talk is as fierce as a thirst. If I tell the whole story from the beginning, everyone's bound to agree with me that

Max's guilt is a moral certainty. Especially Val, who must share the inner shudder of revulsion I have in his presence. Talking about it will give me a better perspective. We may even be able to work out some way in which I can intervene, instead of remaining trapped in the role of passive spectator.

But even as I'm ordering events in my mind the doubts begin. Perhaps it's better to hold my tongue. Max is fireproof. Maybe it's unfair to dump it all on Val when there's not a single thing either of us can do about it. Or maybe the real fear is that there *is* something I can do. And that Val will point it out.

I fill the kettle. The noisy rush of water drowns out thought.

I rouse and stretch a little. It feels different. The mattress less resilient. Then I remember. Jack's sharing my bed. His back is humped in sleep beside me. The night's warm. Even the sheet over us is making me too hot. I push it down to waist level. Without waking, Jack draws it up again. I move a little apart from him. But I don't mind. I like having him here in my bed. Yesterday was such a good day. He was really apologetic about Wednesday's sulk. Said he understood it wouldn't make either of us happy for me to end up a cipher, the way I was with Richard. Only he couldn't help wanting to celebrate the end of term with me.

I think of that other Isabel. Richard's wife. So unlike the person I now am. Even in the warmth of the bed I'm sharing, I shiver at the thought of ever being like that again. It's why I have to keep my own life. My life apart from Jack. I told him about Max. About the way he dropped in, wanting me to go out and eat with him. Not about the way it made me feel, because there's no point. Apparently he turned up at the Sutton Arms afterwards. To a very warm welcome from everyone. So I'm right to be wary. He was on top form, telling everyone about the fantastic week he'd had. Which I'm not going to think about. It's the one step within my power, to forget him for the six weeks of the summer holidays.

Jack's stirring. He turns towards me, murmuring, 'Isabel.'

'At least you got the name right,' I say. When I told him Richard often used the wrong name, Jack laughed. After seconds of disbelief, I found myself joining in. The pain I thought I'd never get over transformed into a shared joke. Part of the way he's healed me.

Still drowsy, he draws me close and begins to kiss me. Richard always wanted sex in the early morning. With him I hated it, my libido at a low ebb. With Jack, I slide into the rhythm of it as easily as he does.

Afterwards we doze again.

It's after nine before we're properly awake. Jack props himself on his elbow and smiles at me. It's his turn to push the sheet down so that he can draw teasing circles around my nipples. As always, he knows exactly how to please me.

'It's never struck me before,' I murmur, 'that Richard had so many partners because he was such a lousy lover. The opposite of what people imagine.'

'How d'you work that out?'

'No one ever gave him the satisfaction he craved so he moved on to someone new. Same result. Whereas you, darling Jack,' – I reach up to stroke his cheek, rough with a night's growth of beard – 'know that only considerate lovers find true satisfaction.'

'Would you be prepared to put that in a reference?'

'Are you seeking another post then?'

'I'm very happy where I am. Trouble is, I'm not sure my post is permanent.'

I laugh a lot at his nonsense. I don't ask him to explain what he means. As with so many things, it's better not to know.

Chapter 18

September 1982

Jack knows he's late. Three days into the new school year and already he feels he'll never catch up. The Italian trip with Isabel seems so remote it might have happened in another life. Today it's like he's living his recurrent nightmare. An unending sequence of kids and staff, demanding instant attention. The familiar dark brick corridors turned unfamiliar. Leading nowhere. The class he never reaches. The frustration which lasts into the first moments of waking.

The tutor group will be waiting, just as the class waits in his dream. Only this is for real. A cover lesson. Introducing new-style Personal and Social Education. He can't help suspecting Simon Clarke's done it on purpose. Another migraine attack. The last gasp of his opposition? Or a signal that the campaign continues? Whichever, Jack's got to teach in Simon's place. And it needs to be brilliant. Because Jack's in charge of the programme and if he can't do it well, how can he expect anyone else to? A fumbled start with cynical fifth years will put them off for good. He knows the topic and the outline of what he has to do but he's had no time to think it through, to imagine how it might run with this particular set of students. To do justice to the subject you need a relationship with the group, the whole point of making PSE a tutor responsibility. Isabel feels her credibility's on the line too. So much so she suggested the two of them could team-teach. Which as it turns out has only dropped him deeper into the shit.

As he hurries to make up time, he tries to collect his thoughts, but they whirl away from him like scraps of paper caught in a gale.

He pushes through a third set of swing doors. The tutor base is in sight. Someone's outside, looking out for him. Clare Henderson. Unmistakeable with that cloud of long reddish hair. A Pre-Raphaelite painting come to life.

Seeing him, she darts forward to meet him. Keeping pace beside him as he strides on, she asks, 'Jack, where's Isabel?'

'She's tied up. I'm doing PSE this morning.'

'You said at registration you'd both be doing PSE. I need to talk to her.'

'Sorry. She's got the Chief Education Officer with her. He dropped in unexpectedly.' At the door he pauses. 'Will I do?'

'No.' It comes out breathy, almost panicky. 'I have to talk to Isabel.'

Jack needs this like a hole in the head. He's late enough as it is. He can hear the chat from the classroom. Swelling as the students find their own entertainment. 'I've told you. You can't. Not at the moment.' Abrupt. Dismissive.

Before he can say anything to soften his response, Clare turns away, deflated, muttering, 'It doesn't matter then.'

Jack has no time to deal with it. He ushers her into the room ahead of him. He's got to get on with the lesson. Choices. How we make them. What interferes with freedom of choice. How to recognise what we really want. Ironic, that. What he really wants is not to be here, doing badly what needs to be done well. They'd made a hasty plan, he and Isabel. And now that's out the window too. It's not like her to let anything stop her teaching. He struggles to let go of his resentment as he gathers the kids' attention.

Half an hour later, it's like coming up for air. Teaching always gets his total attention, everything else forgotten. Now they're in small groups, boys and girls separately. As he'd planned with Isabel, though he's not clear why she was so adamant about the gender split. It's working anyway. Everyone's focused.

Except Clare. She's opted out. The body-language shouts it. Chair pulled away from the tight-knit group. Head turned sideways. In the whole-class discussion he'd noticed it as well. Noticed and not noticed. He wonders if she's sulking because of his response. He knows all about sulking. *See what you've done to me.* Out of character for Clare, the ultimate ideal student. Outgoing. Lively. Not now. He's never seen her looking so miserable. Better talk to her. Find out what's up.

'Jack, Jack.' One of the groups demanding his attention. Then another and another, crowding out reflection. Until it's time to draw the threads of the discussion together. He notices Clare again. Frowning a bit. He'll speak to her at the end. Try to put things right.

But it doesn't work out that way. When he tells the class they can go, a dozen stay behind, wanting to carry on talking. Proving the lesson wasn't a total disaster. He glimpses Clare walking off with the rest. He's half a mind to shout after her. Only it doesn't seem the best way to get on good terms again.

Once the kids let him go, he heads for Isabel's room, to tell her how well he's managed without her. But her secretary Linda says James Greville is still with her. They're having lunch together. Jack feels let down. Which reminds him of someone else who felt let down. Clare. He scribbles a quick note and leaves it with Linda.

Around 1.30, he spots the long lines of the CEO's maroon

Jaguar leaving the carpark. But Isabel doesn't contact him.

When he goes to register 5SC, Clare's missing. She's seeing Isabel, Emma tells him. Which figures. Then he's teaching art. Total immersion again. The phone rings as he gets back to his office. He adds the stuff he's carrying to the clutter on his desk, grabs the phone. Isabel, wanting to see him. Ten minutes, he says. He has things to do. (Or maybe it's his retaliation.) No, she insists. She needs to see him now. Curiosity about what bad news James Greville's brought overcomes any inclination to delay. The governors interfere all the time, but Heads have to juggle two sets of bosses. The Education Authority employs them, decides how many teachers, how much cash each school gets.

When he walks into her room Isabel's standing by her filing cabinet. 'Close the door,' she says.

Dismayed, he does as he's told. He's only seen her as tense once before. He's angry on her behalf. 'What did Greville say?'

'It was nothing. Congratulating me on the exam results. Wants me to run a course for other Heads, on School Transformation.' Her speech is rapid. She can't dismiss it fast enough. 'I've spoken to Clare.' Her voice rises and falters on the name.

'And?'

'She's accusing Max.'

He doesn't want to know. Doesn't want to hear it. But he asks, 'Accusing him of what?' As if he's hoping for some different answer.

'During Activities Week. He took her to the supermarket with him. Stopped the car and kissed her. It happened twice.'

'Happened? Or she says it happened?'

They're both still standing. Facing each other. Confrontational. Isabel's chin goes up. 'She says it and I believe her.'

Max in the pub that Sunday evening. Which he has no wish to remember. It mustn't be the way it seems. Where would that leave Jack? 'So what did she do about it? Slap his face? Jump out of the car? Complain to the other teacher? Suzy, wasn't it?'

'It's more complicated than that.' She shakes her head, struggling with distress. 'Please, Jack. We need to discuss it properly. Not stand here shouting at each other.'

Shouting? He's tempted to shout her down. His own guilt talking? Because he did nothing, said nothing? Or maybe it's a male thing. All women as prick-teasers. While claiming total innocence. But when she sits, he does the same.

'Clare has a crush on Max.' She corrects herself. 'Had a crush.'

There you are then. Fantasy. The diary business all over again. He's convinced himself that was pure invention. But Isabel prefers to believe it all happened. He'll keep it neutral. 'Not unknown, having a crush on Max.'

'Last October he found her in tears. Douglas Blake had bawled her out in a Maths lesson. Told her she was useless. Not a hope of getting a C at O-level, let alone the top grade. She's a high-achiever. Maths is her best subject. She was devastated. Max took her to his room, showed her lots of sympathy, told her to drop in whenever she felt like a chat. So it became a regular thing. Which on one level is fine,' she says, scrupulously fair. 'Or could be suspect.' Her voice has dropped and slowed. 'Depending how you look at it.'

Jack nods absently. Reviewing his own practice. Wondering whether anyone might say the same about him.

'She admits to having a mega-crush on Max. She was over the moon at the prospect of a week away with him. So she didn't object when he kissed her. And she agreed to go with him a second time. That was when he told her it had to be a secret. People would misunderstand. She would only be able to come round to his flat if she promised not to tell anyone.'

To Jack it sounds a bit unlikely. He won't risk questioning it. Says only, 'What did she make of that?'

'It made her uneasy. He'd kind of stepped off his pedestal. But on balance she was more thrilled than anything. She promised to say nothing.'

'So did she go to his flat? Is that what she's claiming?' Allegation, not proven fact. Jack wants to keep it that way.

'No. She went home bursting with her secret. After three weeks she cracked. She told her friend Emma what happened.'

'Christ!' How far has the story spread?

'Emma wasn't surprised. She's got an older sister, Amanda. Amanda had told her about Max. Told her everyone knew Max was *like that*. Clare tried to convince herself Emma was jealous. But it started the doubts. Yesterday Max sent for her, wanting to fix a day for her to come to the flat. The excuse was to prepare a display together. Ready for the Parents Evening. She said suddenly he seemed old to her. And creepy.'

There you are then. Crush over and the fantasy turns vicious. Prince into frog. Or dirty old man. 'She could say no, couldn't she? If she didn't want to go?'

'It's not as easy as that, is it? She put him off. She couldn't manage this week. He was more and more insistent. In the end she did refuse outright. And then he became threatening. Told her if she accused him of anything, he'd not only deny it, he'd get her into serious trouble for making false accusations.'

A double bluff? She's a bright girl. Bright enough to pre-empt the obvious challenge. *You made the whole thing up.* True or false, how's anyone to know? Besides, threats seem out of character. And counter-productive. 'Wouldn't Max see his best hope was to keep her sweet?'

'He changed his tack at the end. Said it was all a misunderstanding. He was sure they trusted each other.'

'So what made Clare decide to tell you the whole story?' Which so far is all it is. A story.

'Max spoke to her in the corridor at break. Asked her to come and see him after school. He was standing close to her, one hand up on the door-frame. Typical Max casual stance. She felt trapped. So she agreed. And then she panicked.'

'Clare accuses Max of kissing her. Twice. Without protest from her. And inviting her round to his flat to help prepare a display. That's what it amounts to?'

'I'm not sure. She was embarrassed. Naturally. I did try to ask for details about the kissing. Whether there was more to it.' She looks at him, dark eyes wide. 'But I couldn't risk putting ideas into her head. In case she has to appear as a witness.'

A witness? Jesus wept, what's Isabel thinking about? 'Hold on. Have you spoken to Max?'

'Not yet. I wanted to talk to you. It all adds up, doesn't it? After everything else that's gone on.'

'Adds up?' What's she talking about? It's hardly the open-and-shut case which puts Max's guilt beyond argument. 'You accused him before,' he reminds her. 'Over Helen and then over Dana. Not Rachel, because she insisted she'd invented the whole thing. I thought you agreed with me. The two of us have to work with Max so it's better to assume he's innocent. Unless there's clear evidence he's done something wrong.'

'I didn't have a choice before. I couldn't make an accusation stick so I had to behave as though I trusted him. I never did. Not for one moment. Did you?'

The question puts him on the spot. He doesn't feel about it the way she does. Only it isn't going to help if he tells her that. 'How do I know what he gets up to?' It comes out too impatient and he sees Isabel frown. 'I guess it's safer not to trust him.'

'No way we can trust him after this. And then there's

Emma's comment. Isn't it likely that what we've uncovered is a small part of something much more serious?'

'What are you saying?'

'That I don't *know*. That I don't see how you can ever *know*. But this time there's no way I can forget all about it. Because I believe Clare.'

She's made up her mind. Whatever happened to innocent until proved guilty? 'You have to talk to Max. Hear his side of the story.'

'You think I should talk to him before I see Clare's parents?'

Jack feels like he's being hustled closer and closer to the edge of a cliff. Like he's grabbing for handholds, tufts of grass, anything to slow his progress. 'You're going to bring her parents into it?'

'What else would I do?'

'They may have all sorts of prejudices. You know how parents can be.'

'I'm a parent too, remember. Clare's upset. I'd want to be told if Laura was feeling like that.'

The conviction in her voice excludes Jack. He's not a parent. Not a real one. He'll never be more than a spectator now. 'At least give Max a chance to deny it before you consider any other action.' It feels personal. 'You'd give me that chance, wouldn't you? You wouldn't just go ahead on the basis of an accusation, without telling me about it?'

'No, you're right.' Isabel slides uneasy fingers between one another. 'Clare doesn't want me to talk to her parents. Not yet.'

He seizes on it. 'Doesn't want you to tell her parents? That's dodgy.'

'Why?'

'If she's making it all up, she wouldn't, would she? They'd know whether she was telling the truth.'

Isabel starts to speak. Then she shakes her head and says, 'I believe Clare.'

So they're back to that. 'Don't you have to keep an open mind? If one student complained about another, you'd do that. And Max is your Deputy Head.'

'Should that make a difference?'

'I don't know about *should*. It sure as Hell *does*.' Jack leans back in his chair, overwhelmed by the difference. Because it's not just any Deputy Head. It's Max Truman, Will Fullwood's anointed son. The guy they might have invented the word charisma for. Isabel's not stupid. She must realise how much she's got to fear if she takes this on. Only maybe it's fear that's driving her. The fear she might do what's expedient. Instead of what's right, according to some fierce standard of her own. Counterproductive to warn her of the danger. 'See Max after school,' he urges. 'That way at least you'll know Clare's safe.'

'Yes, I have to see him, don't I? If he'll only admit it, I can deal with it myself. If he denies it, I shall have to let the governors decide.'

Jack listens in disbelief. They promised they'd never let anything which happened at school come between them. But how the fuck is he supposed to handle this? Safer to walk away. 'Okay,' he says. As he's getting up to go he manages to add, 'Good luck.'

The way she looks at him he knows she feels let down.

Back in his office, he's got a dozen things to do. He needs to sort the stuff from his art lesson. Three phone calls he ought to make this afternoon. That return to finish because it's meant to be back to the Education Office tomorrow. Yet he sits at his desk straightening a paperclip. And going over and over what Isabel said as if he might be able to make it mean something entirely different. It doesn't get any better. She's turning real life into a picture. One of those Caravaggio paintings. Contrast between light and dark exaggerated to the point of distortion. One figure trapped in the glare. Max, the focus of her attention, a complete shit. But what about the murky things lurking in the shadows? If Max is a shit, what does that make Jack? He wants something less absolute. Something which weighs the good against the bad. By absolute standards, how many of them are fit to teach? Max isn't the first teacher to fool around with students. How come it's suddenly a hanging offence? Taking sixth-formers out was quite common a few years back. Jack might have done it himself if he'd ever fancied one of them enough. Will Fullwood joked about it. *What did they mean, teachers had no perks? In comparison, a company car was no big deal.*

Whatever Isabel imagines, Max would never be crazy enough to admit to anything. But there's no way he'll ever convince her he's innocent. It's like ducking a witch. Floating proves you're guilty. Drown and you're innocent. But inconveniently dead. If Max won't confess he has to go. So the school loses an outstanding Deputy Head to save a few girls from sexual harassment. How is she going to convince her colleagues it's worth it? Jack's not convinced and he's in love with her.

It's because he loves her he's got to stop her.

He ought to have suggested they could see Max together. There might have been a chance to nudge her in the right direction. Time's running out. Once she speaks to Clare's parents, it will be too late. Parents have clout. With them backing her, Isabel won't have a problem persuading the governors to act.

The governors. Too bigoted for reasoned argument. Too stupid to understand the real value of anything. Enemies of everything he believes about education. He can hear them now, sitting in judgement on students. On teachers. On everything Thomas Paine High has always stood for. Are they to be the final arbiters of truth?

Chapter 19

Telling Jack. From the moment I understood, it was the one thing I longed to do. As though telling Jack would put everything right.

But Jack asked all the wrong questions.

It made me afraid of giving the wrong answers. So I censored, saying only as much as I thought it was safe to say. If it was hard to face the truth with Jack, how much harder will it be with all the other people I shall have to tell?

I pick up Clare's statement from my desk. Seeing it flutter in my grasp, I put it down again. I lay it beside Emma's. Compare what they say, point by point. What Clare says happened. Emma's recollection of what Clare told her. All the details agree. Not the wording, which would be suspect, but the sense of it. Surely that proves something. Except Emma's testimony is hearsay and I don't think that counts.

Back to the disciplinary manual, to re-read the procedures. I scan the pages. I can't take in the sense because all the time I'm trying to convince myself it won't come to that. But if there is a formal hearing, which is the last thing I want, I can't risk getting it wrong. When I talked to him about Rachel and her dangerous fantasy, as I was careful to call it, he was insisting all the time on his innocence. I understand why. The implications were horrendous. Police involvement. A court case. He was bound to deny everything. More than anything I want him to admit that Clare is telling the truth. So perhaps it's better that this time the accusation isn't as serious.

Perhaps.

Clare's prepared to stand by it. If he acknowledges what he's done, I can talk to him. Make him understand he's betraying the trust between teacher and student. As long as he's in denial, young women are at risk. Will it be possible for us to work together with that admission between us? Knowing the truth. That would give me a hold over him. He's a gambler. He might prefer to face the governors and gamble on getting away with it. Jack doesn't think it's as serious as I do. He thinks I'm making too much of it. I can't be confident the governors will think it's serious enough. I'll have to construct a strong case against Max.

Already I seem to be caught up in a TV police procedural. Keeping the witnesses separate while they were writing their statements. With my secretary Linda's help. She has to know in any case, because she does the typing. Clare and Emma are in Linda's office now, because they dread meeting Max around school.

Jack would say that's because they're lying. I won't listen to him. Rachel's the one who was lying, when she claimed that diary was fantasy. This evening Clare will talk to her parents and give them my letter. If Clare was inventing out of malice, she could have made a far more serious accusation.

Like under-age sex.

In a way, worse would have been better.

What am I thinking of? Wishing a traumatic experience on Clare to make my life simpler? So I could invoke Social Services and the police and leave it all to them. But Max may get away with it yet again. I've uncovered the preliminaries. I bet he's done it dozens of times. This once he's been stopped in his tracks. Not all the other times. Only how could I ever prove it?

Will he see my note? Perhaps I ought to go and wait in his room. I can't carry a pile of documents with me. I have to see him here. He's due any minute. How long shall I give him? Five more minutes? Ten?

I check my watch. The hands haven't moved. It must have stopped. No. The clock on the wall says the same.

'Isabel.'

I swing round from my desk. Max is standing in my doorway. Smiling. When does Max do anything else? *Smile and smile, and be a villain.* My face feels rigid with the gravity of what I have to say. Why doesn't he react to my expression?

'You wanted to see me? Straightaway, you said.' He laughs a bit at that, as though the urgency is a whim of mine.

'Yes. Have a seat,' I say, though I almost choke over the words.

He takes a chair. At forty-five degrees to mine. And close to mine.

I rush into speech, afraid I'll never say it. 'There's been a very serious accusation against you.'

His smile goes. His golden tan has a yellowish tinge.

'What is this very serious accusation?' The way he separates the words is a denial in itself. 'And who's making it?'

Instantly furious. As he would be. Whether he's innocent or guilty. But wouldn't an innocent person ask first who was accusing him? I've become his interrogator. I know nothing about interrogation techniques. I have no expertise in telling truth from lies.

'Am I allowed to know?'

'Clare Henderson came to see me.' Not strictly true. I sent for her, but I can't go into all that. Maybe he flinched at the name. But that could be my imagination.

'Go on.'

Unforgivable to keep him waiting. So I tell him. All the time I'm speaking, I'm listening to my own words, thinking it doesn't amount to enough. And I'm watching his face, trying to work out what he's thinking.

'Do you believe Clare?'

'I have to investigate.'

'So that's what you're doing now? Investigating?'

'Yes.'

'Without giving me a chance to say she's invented the whole thing?'

'Has she?' I ask, knowing as I ask that he won't convince me.

'No.'

He breathes the word so softly I'm not sure what I'm hearing. Something's interfering with my own breathing. More than anything I want him to admit the truth. I wait, too afraid of denial to ask again.

'It's a misunderstanding. Some of it happened, but not the way she described it to you.'

His take on events. Always different from mine. Perception. That's all it can ever be, perception. 'I want to sort it out, Max. To do that I need the truth from you.' I try to make it easier for him. 'She didn't come to make a formal complaint to me as Headteacher. You upset her and she wanted someone to talk to. She's not trying to make a big deal of it.' I want to make it easier but not too easy so I add, 'I'll have to talk to her parents.'

'That's what you intend to do? Get her parents in?'

'I have no choice.' Except there is always a choice.

'Who will the Hendersons be seeing? The Investigating Officer? The Headteacher? Or Clare's confidante?'

There's an edge to his voice. An implied questioning of my impartiality. If it comes to a Disciplinary Hearing, my triple involvement is bound to be used against me. The complexities of it swell to fill my thoughts, leaving no room for me to frame an answer.

'Judge, jury and executioner,' Max says. A ghost of a smile curves his mouth.

He looks shattered. As though something's broken inside him. For the first time in eighteen months all the power is in my hands. I have a shaming second of exhilaration. Then compassion takes over. 'You have to trust me with the truth. I don't want a public enquiry, any more than you do.' Why can't he see I'm trying to help him? 'But unless you're open with me, how shall I ever know our students are safe with you?'

'That's the offer you're making? If I admit to wrongdoing, you'll keep the whole thing quiet?'

Put like that, it doesn't sound right. To avoid repeating his version, I nod my confirmation.

He hides his face in his hands. A gesture so unlike Max I have to look away. 'You must give me time.' His voice is unsteady. 'It's been a shock. I can't think straight. Not at the moment.'

I hesitate. If he leaves now, I'll have lost the advantage. But only a bully would insist on continuing. 'We'll talk tomorrow then. I can't let the matter drag on.'

He doesn't respond. It's as though he's in some world which doesn't include me. He goes, leaving my door open. I hear his footsteps, muffled on the foyer carpet, louder on the parquet floor, then fading into silence.

At home I'm alone with my thoughts. And with the disciplinary manual. I've pored over it like a priest engrossed in his breviary. If Max comes back in the morning and tells me everything, we'll see Clare and her parents together and then we'll both have to put it behind us. If not …

Words. Clare's words. Jack's. Mine. Max's. I go backwards and forwards over them. But I make no progress. More than anything, I want someone to talk to. Daniel? It's tempting. This evening his antagonism towards Max looks like insight. But he's bound to say 'I told you so' and if it's all settled tomorrow I'll regret confirming his prejudice. I can't talk to Laura, who's in Boston with her friend Charlie. Missing my daughter swells to a pain. We haven't even celebrated her exam results yet – straight A's, including the dreaded General Studies. Max and Laura at the kitchen table. The scene, never since discussed, takes on a new significance. Laura a witness for the prosecution? I don't want her dragged into it. She's in the States. The choice is out of my hands.

'Mother.' Dan's voice. He sounds angry, but that's because he's shouting. 'Max to see you.'

My heart seems to shift and settle again in the wrong place, beating at double speed. I don't know when I have been so afraid.

I'm being ridiculous. He wouldn't have come unless he'd decided to talk to me. It's positive. It can be settled tonight. Of course I must see him. Not up here though. I hurry out of the room and down two flights of stairs. Reason enough for my rapid breathing.

Daniel has disappeared, leaving Max alone in the hall.

'Good evening,' I say, with new formality.

'No way,' Max says. The brilliant operator is back. The balance has swung again. His crystal-clear vision of the way things are, set against the misty world of doubts which I inhabit.

But I can't give up. 'Clare is absolutely consistent in what she's told me.'

'Poor kid. I knew she had this massive crush on me.'

'It's not about her feelings. It's about your behaviour.'

'My behaviour? What Clare claims I've done, you mean? I saw the risk, of course I did. After that crazy business with Rachel.' His eyes widen. 'All that crap she wrote in her diary. Pure invention, as she admitted to you. Didn't she?' Challenging me. Demanding a response.

It won't help to get drawn into an argument about the past. 'That's what she told me, yes.'

'And you believed her. Obviously you did. Or you'd have taken action.' Again he seems to demand a response.

This time I stay silent.

He compresses his lips. 'So I was more scrupulous than ever not to say or do anything which might be misinterpreted. But I can't be brutal, Isabel. It's not in my nature.'

'Clare's made a complaint.'

'Christ almighty!' He loses his cool a little. 'I'm telling you she invented the whole scenario.'

Using the same excuse. Hoping to get away with it again. I say stubbornly, 'If I'm presented with contradictory statements, I have to investigate.'

He shakes his head. Spreads his hands in a gesture of bafflement. 'An investigation would crucify me, no matter what the outcome.'

He is afraid then. It's worth repeating my offer. 'If you both agreed on what happened, there'd be no need for a formal enquiry.'

'Confess to something I haven't done? I tell you it's total fantasy. I've done nothing wrong and her lies are dropping me in the shit.'

Silence. I wait for him to break it.

'Look,' he says. The soft drawl, the charm offensive, so hard to resist. Because no-one does it better than Max. 'I agree with you, Isabel. We can't ignore it now it's gone this far. You've invited her parents in tomorrow. Let me talk to them first. With Clare as well. You see them afterwards. If they're not completely satisfied then you must do what you think is right. I'm the last person to try and stop you.'

A way out. Max talking to Clare and her parents. More potent than any conversation I could have with them.

He leans forward, eager to persuade me. 'Nice people, the Hendersons. I've met them. That'll make it easier.'

Met them? That time when it was vital for me to go to the meeting. According to Max. Another piece in the jigsaw. He met them. So I didn't. 'What would you say to them?'

'I'll explain …'

I stop listening. Because I know Max's explanations. Explaining black is white. Only if I refuse to hear can I hang on to my certain knowledge that black is black.

Coffee. The third cup already this morning. Probably not helping the headache three Anadin have failed to shift. My mouth parched with the dryness which follows a sleepless night. Tiredness gritting in my eyes like sand. Linda's here already, almost as early as I was. Everything is on hold until I speak to James Greville, which I can't do before the Education Office opens at nine o'clock.

Linda buzzes through. Leo Stewart wanting to speak to me. I'm on the point of saying no. Except he's been a Head much longer than I have. He's bound to be familiar with the procedure. So I say yes.

I dispose of his query with unseemly haste and launch into my own dilemma.

'Forget it,' he says.

My hand tightens on the phone. Disbelieving, I echo his words.

'Isabel, it will only give you grief. Persuade little Clare she misunderstood. Encourage Mr X to apply for promotion, write him a brilliant reference and get rid of the problem.'

I end the call as soon as I can. It's disgust I feel, I tell myself. But it isn't. The fears knot together, a hard ball filling my stomach. Who's going to take Isabel Lincoln's side against Max Truman when even Jack, who loves me, is wavering?

Which brings me to that other, deeper layer of fears. The ones I'm ashamed to look at. The fear that Clare is a liar and I am her dupe. The fear that I'm acting out of spite, because Max was, is, always will be, better at everything than I am. The fear that staff and students will unite in rejecting me. The fear that Jack won't love me any more.

Separated, each individual fear looms larger.

I won't let them alter my decision.

I draw towards me my list of questions for the Chief Education Officer. James with his sexist banter. An unlikely ally. But I have to persuade him to take it seriously or it's a lost cause. I rehearse my pitch with growing desperation.

At the first shrill sound I snatch up the phone. Linda's done her best but they've fobbed her off with Dennis, an underling. Tension peaking, I talk to Dennis myself, insisting the matter is urgent and highly confidential.

Finally, James Greville. 'Isabel. I'm flattered by your determination to speak to me personally.'

If I answer in the same vein, I'll choke. As calmly as I can manage, I begin my tale.

He listens without comment. He issues crisp instructions while I scribble: 'Cancel p.m. meeting with Max. Suspend him as a neutral act during investigation.' The list lengthens.

When I think he's finished, he says, 'One more thing.'

I pick up my pencil again.

'It's not going to be pleasant, Isabel, but I expect you already know that. Congratulations on having the courage to do the right thing.'

The warmth in his voice is so wholly unexpected that I choke a little on my thanks and blink to clear hot tears from my sore eyes.

At least the waiting's over. Max first. Last night he didn't understand where his stubborn denials of any wrongdoing were leading us. Even though I told him he couldn't see Clare's parents, he still thought I might be persuadable. So he agreed to stay at home this morning. He answers his phone on the first ring. He reacts to his suspension with angry disbelief. His promises of support, my fantasies of cooperative management, all as insubstantial as breath on frosty air. We are enemies now.

Next the Chair of Governors, Gordon Lindsay. However uncomfortable I feel about tackling him, I can depend on his readiness to condemn his old adversary, Max Truman. Then I remember his warning: 'Fullwood's system of education is worse than nonsensical. It's dangerous.'

'Dangerous?'

'Yes. Blurring the boundaries between teachers and pupils. All these young men around. All these out-of-school activities. Why would the teachers be so ready to give up their own time, unless there was something in it for them?'

What am I doing? Gordon will seize the opportunity to condemn not just Max, but the whole system. It will confirm his worst prejudices, offering him the evidence he wants to insist Thomas Paine High School must abandon the principle on which it was founded. The Equal Value principle. Teachers and students working together on equal terms.

I have no choice. The procedures are laid down. Agreed with the teacher unions. I tell Gordon. Or I do nothing.

There's a delay before I can speak to him. It makes it even harder to tell my story. How many more times shall I have to repeat it?

'Disgraceful. Disgraceful,' he says each time I stop to draw breath.

I tell him Max denies it ever happened.

'Deal with it. It's the excuse you need to get rid of the man, isn't it?'

'There'll have to be a formal disciplinary hearing.'

'No, no. We don't want that. Washing the school's dirty linen in public. Last thing we need after your efforts to improve the school's reputation.'

'It's unfortunate but there's no alternative.'

'Happens all the time in business. Need to get someone out. Put the right pressure on and they go with no adverse publicity.'

'It doesn't work like that in the public sector. The disciplinary procedures have been agreed with the unions.' I get no further.

For some minutes I listen to Gordon's view of the unions and their pernicious grip on the country. I am not to allow myself to be intimidated. I deny being intimidated. I have already done my best to persuade Max to go quietly. A disciplinary hearing cannot be avoided.

The edgy discussion goes round in circles until at last I ring off convinced he condemns Max's actions less harshly than my fixation with procedure.

Where's Jack in all this? Why hasn't concern, or even curiosity, brought him to my door?

The Hendersons are here and I have no time to pursue the thought.

Max is right. They are nice people. Articulate. Polite. And unhappy. The mystery of their November visit is revealed.

'It was delicate,' Caroline Henderson says. 'We didn't want to make unsubstantiated allegations, did we, Angus? We thought if we had a quiet word with you, the risk could be avoided.'

I apologise.

'No blame attaches to you. How could you know? We should have had it out with Clare. You were so desperately keen on the Field Archaeology, weren't you, darling? You didn't see it our way.'

Clare nods. Dark shadows under her eyes suggest she's had as little sleep as I have.

'Thought the chap was encouraging her, didn't we, Caroline? Irresponsible, that.'

'Unprofessional,' she agrees. 'But he was so plausible. He convinced us we'd got it all wrong. And now this business. It's upset you, hasn't it, darling?'

'It's made me feel horrible. How can I ever face him again?'

Her mother stretches out a reassuring hand. 'You won't have to, Clare.'

'I can't leave. I love it here. Anyway, what about my exams?'

'I'm quite sure Isabel understands that.' Caroline turns to me for confirmation. 'You won't let him stay, after what's happened, will you?'

So then I have to break it to them. It won't be my decision. The governors will hold a Disciplinary Hearing. Procedure again. As I describe it to them, they look more and more dismayed.

'You mean it's possible they might not believe Clare?' her mother asks.

I have to admit the possibility.

Mr Henderson mutters that justice has to be seen to be done, but there can't be any doubt about the chap's guilt.

I explain that since Max denies everything the governors will have to decide.

'Clare wrote a statement, didn't she? We thought that was

just for your benefit,' her mother says. 'Will it be evidence at this hearing?'

'Yes. Max will dispute it. It would help if Clare's prepared to tell the governors what happened.'

Outrage. All the Hendersons' protective instincts come to the fore. Max has upset Clare enough. The prospect of her integrity being questioned, even her reputation being attacked, is beyond bearing. Obviously the man is a menace. He should be forced to leave the school. The teaching profession. But not if it requires their daughter to be pilloried.

I do my best to persuade them it won't be as bad as they fear. Though I don't know, do I? It might be as bad. Or worse.

Angus Henderson is frowning. 'This Max guy deserves to have the book thrown at him. But you see the problem, Isabel. What are the limits of your powers, as Headteacher?'

'There are stages, with built-in delays. Counselling. Written Warning. Final Written Warning. Only the governors have the power of dismissal. Which the Chief Education Officer expects them to exercise, in a case like this.'

He nods understanding. 'It's unsatisfactory. But the governors will have to be kept out of it. We can't expose Clare to some ghastly public grilling. If that's the utmost you can do, so be it. We shall depend on you to keep our daughter safe. No doubt you'll be keeping a close eye.'

I confess it's no longer a choice. I've set the wheels in motion. I have no power to stop them now. Their concern for Clare is growing by the second. I can't help putting Laura's face on Clare, which undermines my attempts to reduce the ordeal to rational proportions.

Caroline and Angus agree the highest priority must be to protect their daughter. There is no question of her speaking out against Max.

'I want to,' Clare says. The three of us turn towards her, surprised. 'It's true, what Amanda says. It's happened to loads of people. Max made me feel special. But that's just the way he does it. I hate him now. I don't want him to get away with it ever again.'

Which starts an argument. I understand where her parents are coming from, God knows I do. But I need my star witness. So I keep quiet. Not offering encouragement to Clare. Not backing up her parents either. The Hendersons want her to come home with them, to discuss the matter further. Clare wants to stay in school, now she knows Max has been suspended. I offer them a room, to talk on their own. Clare remains adamant, insisting there is nothing more to discuss. Her determination shames me. Only I worry it's ignorance. She can have no concept of how it will be. I ought to warn her. But I need her.

On one point I'm in total agreement with Clare's parents. At all costs she must avoid discussing the matter with anyone in school.

The Hendersons leave, unhappy and dissatisfied. Clare wants to get to her lesson. As she leaves me I hear a voice I recognise asking if she's okay. If she makes any response, I cannot hear it.

Then Jack walks in. The door slams shut behind him. He strides across the room. He's smiling. Not because he's happy. His face is shadowed with concern. Not to beguile me. There's no pretence in him. The smile is a lover's smile.

So it's all right. I can even manage to smile back.

Chapter 20

Quarrelling with Isabel won't help. Jack can see that now. It's just as well yesterday's quarrel was mostly in his head. What he didn't say. What he failed to offer. Reassurance. Him telling her she was doing absolutely the right thing. Which from the way she's looking at him is what she's still hoping to hear. So if he wants to get her to see things differently he'll need to tread carefully.

He closes the door behind him and walks straight across to her. Sitting close to her he takes her hand and holds it in both of his. Not for long – they're in school after all – but it's long enough. Her smile widens.

'Are you okay?' he asks.

'Better now.'

'How's it going?' A natural enough question. And he needs to know.

'It seems to take forever. There are so many hoops to jump through. So many days' notice before we can move to the next stage. It might be after half-term before the hearing takes place. I want it all to be over, Jack.'

'You're not the only one. But maybe it's better to give it time.'

She's looking at him as though she can't believe he's said it. 'Why?'

'Something might happen. So there was no need for it to go to the governors.'

'Like what?'

He's vague. 'There might be a way round it.'

'There is no way round it. No other way to stop Max.'

Jack chooses his words carefully. 'You think they're sure to find him guilty?'

'How can I be sure? But James Greville doesn't seem to think there's any doubt about it.'

'Max will have the union to defend him.'

'Yes, but our governors are unlikely to be impressed by that. Gordon's already impatient because I'm insisting we have to follow the rule book. He can't understand why I don't just boot him out, the way he would if it happened in his firm.'

'Or turn a blind eye. Wouldn't that be more likely?'

'Probably. I doubt the financial sector takes sexual harassment very seriously. But then they don't have children to protect.'

Jack doesn't comment. Instead, he says, 'It's what the governors have been waiting for. A stick to beat Max with.'

'Max has provided the stick himself.'

'It's not what we want though, is it? Giving them a weapon to attack the school, not just Max. They'll argue it proves their point. The way the school's run makes it inevitable.' Then he wonders if he's said too much.

But Isabel is nodding vigorous agreement. 'Exactly. I knew you'd understand. That's the worst thing about it. One of the worst things. I thought I was winning. Persuading them that the system was delivering academically so it couldn't be so wrong-headed. Getting shot of Max won't be the end of it. I shall have the battle to fight all over again and at every opportunity they'll use Max as the ultimate weapon. If only he'd resigned before the governors knew anything about it.' She's looking at him with sudden hope. 'Is that what you meant? When you said something might happen. That he could still resign?'

'How would that help? It's too late, isn't it, now you've spoken to Gordon? Or could you still stop it?'

'If he resigned, that would stop it, I guess.'

'Or if the accusation was withdrawn.'

'Yes, but that isn't going to happen, is it? Thank God.'

'Why do you say that?'

'Jack, it would put us in an appalling situation. Stuck with a Deputy Head we can't trust around adolescents.'

'Doesn't the school matter more? How will you feel when the governors insist on dismantling everything we've worked for?' He's saying too much but his passionate conviction has taken over. 'Can't you see it coming? Compulsory uniform. Streaming. Calling teachers sir. The lot.'

'It's what I'm afraid of, yes.' Her voice is small and quiet. 'How long would our caring, sharing community survive that sort of regime? No more co-operation. Us and them. What would happen to mutual respect and trust?'

'Not much of that left by the time the governors have finished.' He hears himself, loud and angry.

'And all thanks to Max. I can never forgive him.' Now she's shouting too. 'Using our students for his pathetic sexual gratification! Where's the trust and respect in that? Undermining the principles on which the school is founded. Or perhaps the governors are right. Perhaps we're asking too much of human nature, of male human nature anyway, and someone's bound to take advantage. It seemed all right only as long as there was a Head who closed his eyes to the exploitation. The way Will Fullwood did.'

Jack hates to accept there's any truth in her accusation. But he can't quite get his tongue round a furious denial. He turns his anger on Isabel for being unrealistic. Why does she have to be so starry-eyed in her expectations? 'Maybe when teachers and students treat one another as human beings you have to accept there's a down side. They'll have human feelings occasionally. Sexual feelings.'

She draws breath to speak. And stays silent. It's like there are no words to express her fury. At last she says, 'You mean our system's so wonderful I shouldn't bother about minor problems? Like a Deputy Head having sex with a fifteen-year-old? You're as bad as he is, Jack.'

How have they got here? With a gulf between them it seems impossible to bridge. Jack shakes his head. 'Is that really what you believe?' It comes out as a whisper.

She's the one who reaches out then and takes his hand. Despite the anger, the current of desire flows as soon as she touches him. So he waits, ready to listen.

'It's the nightmare. More than anything I want you to convince me that's all it is. A nightmare.' Her hand squeezes his. 'I want you on my side. Not just because I love you and I hate disagreeing with you. But because if I can trust you it changes everything.'

'You can trust me. Of course you can.' What else would he say? 'Only I'm worried for you. It's not enough to be right. It never is, is it? You have to persuade everyone else you're right.'

'So were you putting the arguments you think the other side will use?'

'Something like that.' She still looks doubtful. Shifting to safer ground, he says, 'We promised nothing that happened at school would ever come between us.'

'Yes.' But it comes out hesitant.

'We need some proper time together.'

'You'll come tomorrow evening, won't you?' Now she sounds like his lover. Anxious in case he's going to refuse.

'Course I will.' Her hand still rests in his. Could be they're both afraid to let go. 'Let's enjoy our evening together. Forget about all this for a few hours. There'll be plenty of time to talk on Saturday.'

An uncertain frown. Then her brow clears. 'Whatever you want, Jack.'

It's only a form of words but he likes to hear her say it.

Jack's never done it before. Never undressed Isabel until she stands before him naked. He's undone buttons. Unhooked her bra. Seen her undressed many times. But never performed this ritual act. He's not sure why it seemed so necessary tonight. He draws her towards him, bare skin against bare skin, feeling her little shiver of arousal, matching his own. His hands slide down her back and hold her hard against him. She raises her mouth to his and he bends to kiss her. Her lips part and he slides his tongue between them.

It's not enough. It's nothing like enough. As though he's her partner in some old-fashioned dance, he steers her towards the bed. She yields at once to his guidance. She lies back, inviting him. He doesn't need inviting twice.

Saturday morning. A September day warm enough for midsummer so Jack's driven Isabel up to Kenwood. Too many people with the same idea. Parking at a premium. Finally they're walking down towards the lake. He takes her hand, chilly even today. How to start? Apologising. A good way to begin even if he doesn't quite mean it.

'You know the worst thing about this Max business? I've let

you down, haven't I?' The tenderness in her expression tells him he's got it right.

'You haven't let me down. That first day we got off on the wrong foot.'

'I guess I couldn't help seeing it from the male point of view.'

'Which is?' Less friendly.

'That it's possible to get it wrong without meaning to.'

'Like when you kissed me the first time? I might have been furious?'

They pause, gazing at each other. Lovers remembering.

Until Isabel says, 'You always know. The chemistry or whatever.' They stroll on, side by side. 'A teacher getting that feeling with a student knows it's sexual. And that's off-limits.'

'So Max would have known? If it happened.' He doesn't stress the conditional and she lets it go. 'Okay, but keep it in proportion. There are plenty of other things just as important.'

'Such as?' Instantly challenging.

He back-pedals. 'Such as your peace of mind.'

'Oh that. What about Clare's peace of mind? Mine has to take second place.'

'And it changes the way people see you. Bound to.'

'I realise it's damaging my relationships with colleagues. But this matters more.'

'I understand that.' Though it's arguable surely. 'Maybe there are ways to limit the damage.'

'I can't see how.'

'You've made such a difference in eighteen months. Getting staff on your side. Changing attitudes.'

She laughs without amusement. 'I haven't changed attitudes enough, clearly.'

'Long-term it's what matters though, isn't it? And Max is undoing all your good work. Setting everyone against you.'

'Do you think I don't know that?'

'Why don't you talk to him?'

'Talk to Max?' The way she drags out the name says it all. 'I have nothing to say to him. I doubt it's allowed, anyway.'

'You could check that out. And who's to know? You talked to him before. Why not try again?'

'I wanted him to admit what he'd done. As a first step to changing his behaviour. But he's still in denial.'

'He denies it happened the way Clare says it did.'

She stops. Turns to face him. 'What are you saying, Jack?' Her voice trembles a bit.

'He has to deny it. You must see that. He says he has no choice.'

'You've spoken to him?' Eyes wide.

He feels like a traitor, admitting he has. Wednesday night. In the Sutton Arms.

'So that's where he found his courage.' Scornful.

'We had a pint together.'

'You agreed to meet him?' She makes it sound like a betrayal.

'No. We happened to be in the same place at the same time.' The pub just after opening time. Cheerless. Empty. Except for the two of them. 'I wasn't supposed to refuse to answer when he spoke to me, was I? Be reasonable.'

'Okay, so you answered him.' And then, curious in spite of herself, 'What did he say?'

'That you'd talked to him about a complaint from Clare. It was a mess.' *You know how it is, Jack. You get a bit carried away. Find yourself where you never meant to be, wondering how to extricate yourself without too many hurt feelings.* And Jack knows exactly how it is. 'One of those situations you wish you'd never got into.'

'I bet.'

'He found it tough to explain. Because he feels bad about it. Wasn't surprised you were indignant on Clare's behalf. Only it wasn't the way she'd apparently described it to you.'

'No?'

'No. There was so much going on in his head. Not wanting to drop Clare in it. You having so little trust in him. Getting hold of the wrong end of the stick.'

'It didn't occur to him to try telling the truth for once?'

Jack stays patient. 'He asked me if I thought you'd listen if he tried to talk to you again. I said I was sure you would. So that's why he came round to see you. Only it didn't work.'

'He was very persuasive. Very eloquent. He's a very polished liar.'

'Isabel, it's you against him all the time. It's not helping your case. What harm would it do to show him a bit of sympathy? Come to some agreement to make it easier for each other? The way things are, he can accuse you of pursuing a personal vendetta.'

'He's the one who's in the wrong. I'm only doing what I have to do.'

The look on her face tells Jack he's fucked it up. Why can't she see he's trying to protect her, for Christ's sake? But even in his anger he loves her. He has one last try. 'Max thinks it's all you. Why don't you tell him the Hendersons are pushing it?'

'Because it happens not to be the truth. That may not matter to either of my Deputy Heads. But it matters to me.' For one second she hesitates. Then she says, 'I can catch a bus home.'

He's left watching Isabel as she dashes up the slope. As though she can't get away from him fast enough.

❏ ❏ ❏

Sod Isabel. Jack's tried to convince himself he doesn't care. Only his thoughts keep looping back to their row. To his clumsiness and her fury. She might have phoned. Or come round, like that evening when she'd waited outside his house. He could have rung her, but what if she slammed the phone down on him? Safer not to risk it. He hung about yesterday afternoon and most of today half-expecting her to contact him. He has to accept it's not going to happen. It's after six, the evening still sunny enough to mock his gloomy mood. He yawns and stretches with the weariness of boredom. He needs a drink.

Without conscious decision he gets into the car. Not the pub down the road then. Pulling away from the kerb, he accepts he's going to the Sutton Arms. He needs company. People to take his mind off his problems. Though he may be heading for a few reminders. Maybe it's a bad idea. A couple of right turns would bring him back to his own street. But at the lights he goes straight on. He has to do something to put a stop to this obsessive re-cycling of his doubts. Is there any such thing as The Truth? When everyone has a different take on things. Clare telling one story. Max telling another. Each of them equally definite about their own version. He knows Max can be devious. Offering the inter-pretation of events that suits him. He's dropped Jack in it some-times. Only everyone does it. All the time. Rounding out the picture with light and shade. Jack does it himself. A few high-lights, improving the way his own actions look. A few deeper shadows, darkening other people's. Not with any particular intent to deceive. Just because it doesn't seem possible to face his own actions in the unflattering glare of total accuracy. It would be much safer not to believe the worst of Max. Why can't Isabel touch up the picture?

The pub's almost empty so he sees them as soon as he walks in. Simon Clarke. Tim Mayhew. And Max Truman. They're sitting at a table in the far corner. They spot him and raise their hands in greeting. Simon says something and there's a burst of laughter. What does he care? He heads for the bar. He's watching the barmaid pull his pint when he feels a hand on his arm. Max.

'How about a whisky chaser?'

Another Sunday evening. Another pub. But this time he says, 'Why not?' After the weekend he's had, he needs something to lift his mood.

Max orders more drinks. Insists on paying for them all. Together they carry them across to the table in the corner.

'What did you think of the Spurs result?' Simon asks. He's a lifelong Tottenham supporter.

Football. A safe subject. Jack's glad he came. He has to work with these guys. For Christ's sake, it's not a betrayal to have a drink with them.

In minutes he'll see Isabel again. Jack's hung about deliberately so she'll get to the Monday morning briefing ahead of him.

He spots her at once. As he always does, wherever she is in a room. Some magic between them drawing his gaze. She's sitting up very straight. There's space around her, a deliberate distancing. Leaving her isolated. She's wearing that grey silk skirt and jacket. With a black top underneath. She's too pale for that today. He heads straight for her and takes the seat on her left. Whatever she thinks about him he's not a coward. He mutters a formal good morning. She responds with matching formality.

No Max of course. Management doesn't have reserved seats, not even unofficially. So there's no empty chair. But there might as well be. An absence filling the room with its disturbing presence. Any other Monday there'd be a swell of chatter. A hundred plus staff, catching up on one another's weekends. Sorting problems. Making arrangements. Today no one seems to have anything to say. No need to call for quiet. Isabel's voice is instantly audible. She's got it under iron control. But he hears the tightness of tension in it.

Before she's properly started, there's an interruption. Tim Mayhew.

'Max Truman is our Deputy Head. It's totally unacceptable to let his absence pass without comment. I insist on a formal, public explanation.'

'Very well. There has been an allegation against Max Truman. He has been suspended, as a neutral act, while I investigate on behalf of the governors.'

'That's not good enough.'

'It will have to be good enough. There is nothing more I can say. A public discussion of the matter will not help Max.'

Isabel's attempt to get back to the agenda is thwarted by a dozen voices. Simon Clarke, the loudest, wants to know why Max has been suspended. Isabel explains it's normal procedure, as their union reps will confirm.

'Surely,' Simon says, outraged disbelief dragging out the word, 'some judgement is called for. No one in their right mind would listen to such a crazy accusation. We're all convinced that Max is innocent, aren't we?'

Plenty of loud male agreement.

Isabel's voice rises above the racket. 'Whatever the strength of our personal convictions,' she says carefully, 'it has to be wrong to pre-judge the issue.'

'Come on, it's an open-and-shut case.'

'The procedures have been agreed with the unions. I have to follow them. Suspension is a neutral act which carries no implication of guilt.'

You have to admire her. Jack does anyway. Keeping her cool under attack. Maybe he ought to back her up. But he doesn't.

All around her the indignation boils up like milk in a pan. He watches, catching a puzzling exchange. Val Stephens, indicating she'd like to speak. Isabel frowning her into silence. No one speaks against Max. Not even the few who were out to get him when he was Acting Head. The reactionaries.

'We're all at risk,' Douglas Blake declares, 'if you are prepared to accept unsupported, malicious allegations from a student against the word of a teacher.'

The NASUWT position? Innocent teachers, malevolent kids? It's not the way they are. Not here at Thomas Paine High where relationships are key. Yet there's loud agreement. And Jack understands why. Because he feels the shiver of it too. Suppose a kid accused him? When he hadn't done a thing? How do you prove a negative, for Christ's sake?

Isabel's chin goes up, mouth set. Headteacher. In charge. 'I hear the strength of feeling. But there is still a school to run.' She goes rapidly through the bulletin. Looks at the clock. 'Your tutor groups are waiting.' Gets to her feet. Jack does the same.

'Hang on.' Tim again. 'Students are bound to ask. How are we to explain Max's absence?'

'Admit the fact of his absence. Offer nothing which encourages gossip.'

'That's all very well but—'

'I acknowledge the difficulty. I have no further suggestions. Except that lateness will increase student excitement.' Another pointed glance at the clock.

Jack waits. Half-expecting outright refusal. Then Isabel's resolve prevails. There's an angry buzz as they file out. But they go. He has a student to see. He's not sorry to have a reason to leave her. Only if she'd weakened, if she'd turned towards him with a glance of appeal ... But she hasn't. So he follows the rest.

Chapter 21

'We should have talked months ago.'

'Perhaps.'

'At least you know your response is absolutely the right one.'

'Is it, Val? I'd give a great deal to be certain.'

'You don't doubt that, do you?'

'I doubt it every minute of every day.'

She stares at me in astonishment. 'You believe Clare, surely?'

'Believe her, yes. But belief isn't knowledge.'

'I told you. I've known it was going on for years. Only I had no way of proving it.'

'Exactly. You couldn't prove it. We don't have proof.'

Val's mouth tightens into a hard line. 'I recognise the breed.'

I lean back against the cushions. As though I'm trying to distance myself from her words. We meet at the Women's Group. We've eaten together half a dozen times. I've found her a useful ally. But I've never been to her house before. We're not on the sort of terms where we drop in on each other. I'm here tonight because I couldn't stand the isolation any longer. After three days it was enough to overcome my hesitation about confiding in her. Now the misgivings come flooding back, silencing me.

'Come on, you know Max is guilty,' she urges.

Her absolute confidence crystallises all my half-formed misgivings. Two women. Both divorced. I hear the accusation. *They would think that, wouldn't they?* Jack too reluctant to believe, Val too ready. I need someone like myself, poised between doubt and certainty. 'Suppose Clare invented it? She admits she had a crush on him. A fantasy she half-believes herself?' I put the case for the defence, wanting it demolished. 'That's possible, isn't it?'

'Is that your considered opinion?'

I hear it as a jeering comment, not a serious question. Yet I choose to answer it seriously. 'No, in my opinion it's not fantasy. Because it's the second time around.' And I tell her about Rachel's journal.

'Her mother was concerned enough to come and see you. Was there no way you could pursue it?'

I feel accused. 'I don't see how,' I protest. 'Not after I'd talked to Rachel. She was adamant. She'd invented the whole thing. Her mother backed her up.'

'Houdini. Max ought to be in the *Guinness Book of Records*. He escapes from the most impossible situations.'

At least Val's acknowledging the problem. 'How has he got away with it for so long? Why didn't someone put a stop to it years ago? It makes it seem as if I'm imagining it all.' I laugh as though I don't quite mean it.

Val doesn't respond to my laugh. 'Men don't take it seriously. They'd argue we're not talking children, but nubile young women. Around the age of consent. Which is arbitrary, anyway.'

My unease gets me to my feet. I walk across the room. I turn my back on her, gazing at the lengthening shadows in the street. I don't have the nerve to look at her as I say, 'How wrong is it then? In the whole scale of things? With a fifteen-year-old? It's wrong here and now in our society. But absolutely wrong?'

'What are you saying?'

I swing round to face her then. I lean back against the

window-sill. 'Sexual attraction happens. We can't switch it on and off. At Thomas Paine High we put a lot of energy into breaking down barriers between teachers and students. Which makes it even more likely. Not that it doesn't happen in other schools. It's happened to me. Boys being attracted to me.'

Val's staring at me, dark eyebrows lifted.

I won't be put off. 'It must have happened to you.'

'Of course it has,' she says coolly. 'It's what we do about it that matters. Neither of us would dream of starting a relationship with a fifteen-year-old boy. Because we know it would be total exploitation.'

'It's not bound to be exploitation. It could be a genuine partnership.'

'Are you suggesting it might be a genuine partnership between Clare and Max? With a man twenty years older? In our patriarchal society? Sex and power.' She jerks her hand, an abrupt, angry gesture. 'The familiar, unholy combination. Why do you think Clare complained to you?'

'She hated it. She couldn't face Max.' The strong sense of her alarm and dismay rushes over me again. I have to accept there is no way of doing good without doing harm. She came to me asking for protection. 'She was afraid,' I say. 'Max was in the wrong. Which put him in her power. Yet she was still afraid.' I hesitate, puzzled. 'It should have made her feel she had the upper hand.'

'It doesn't work like that.'

I've sometimes wished I looked as serene as Val. Instead of having the kind of face which flags up every passing thought. Now all her serenity has drained away. She looks stricken, speaks haltingly. 'The victim always feels guilty. The paradox of sex. Such delight when it's mutual desire. So much disgust where there's coercion. Disgust with oneself.'

Personal experience? I don't ask. I'm too busy with my own

feelings to worry about hers. Richard's infidelity was always my guilty secret, not his. The shame of it possesses me now. But my past has nothing to do with this urgent present. 'So Max has to be stopped?' I intend a statement. Ask a question.

The name seems enough to energise her. 'Yes.' Vehement. Emphatic. 'You're not backing off that, surely?'

The question demands an equally emphatic answer. But I can't give it. I sit down again, facing Val. 'I still wonder if there might have been another way to do it. Whether it had to be the disciplinary hearing.'

'What's the alternative? Talking to him? To persuade him of the error of his ways? He's more likely to persuade you that black's white.'

It brings back the moments when I believed Max. Almost believed him. Wanted to believe him. 'I'll never be quite sure.' A murmur. Half to myself.

Val's impatience turns to concern. 'What is it, Isabel? Why is it so hard for you to accept the truth?'

'Max is right. It will destroy him.'

The familiar Gallic shrug, hands spread. 'So be it.'

No compassion. 'If he's not guilty?'

'His luck's run out. Rough justice for all the times he's got away with it. Face it, Isabel. The man's a paedophile, abusing his position to get access to young girls.'

'All our male colleagues are against us. Even Jack.' The words escape in spite of me.

'Oh, Jack.' A scornful dismissal.

I don't want to say it. I don't want even to think it. Yet I have to ask. 'You're suggesting Jack ...?'

'Is having it off with students? I doubt that. He's a flirt, of course, but very safe around students, in my observation.'

Her shrewd glance makes me self-conscious.

'I thought he was going to back you up when he sat down beside you,' she goes on.

'So did I.' The pain of that disappointment throbs afresh.

'Too much to ask of any man, I guess. They're all working themselves up with stories of innocent victims maliciously accused. Asking one another who'll be next.' She clicks her tongue dismissively and changes the subject. 'Why wouldn't you let me speak at the Monday briefing?'

'I didn't think it would help. I don't want men on one side, women on the other.'

'It's what you've got, whether you want it or not.'

A bleak division of the genders. A waste of precious energy to fight against it any longer. She may not be the ally I'd have chosen but I have no other. I am too dismayed to reply.

Val is studying me doubtfully. Then she leans forward and says, 'Look, I have absolute proof.'

I feel a surge of hope. Evidence? Uncontaminated by any prejudice I could be accused of? 'That Max is guilty?'

She nods. 'My first year as Deputy. Two fifth year girls rushed into my room to tell me their friend Vanessa was having a fit in the toilets and refusing to come out of the cubicle. When I got there she was sobbing out lots of incoherent stuff. Her parents would kill her. What was she going to do? Garbled, a lot of it. But I heard her say, "Max promised it wouldn't happen." I heard that distinctly. I coaxed her out and up to my room. She told me she was sure she was pregnant. Her period was four days late. She was calmer by then and she clammed up completely when I questioned her about having sex.'

I want to ask why on earth didn't Val tell me before. But hearing the rest of the story seems more urgent. 'So what happened?'

'I told her I was worried about her. I'd have to contact her parents. She was frantic. I agreed I wouldn't tell them why she was upset. She had to tell them though. And I'd need a phone call from her mother to reassure me she wasn't at risk. When she'd gone, I found something which must have dropped out of her bag. A birthday card. From Max. "To my little Vanessa. Thank you for everything. Love, Max."'

'Let me get this straight. You're saying Max had had sex with this girl and made her pregnant?'

'It's obvious enough, isn't it?'

'You're positive you heard her say his name?'

'For God's sake, I'm a linguist. My ear's attuned to nuances of pronunciation you'd never notice. No way I could be mistaken about a name.'

'Did you confront him with it?'

'No. I decided to await developments. Then Vanessa's mother came to see me. Very sweet. Totally unworldly. They belonged to one of those extreme Christian sects. Vanessa wasn't pregnant after all. Her mother blamed herself. For a failure of sex education. Her daughter led a very sheltered life. She'd convinced her mother she'd thought French kissing could give you a baby.'

'Good grief, was she really so naïve?'

'In London? In the Seventies?'

'No, it's unlikely.' Absolute proof? It's like trying to build a castle from dry sand. It slides away, blank and featureless, as you try to fix the detail. Disappointment makes me sharp. 'You could scarcely hope to convince a jury, could you?'

'I had to accept the police wouldn't be interested. But if you'd been Head then it would have rung alarm bells, wouldn't it?'

I try to imagine it. A clean slate. No preconceptions. 'Yes, definitely.'

'I took it to Will Fullwood. He made fun of me. Asked

whether sending a birthday card was Max's equivalent to sending the Archangel Gabriel. When I persisted he advised me to
keep my warped menopausal fantasies to myself in future. I
didn't want my colleagues to think I was unbalanced, did I?'

'That's outrageous.' I'm angry on her behalf. And it helps. I
won't misjudge her, the way Will did. Which means I accept
her interpretation of events. 'What did you say?'

'I asked him what action he was going to take. He told me he
would warn Max.' Val gives a small, mirthless laugh. 'About me
rather than about his behaviour, I gathered.'

'Supposing something else had emerged? A girl who really was
pregnant? And Will had had warning. He was taking a terrific risk.'

'Risk never worried him. Will against bourgeois society.
That's how he saw himself. The mission was what mattered, not
some silly little girl's bad experience.'

'Was there nothing you could do?' A reversal of roles. Why
is it always so much easier to see what someone else ought to
have done?

'I spent hours wondering, believe me. I wouldn't wish an
unwanted pregnancy on a fifteen-year-old but I couldn't help
regretting the absence of hard evidence.'

'Couldn't you complain to your union about the way Will
treated you?'

'Hardly. In this area it's dominated by the left wing. Will
Fullwood was a major hero. Up there with the Heads of Rising-
hill and William Tyndale. The two martyrs of the revolution.
No way they'd help me martyr Will.'

'The governors? They'd appointed you. They must have
been on your side.'

'I considered that very carefully. In the end I decided they
wouldn't take it seriously enough. I needed a better issue. More
evidence.'

My pulse rate rises. What if the governors don't take Clare seriously? 'Why did you think they wouldn't take it seriously?' I have to ask even though I'm unlikely find any comfort in the answer.

'*Women's lib nonsense. They're just anti-men.* Can't you hear them?'

The trouble is I can hear them. All too clearly. Changing the subject a bit, I ask, 'Did you consider resigning?'

She looks astonished. 'Not for one moment. Why should I give anyone that satisfaction?'

'But you must have felt completely isolated.' Months of it, when seventy-two hours has seemed endless to me.

Another Gallic shrug. 'One of those things. I stayed as a witness. In the hope that one day my testimony could be put to good use.' She smiles. 'Max has never forgiven me.'

'For taking it to Will?'

'For knowing, most of all. The dark side of the dazzling Max Truman.'

'Do you think any other staff know?'

'About Max and his fan club? The girls who go to his flat to water his potted plants? At least half our male colleagues know, at a guess.'

'You're not suggesting they're all complicit?'

'The ones who share his tastes are. Like Tim Mayhew. And Simon Clarke. The others don't see any reason to get worked up about it.'

I don't want to believe her. It's not the way I want the world to be so it can't be true. 'You don't know that.'

'It's obvious enough. Girls in their offices after school. The way they let them hang around. The way they bask in adoring glances. Why do you imagine Simon fought such a desperate rearguard action about his precious PSE?'

'It was his empire. He wanted to hang on to the power it gave him.'

'Did you ever look at the sex education?'

'I've glanced at it. No more than that.'

'A lot of stuff about relationships. Some of which comes close to being a defence of paedophilia.'

Val must be exaggerating. I'd have noticed. 'That would draw attention to it. Why would he do that?'

'A method of selection. Dirty talk. A turn-on in itself. The start of the grooming process.'

'That's nonsense, Val.' Though I'm making a hasty resolution to hunt out the material and check it. 'You're not suggesting half the staff are active participants?'

'You forget. PSE was taught by Simon's precious team.'

My agreement is reluctant. 'I suppose so.'

'Have you never wondered about Tim and his Photographic Society?'

At once I feel I ought to have done. Max has filled my thoughts, to the exclusion of anyone else. 'Is there something suspicious about it?'

'For a start, there are almost no boys in it. I've no time for sexual stereotypes but photography tends to be a male interest. The members are hand-picked.' She states it as a fact. 'Fun in the darkroom, I guess. Max and Simon can provide models. And enjoy the prints.'

'You mean Tim takes photos of them with students?'

'Well, what do you think?'

'You've seen them?'

'No, I'm not on the circulation list.'

I cling to uncertainty as though it's a lifebelt. 'There's no evidence then.'

'I bet there is. In Master Mayhew's filing cabinet. It's why

I've always wished there was something serious enough to report to the police.'

My brain resists. Val's distorting the facts to support her belief-system. I ought to be insisting she's got it wrong. I bow my head, pressing my hand against my forehead, as I murmur, 'Dear God.'

'It's crazy to have any qualms about what you're doing to Max. He deserves everything he gets. And more.'

I think she intends to be comforting. 'If so much is wrong, I can't see how it can ever be put right,' I say.

'At least you've made a start, taking this business of Max to the governors.'

My thoughts run in dark channels. Is the corruption there for anyone to see? Have I been averting my eyes from unpleasant truths when I thought I was fearless in facing them? Maybe Val is the clear-sighted one, seeing the world as it really is, while a haze of romantic ideals obscures my view. 'I blame myself,' I murmur. 'For being too quick to accept there was nothing I could do. I go over and over what's happened. My uneasiness. Suspicions I ought to have followed up. Action I should have taken.'

'Guilt. The default position of most women. Not to be recommended.'

'If all you say is true ...' I have to stick to the conditional. 'If it's true, does that affect your approach to education? Should it make us wary of being ourselves in the classroom?'

'It's high-risk. I think it's the only way to teach well. But there's no denying it's high-risk.'

'As the governors keep telling me.' How have I got here? Agreeing with Gordon and Colin, quarrelling with Jack. 'Our overwhelmingly unreconstructed-male governors. I must be mad to expect them to take Clare seriously.'

'Your salvation is that they loathe Max Truman.'

My agreement is half-hearted. We catch each other's dismay. We go through the governing body one by one, gloom deepening.

It's nearly nine when I leave Val to drive home, a mountain of work in my briefcase awaiting attention. Half the arguments I used were Jack's. I hate disagreeing with him. I have to get angry to find the courage to do it. Otherwise the urge to please him is overwhelming. But that's the past. Only the most formal contact since last Saturday's row. Nothing has ever divided us for so long before. We shan't make it up now. How can I bear it, when I need him more than ever? Absolute certainty would simplify everything. The kind of certainty Val has. While I was with her, suspicions hardened into solid fact. But that's all they are. Suspicions. If I saw stark black and white, instead of subtle shades of grey, it might all seem worth it. Because nothing I've achieved in the last eighteen months is likely to survive the destructive power of calling Max to account.

Supposing I can't make the charge stick?

Fail to convince the governors and he escapes scot-free. Winner takes all. Maybe there is wisdom in knowing what to overlook. Jack thinks so. Even the Hendersons would have been happier if I'd hushed the whole thing up.

But not Clare. Max and that insidious charm of his. Impossible to quantify the damage he's done. The shame and guilt he's induced. The victim's secret. Children never rush to complain about parents who beat or abuse them. When it leaks out, they confess reluctantly. As though the crime is theirs.

Indoors, I head for the kitchen. There's white wine in the fridge. Alcohol, taking the edge off my anxieties. It's too inviting. I opt for tea. As the kettle boils, Dan comes in.

'Are you okay?' he asks, concern for me knitting his brow.

Richard's voice. Richard's expression. His father's son. For a moment I doubt even Daniel. Then recovering, I say, 'Fine. Want a tea?'

The doorbell interrupts us. A shrill alarm. I turn to Dan for help. 'If that's Max, I'm not here.'

'Got you,' Dan says. And heads for the hall, letting the kitchen door thud shut behind him.

He's back, caught up in conspiracy. 'Jack,' he hisses. 'I told him I wasn't sure if you were in though he must think it's weird I—'

I whirl out of the room. Jack may already be convinced I don't want to see him. He's there in my hall. A solid, reassuring presence. Though he looks a little uncertain. I run into his arms, repeating his name like a charm.

He holds me close and kisses me. I forget all the guarantees I meant to ask for. Now he's here our embrace is the only thing that matters.

Dan's retreated to the kitchen. We follow him there. We accept his offer of tea, though I'm tempted again by the wine, and its power to make opposed standpoints a little hazier. When Dan departs, muttering about the work he has to do, the awkwardness takes over.

Finger tracing the pattern on my mug, I say, 'I'd like to ignore what's happened. But we can't, can we?'

'No. I came to tell you something.'

Not to make up then? Lacking the courage to ask, I stay silent.

'Will you hear me out?'

'Of course.'

'You'll be angry. But I want you to listen to the end.'

God, what is he going to say? My stomach hollow with apprehension, I tell him I'll listen.

'I want always to be on your side. To back you up. But not

mindlessly. You wouldn't want that, would you?'

My agreement is half-hearted.

'With Max I wasn't convinced it was the right way to go. Neither of us knows exactly what happened with Clare. I wanted to believe it was nothing too serious.'

At least he's putting it in the past tense.

'You seemed to want to put the worst possible interpretation on it.'

I swallow down an angry denial. I agreed to hear him out. It may be the last time we ever talk as lovers. If we are lovers. I can't be sure how much our embrace in the hall meant to him.

'So the way I saw it you were putting a lot at risk on quite dodgy grounds. Things which matter to me. Your success as Head. Relationships with colleagues. The whole future of Thomas Paine High. Because it's exactly what the governors have been waiting for. Proof that the way we do things is worse than ineffective, it's immoral. A chance to crucify Max. Tough, even if he's guilty as charged.'

It makes it worse that these are my doubts. I try to detach myself, tracing the pattern on my mug obsessively.

'That's if the governors find him guilty. They're an unpre-dictable lot. Who knows which way they'll jump?'

His question feeds my uncertainty. I can't answer him.

'No point in doing it if it doesn't work.'

If the governors decide there's no truth in the accusation, will that make it less true? My mouth is too dry for speech but the question is loud in my thoughts.

'To me it looked like you'd dug yourself into a hole and I might be able to help you out of it. You insisted there was no way it would help to talk to Max. I disagreed.'

This time I can't hold the words back. 'You've talked to him again?'

'I said you'd be angry. I talked to him in the pub a week ago. You know about that. And twice since.'

'To hear his side of the story, I suppose.' I make no attempt to keep the sneer out of my voice.

'That was only the first time. The second time, Sunday evening, he was with Tim and Simon.'

I shiver at the names. They seem to prove Val's case. 'Go on.'

'I had a drink with them. We talked football.'

'Male bonding?' Another sneer.

'Something like that. I thought I was proving the business with Max wasn't too serious. We could get over it and carry on as before.'

Again the past tense. It gives me a flicker of hope.

'Yesterday Max phoned. Asked me to meet him at the sports club he belongs to for a game of squash. I didn't see any harm in it so we fixed it for this evening. That's where I've been. Playing squash with him.'

I shake my head in disbelief.

'I won.' Mildly triumphant. 'And then we had a drink in the bar. That was when I realised why he'd invited me. You need to understand where I was coming from. Hoping there was some way out. Max hoped that too. Only not quite the way I did.'

To my astonishment Jack reaches out and captures both my hands. I find the courage to look at him. He's frowning. But the warmth of his hands enfolds mine.

'He started talking about you. Said he knew I had influence with you. Couldn't I persuade you it was a big mistake to go ahead? He was sure I agreed with him. I admitted I did. But I told you you were convinced you were doing the right thing. Unless he had something new to offer, there was no way I could change your decision. Then he got threatening. You'd be in a mess when the truth came out. He'd use it at the disciplinary hearing. How you weren't fit to be in charge of a school. You were too busy having it off with me to do your job properly.'

'What?' All my horror compressed into a single word.

Jack presses my hands. 'I got up and walked away before I hit him.'

'So you're not on his side?'

Jack grins. 'Not exactly, no.'

'Because you're furious with Max? Or because you think I'm doing the right thing?'

'This is the hard bit. He was desperate. I've never seen him like that before. It was like I'd never looked at him properly. He's said stuff to me, I've seen things, but until tonight, in that bar, I've always managed not to understand. I've known and not known. Can you accept that? And forgive me?'

'Why didn't you tell me the moment you arrived?'

'What do you mean? I kissed you, didn't I?'

I'm pointing out that Judas could have said as much when he leans forward to kiss me again. I have to admit the way he does it saves a lot of words. But it's awkward, sitting on kitchen chairs. So we head for the sofa in the sitting-room and start again. After a while I draw away to say, 'Do you think there are other people like you? Who know and don't let themselves know?'

'Most of the staff, at a guess. It's making sense of the contradictions. Accepting that Max can be brilliant in so many ways. And an absolute shit in the way he exploits young women.'

'We want villains or heroes. Not both in one man.'

'But it's what we've got.'

'I've been talking to Val Stephens. She thinks it much worse. A web of corruption. Involving Tim Mayhew and Simon Clarke. A ring of paedophiles.' I hesitate, nerving myself to ask the question. 'Is that something else you've known and not known, Jack?'

'They're his mates, yes. I guess they'd cover up for him. But more than that? Did Val offer any evidence?'

'No hard evidence. Maybe I don't believe her because I don't want to.'

'Tim's a disciple. In his eyes Max can do no wrong. I doubt he'd do much on his own initiative. Simon's a burnt-out case. Early promise unfulfilled. He can imagine he's still going places if he can hang on to Max as his best mate. I don't think there's any more to it than that.'

'We're optimists, Jack. In our eyes the glass is half-full.'

'It's not empty, though, is it? Pessimism can distort the truth just as much as optimism.'

'Max is the key to it then?'

'No question.'

I fidget with a button on his shirt. 'Do you think he will use our relationship to attack me at the disciplinary hearing?'

Jack gives me a reassuring hug. 'Let him. Don't try to cover up. Why should we? There's no way he can produce evidence it's doing any harm, because it isn't.'

My nod is uncertain. 'He was taking a risk, wasn't he? Talking to you like that.'

'Risk never bothers Max. He always wants to live life on the edge. Part of his wonder-boy image.'

'Wonder-boy? Clare called him old and creepy.'

'It's a bit pathetic when you think about it. A couple of hours ago I could have murdered him. But he's like Peter Pan, isn't he? He doesn't want to grow up. And forty's staring him in the face.'

'I always thought Peter Pan was pernicious. His only saving grace was that he stayed in Never-Never Land.'

Jack laughs and I join in. His tolerant kindness reassures me. My action is proportionate. I am doing only as much as I have to do. It's like finding a sunny corner, sheltered from the bitter wind I've shivered in. I relax, even though it's only a very temporary shelter.

Chapter 22

November 1982

A classroom. E4, where I teach sometimes. Chairs, grey plastic and metal. Tables with grey plastic tops. Eight fluorescent strip-lights, one buzzing. Chalkboard, cleaned to leave only a whitish residue. Noticeboards, with tidy displays. Clock on the wall, hands pointing downwards at 7.27. All utterly familiar. Yet all dauntingly different. On three sides, tables and chairs pushed back against the walls, so there's hardly space to edge behind them. On the fourth side, two tables as far apart as possible. Two chairs at each. Two unoccupied. The witness stand. Two occupied. The Area Union Secretary, Lisa Whitworth, in one. In the other, Max Truman, the defendant. Classroom transformed into courtroom.

I've met Lisa. Nice woman. I smiled at her as she walked in. She ignored my smile, blocked my attempted greeting. Acquaintance turned enemy. She's here to support Max. My Deputy Head. I can't look at him. What I know he's done. What he may have done. What I'm doing to him. It's all too much. Who's on my side? Across the corridor in E3, Jack sending encouragement through the ether. Here, James Greville, Chief Education Officer. Shrewd. Professional. And totally support-

ive. Will it be enough? No encouraging glances from Gordon
Lindsay, studiously neutral as Chair. Or so I hope. I suspect he
blames me. He enjoyed his dark suspicions. Giving them substance is overkill. Colin Blaine will follow Gordon's lead. Five
more governors, solemn in their suits. Seven men. Gaynor
Jones, Parent Governor, the only woman. The waiting's the
worst. We're all here. Why doesn't Gordon start? He's muttering to Dennis Green, Clerk to the Governors, at his elbow.
Nodding. Shuffling of papers. Checking the procedure, I guess.
I've read it so many times I could recite it in my sleep. Gordon
looks up. At last!

The preliminaries are interminable. Introductions. An
explanation of the purpose of the hearing and the form it will
take. I sip water, my tongue drying in my mouth.

Gordon turns to James. 'Mr Greville, perhaps you would
clarify the points at issue.'

'Certainly. Clare Henderson, a student at this school, has
made a serious allegation of inappropriate behaviour on the
part of Max Truman. Such behaviour would be a clear breach
of the code of conduct for teachers laid down in the disciplinary
manual.'

Lisa shifts in her chair.

James continues smoothly. 'I stress the behaviour is alleged.
The Chair of Governors has responded correctly by asking the
Headteacher to act as Investigating Officer. It will be up to
the governors to decide whether the allegation has been sub-
stantiated.'

A fog of jargon. Is everyone following? Not James's fault.
He has to stick to the procedure.

More from Gordon. How's Max taking it? I nerve myself to
check. Intercept the rueful smiles he and Lisa exchange. Note
the way her gaze lingers on him. She's succumbed then.

Another sucker for his charm. No chance of female solidarity there. I'm too occupied with the two of them to follow the proceedings. Until I hear my name.

'Mrs Lincoln telephoned me. I requested her to undertake an investigation on my behalf.'

Actually I told him that's what he had to do. I meet his gaze. He's asking me to explain what I discovered. I'm conscious *discovered* is inaccurate. It all came from Clare, wanting to talk to me. Because I teach her English and she knows me. Because I'm a woman and she wanted to accuse Max. Before I can answer, Lisa Whitworth intervenes. She questions the order of events. Was it Thursday when I spoke to the Chair of Governors? I admit it was.

'Is it not the case that this allegation was made directly to you?'

'Yes.'

'I understand you sent for Mr Truman on the Wednesday and charged him with improper behaviour. It seems you had made your mind up before you were requested to act as Investigating Officer.'

'Max Truman is my Deputy Head.' Hesitation. A switch to the past tense. 'He's been a trusted colleague. I hoped a conversation with him might clear the matter up.'

'Was that for his sake or for yours?'

'It was unpleasant for both of us. But for his sake most of all.'

'The ambiguity of your own position didn't alarm you?'

Alarm? It makes it sound serious. But I deny any alarm.

'You listened to Clare Henderson's story. You told my member you believed her. You became his accuser. Yet you accepted the role of Investigating Officer.'

'Yes, I ...'

Lisa interrupts my attempt at explanation. 'So much for impartiality. You advised Mr Truman that it would be better for him not to deny these serious allegations, did you not?'

I've been restrained in an attempt to demonstrate impartiality. I've failed. Obviously. I come back fiercely. 'If the allegations were true and if Max Truman admitted they were, counselling would have been the appropriate response.' I glance around. 'Instead of all this.' A single word to encompass the weeks of waiting, the endless exchange of correspondence, the corrosive distrust spreading like an infection, and tonight our submission to the governors' verdict. 'I was acting in his best interests. He denied the allegations. I pointed out the governors would have to decide.'

Lisa looks as if she's about to attack again. Gordon steps in belatedly. I take the opportunity to refer everyone to the statements from Clare and Emma. There's a rustling of papers. Minutes of silent reading in which I can draw breath.

Fitzroy Buchanan tosses down his copies. Indicating what? Disgust? Disbelief? 'Clarification, Mr Chairman. How are we to establish the veracity of these statements?'

'That is what we are here to do, Mr Buchanan.' Gordon betraying the irritation an intervention from Fitzroy unfailingly provokes. 'With your agreement, ladies and gentleman, I propose to invite Clare Henderson to speak to us now. Any further wait will add to the stress on her.'

For a second I think Lisa may object. But she says nothing. The Clerk to the Governors sidles behind chairs to the door and leaves to fetch Clare.

What have I done? How will Clare cope with hostile interrogation? I have far too long to worry before the Clerk at last reappears with Mrs Henderson and Clare. They take the seats he indicates. Clare flashes a glance sideways. The distance between the two tables shrinks to an uneasy proximity. She settles herself, shaking back the cloud of auburn hair. Crazy to wish her less striking. Less attractive. But I fear it will be held against her. Some warped male logic. *What does she expect, when she looks like that?* Why should appearance matter so much? Though I've bought into it myself this evening, softening my grey skirt and jacket with a rose-printed blouse. And I hope they're all noticing Max is far too good-looking.

Gordon's speaking. I can tell by his voice he's made his judgement of the Hendersons. His sort of people. Deserving of urbane courtesy. Surely that must help my cause? He's talking to Clare now. 'I know how difficult this must be for you. We have your written statement. We'd like you to go through what happened and then you may be asked some questions. Is that all right?'

Her response is perfect. A glance towards her mother, here to support her daughter despite her own misgivings. Then, 'Yes, thank you,' hesitant but clear. Her account is spontaneous, adding a little about how she felt, not deviating from her statement in any particular. I breathe out in my relief. No one can doubt now.

Gordon is inviting questions. I hold my breath again through seconds of silence.

Lisa first, smiling. 'Thank you, Clare.' As though the accusation has done her a favour. 'This Field Archaeology trip – you were keen to go?'

Puzzled agreement from Clare.

'Not a particular interest of yours though, is it? I understand you're a mathematician?'

'Yes.' Affirmative on a rising note of interrogation.

'So you wanted to go because Mr Truman was running it?'

Clare exchanges a frowning glance with her mother. 'At the time we were choosing, yes.'

'And at the time when you went?'

'I suppose so, yes.'

Three extra words making the agreement reluctant. Suspect.

Lisa's smile is wider. '*You suppose so. Yes.* Thank you, Clare. No further questions, Chair.'

Aware she has been wrong-footed, Clare looks around in anticipation of other questions. A natural reaction. But I wish it didn't look as though she was avoiding meeting anyone's eye.

No questions are forthcoming. Gordon is thanking the Hendersons. They're leaving. No prolonged interrogation. I should be relieved, for Clare's sake. I feel a deeper disquiet.

Gerald Findlater mutters, 'Striking-looking girl. Bound to attract attention.' His comment dies upon the air in the shuffling as the meeting settles itself again.

Max now. His chance to tell it the way he sees it. Looking at us all with that frank, fearless gaze of his. Taking us into his confidence. Though beneath the table I see his feet shift.

He begins in a gentle, unthreatening drawl. How much he regrets that it's come to this. Clare, a student for whom he had a high regard. For her to make such wild accusations. He has the same sense of astonished disbelief, of total shock, which he felt when the Headteacher, his friend and colleague Isabel Lincoln, summoned him.

'It was the unquestioning acceptance of a student's word against my denials which hurt most of all.'

Lisa interrupts him. 'Max, I know it seems self-evident to you. But you need to make a public declaration of your total innocence.'

He nods. As though he's overlooked it. Because it's inconceivable to him that anyone could take the girl seriously.

Dear God, the governors are nodding with him. Chaps who understand the way things are.

'I assure you all.' Max, voice steady, the drawl gone. 'There is not one word of truth in these extraordinary allegations.'

Lisa prompts again. 'And that's why there could be no question of accepting the Headteacher's bizarre suggestion that you ought to settle the matter by confessing to an offence of which you are entirely innocent?'

'Absolutely. No way was I going to confess to such an appalling betrayal of trust.'

They've rehearsed this. It's so unfair. When I was trying to help Max.

James says, 'Chairman, with your permission. The Headteacher has already given us an accurate description of the offer she made. Best practice. Agreed with the unions. As Area Secretary, Ms Whitworth, you will be well aware of that.'

But what chance does the truth have against the distorting magic Max can always command?

Lisa's not put off. 'Max, I know Isabel Lincoln's attitude disappointed you. Did it surprise you?'

He mimes reluctance. 'It's been so hard for her. Taking over as Head after someone as outstanding as Will Fullwood. Someone with so much charisma, who commanded such loyalty. I've done my utmost to back her up but I'm afraid she resented me. Especially when colleagues looked to me for a lead.'

I detach myself, analysing. It could have been worse. He hasn't brought up my relationship with Jack. Though there's still time. High risk, talking about Will Fullwood. It provides me with a motive. But it links him with the old enemy. Gordon hunches his shoulders, face brick-red. Good.

Fitzroy again. Indicating a wish to speak. A curt nod from Gordon. 'Mr Truman, have there been previous complaints about your conduct?' To my surprise, Fitzroy sounds belligerent. As though he's addressing a favourite target, some member of the Militant Tendency perhaps.

Max looks shocked. 'No, certainly not. Isabel Lincoln is the first person who has ever questioned my integrity.'

Yes, he's always got away with it. I cross-questioned Jack, but none of his knowing-and-not-knowing added up to evidence. I thought of bringing up the Dana business. I wanted to photocopy sections of Rachel's journal. But James said neither would help. Better to focus on the single issue where the student has made a specific complaint.

Fitzroy remains aggressive. No smoke without fire. Has Max been up to something?

Even to me, it's unacceptable. Lisa leans forward. Max gestures to restrain her. 'I'm afraid the girl saw her opportunity. A woman as Head. A few lurid stories in the tabloid press ...' He lets his accusation die away.

Perfectly judged. Fitzroy swallows the bait. 'Point taken.' He laughs a man-of-the-world laugh. Max has the sense to stay grave. I seethe.

Gaynor Jones, Parent Governor, raises her hand. Female. With a daughter. But unpredictable. 'This Clare Henderson.' Not an encouraging start. 'She was keen on you, was she?'

'It seems so.'

'You knew that, didn't you? I'd guess you get quite a lot of it, a young man like you.' Max grimaces. Gaynor persists. 'So you could tell, couldn't you?'

Yes, he could tell.

'What did you do about it?'

The question appears to please him. 'I took care to give her no encouragement. To behave with scrupulous professional detachment.'

'That's unusual here, isn't it? There's a lot of pally stuff between teachers and kids, isn't there?'

I want to explain how it really is. Except Gaynor isn't waiting for answers. 'Knowing the way she felt, wasn't it risky to take her away with you for a week?'

Max has more to say about that scrupulous professional detachment of his.

I've seen my opportunity. It's only hearsay. It may be disallowed. But the governors can't forget what they've heard. I sign to Gordon. He invites me to speak. 'The arrangement alarmed the Hendersons. They made an appointment to see me, referring only to concerns about Activities Week.' I ignore Lisa's attempt to intervene. 'Max persuaded me he should deal with it, as he was in charge of the whole programme, while I went to a meeting about the new exam. The Hendersons told me Max convinced them their fears were unfounded. So he had warning.'

Lisa is asking how I can claim to know what occurred when I wasn't present. A rearguard action. I've made my point.

Gaynor has more to say. 'Why would Clare want to get you into serious trouble, seeing as she's keen on you?'

He's ready for this one. 'She sought me out with some tale about helping to prepare a display. In my determination to offer her no encouragement, I was sharp with her. I could tell she resented it.'

James has a question for Max. 'Clare must indeed have felt resentment. Resentment strong enough to prompt her to make allegations which may destroy your career. You claim they are a malicious invention. If the governors agree, I assume you would expect them to exclude Clare permanently as the only sufficient punishment.' He's offering a stark choice. Dismiss Max or expel Clare. Brilliant. 'Schools cannot afford to harbour a student who has no scruples about damaging innocent reputations.'

Max looks ashamed. For the first time, he looks ashamed. He can save himself only if he lets Clare suffer. He leaves it to the Area Secretary to demand the stiffest penalty. Recognising it's not the best note to end on, she brings up my bias again. Girls know I am ready to listen to spurious complaints. She invites me to deny I am an active feminist. A member of a Women's Group.

I hesitate. That unlucky summer evening when Max dropped in, fresh from his week with Clare. Yet he can maintain his innocence and I've no choice but to admit guilt. 'Yes. I'm a feminist.'

Lisa Whitworth, the hypocrite, exchanges glances with the governors, as though she's proved her point.

I'm stung into confronting her. 'Why would I, as the Head of a mixed school, want to deny that I subscribe to a philosophy which advocates equal treatment for both genders? I understood that was your union's official policy. Don't you support it, Ms Whitworth?' Myself, I've never gone for the Ms. Too hard to pronounce, I claim. Too challenging, maybe. But Lisa does. I've scored a point. Only that's not what it's about. It won't endear me to the governors. I half-wish Max had accused me of allowing my passion for Jack to distract me from my duties. In their eyes evidence of a healthy attitude to sex. Not the warped anti-men stance of a *women's libber*, with its dark overtones of lesbianism.

Max and Lisa leave. The tension slackens. I tell myself it has to be a good sign. Gordon is asking if they have any more questions for me. Within minutes I'll be able to leave too. While they make their minds up. They ask me to go over what Clare told me. Shades of meaning. I have to get the emphasis exactly right. General discussion. Arguments circling inconclusively. If only I'd been able to charge Max with something more serious. Something no one could excuse. I had to rely on Clare, the only one to speak out. They seem to have forgotten me. I'm a willing eavesdropper, desperate to judge their mood. The Chief Education Officer is restless. Dismayed by this amateurish disregard of procedure, I guess. Aware the outcome depends on keeping them sweet.

Fitzroy delivers his verdict. 'It's been blown up out of all proportion. A minor incident. Girl led him on. Then she changed her mind. Got annoyed and decided to drop him in it.'

'Mr Buchanan.' James, coldly authoritative. 'We are talking about a teacher and a pupil. There is nothing a pupil can do which absolves a teacher from the absolute responsibility to maintain professional detachment.'

James is right. And wrong. The education expert, putting a governor in his place. Fitzroy resents it. Worse, the rest resent it on his behalf. What chance does the truth have against human passions?

Gerald Findlater says at his public school there was a man in charge. Do I think I'm seeing things differently because of my sex?

And how, I think. But I seek a diplomatic response. 'No doubt girls find it easier to talk to a woman. They'll tell me when they might not tell a man.'

'Exactly,' Fitzroy sneers. 'They'll run to you with any tale, as Mr Truman suggested.'

'Not at all.' I'm too impatient to play this game any longer. 'The reluctance to report sexual harassment is the problem, not frivolous accusations. I'm delighted if my gender makes a difference.' I can tell by their reaction it's not what they want to hear. There's general chatter. In which I hear 'Women's Lib' several times.

The room is airless. My fears, their prejudices, filling the space, crowding out the oxygen. I attempt to signal to Gordon Lindsay that I ought to have left. He seems to have abandoned his responsibilities as Chair. He's deep in discussion with the Clerk to the Governors. At last he makes a peremptory demand for order. He addresses James Greville, requiring clarification of the penalties available. Does that mean he's made up his mind Max is guilty?

'The governors have the power of dismissal,' James says. 'They can also give a Final Written Warning. But dismissal is the appropriate penalty for such a serious breach of the code of conduct.'

Gordon nods slowly. Gordon, ever-decisive. But for once apparently wavering. Then he remembers me. The momentary relief of escape. Short-lived. Because it brings the decision nearer.

Across to E3 where Jack sits at a table strewn with paperwork. 'Isabel! At last.' He gets up and takes both my hands. The contact soothes me. He's been heroic. Told everyone he backs me one hundred percent. With predictable consequences. Ostracism. Doubt Max? Who wants to give up a hero? Or maybe a partner in crime? The few who support us are outcasts. Without Jack, I don't know how I'd have survived the past weeks. 'Christ, what are they doing in there?' he says.

'Eleven o'clock! I thought it was my imagination I'd been in there for hours.'

'How's it going?'

I indicate the need for low voices. Max and Lisa, next door, in E2. 'Can't tell. They veer one way and then the other.'

'They have to find Max guilty. Don't they?'

We're both whispering. Conspiratorial. 'Or expel Clare for making malicious accusations.'

'Shit!'

'That's the choice James gave them. It helps. They may not want to sack Max. But expel a nice middle-class girl like Clare?'

'We're home and dry then.'

'Possibly.' Supposing I have to face the alternative? I begin a dreary computation of the consequences.

'You're not convinced.'

'I know what matters is protecting Clare. And stopping Max. He's abusing his position to satisfy his own warped needs. Only I can't help thinking what it means for me. If the governors choose to believe Max, not Clare. The truth doesn't count. They have the power to make it a lie.'

Jack attempts encouragement. I'm trapped in my own negativity. Our whispered conversation dies to an uneasy silence as the waiting lengthens.

Footsteps: the Clerk come to summon me. As he alerts Max and Lisa, I hurry into my place, avoiding an awkward encounter. Clare and her mother have long since gone home. I glance around, attempting to interpret the mood of the meeting. I'm too fraught to make a rational assessment.

Gordon, looking sombre. 'After the most careful deliberations, we have reached the decision that Mr Truman is guilty—'

Guilty. The only word I need to hear.

Gordon is still speaking. '—of breaching the code of conduct by inappropriate behaviour with a female student.'

A whirlpool of thoughts. Clare vindicated. My action upheld. Finally the staff will have to trust me, not Max. I can't look at him. He can do no further harm at Thomas Paine High. But I've destroyed him. Dismissal. Disgrace.

Gordon's addressing Max directly. 'Mr Truman, the governors take a very serious view of this unfortunate incident. You will receive a Final Written Warning.'

It's a mistake. He'll correct himself. Guilt means dismissal. James made that clear. I look towards him. He is stony-faced.

I know then there will be no correction. No dismissal. I have lost.

Chapter 23

In less than a day everyone knew not so much what Max had done as what I was doing to him. Antagonism sifted in the air. I drew it in with every breath. In the corridors I faced hostile stares from the more partisan amongst my colleagues. Most of them failed to see me, avoiding the issue of smiling or not smiling, speaking or not speaking. Though perhaps some of it was my fault. It's no longer easy to look people in the eye. I assumed, without analysis, that if the governors found Max guilty it would make a difference. On Friday everything was distanced. The hearing hadn't finished until after one that morning and the hours of tension left me spaced out. The unexpected outcome bewildered everyone. This morning I can no longer pretend that my catastrophic school transformation was a temporary phenomenon. The growing confidence that Thomas Paine High would flourish under my stewardship has gone for good. Like a child tearing up her work because she's spotted a single error, I've smashed to fragments all the delicate relationships I spent patient hours building.

Was it a concerted plan or did each one of my colleagues come individually to the same conclusion? Whichever, I conducted this morning's briefing in a silence so absolute the creak of a chair was as loud as a cry. As for the student reaction, maybe there's an unexpected gender divide. An attack on Max was sure to make his female fan club spring to his defence. But at morning break two fifth-year boys brought me a typed document. **THE DOSSIER.** Two words in heavy black capitals on the top sheet of a pile of sheets, hole-punched and linked with a treasury tag. When they left, I took the time to read it, not knowing what to expect. Statements from twenty-three boys which one of them had taken the trouble to type. Or maybe he's got his own computer and used that. Each statement described an incident. Max behaving inappropriately around girls. Hope flaring up again, I read them with forensic attention. They back the judgement I've already made. But there's nothing serious enough to justify fresh action. The boys' motives would be questioned at once. Like Clare, they must be resentful of some imagined slight. Or they are jealous of a teacher who enjoys so much popularity. Yet for all that it cheered me and I left it on view in my pending tray.

It's there now as I wait for this afternoon's uncomfortable little ceremony. Gordon Lindsay and I have to deliver the Final Written Warning to Max. Gordon tried to get out of it but James insisted he had to be present. Maybe if Gordon had known about it before he might even have gone for dismissal. Maybe. In fifteen minutes I shall come face to face with Max for the first time since the disciplinary hearing. Until we've performed this ritual the suspension remains in force.

Gordon. Arriving first by prior arrangement. We exchange an unsmiling greeting. Quite a difficult trick, that, as the smile slides into place and must be consciously resisted.

He sits down, hunching his shoulders and muttering that it's a bad business.

I agree with him. 'The Hendersons are very unhappy. Mrs Henderson phoned me this morning. As she reminded me, they have always been very supportive parents. They cannot understand the school's failure to take effective steps to protect their daughter.' I've planned this speech and it comes out rather fast. I'm determined to put my Chair of Governors on the spot. 'They're asking for an appointment with you as soon as possible.'

Gordon clicks open the fasteners on his black leather brief-case and thumbs through his Filofax. 'Not this week. Don't have a spare moment.'

'I realise how busy you are but it should be tomorrow or the day after at the latest. Postponement suggests we're belittling their concerns.'

He looks astonished. It's not my normal complaisant style. 'I don't know when—' he begins.

'Tomorrow evening? It doesn't have to be during the work-ing day.' I keep my pen poised above my diary until I pin him down to half-past seven Tuesday. I hand him the Formal Written Warning, which Linda has typed, and a photocopy of the page from the disciplinary manual which explains its significance. While he scans them, I ask him what he's going to say to Max, on the pretext that I want to back him up.

'I'll leave it to you.'

'I should find that difficult. I'm not clear what message the governors intended. Is his behaviour acceptable or not?'

'It's unfortunate. He upset the girl, which was wrong. Nothing too serious though, was it?'

'That's what you'll tell him? And you intend to say that to the Hendersons as well?'

He frowns, his face reddening. 'Women make too much of these things.' He's come out with it at last. 'Blow them up out of all proportion.'

I promised myself I'd keep calm but my pulse-rate's rising and my voice trembles as I say, 'You are at liberty to take that view. I'm not. The education authority which employs me condemns such behaviour.' I ought to leave it there but I can't. 'And so do I. Unreservedly.' The words aren't so bad. It's the way I shout them.

At that moment Linda knocks and pops her head round the door to say Max has arrived. Since there's little chance of putting matters right between me and Gordon, delay is pointless. I thank her and say we're ready to see Max. My Chair of Governors doesn't contradict me.

I study Max as though there is still some possibility of understanding him. Does he look subdued or am I seeing what I want to see? He takes the seat Gordon indicates with his usual elegant economy of movement. Apart from one grave glance in my direction, he fixes his gaze on Gordon. I wonder if it makes any difference that they are old adversaries.

The second fraught silence of the day. I'm surprised that the rustle of paper can sound so loud as Gordon separates the two sheets I've given him and hands one of them over to Max. Max holds it at a little distance, as though it doesn't belong to him. The Chair of Governors reads from the second sheet. He too has the knack of denying ownership, making the words from the disciplinary manual a recital to which he may or may not give wholehearted assent. I wait for the two questions at the bottom of the sheet.

'I have to ask you whether you understand the significance of the disciplinary procedure and the action the governors have taken,' Gordon says.

'Yes, thank you.'

'Do you wish to say anything?'

'Yes. I want to make it clear I continue to deny the truth of the allegations made against me, in the strongest possible terms. But after very careful consideration I have decided not to appeal against the governors' decision.'

I hear my own sharp intake of breath. I wasn't expecting this.

Max isn't looking at me. He's still meeting Gordon's gaze, keeping up his display of fearless innocence. 'I regret the decision. But I understand it. The Chief Education Officer put the governors in an impossible position by presenting the issue as a choice between finding me guilty, or finding Clare Henderson guilty of deliberate malice. Everyone who knows me will confirm that for me the students always come first. I find myself unable to pursue a case where my victory would be at the expense of destroying Clare Henderson's future.'

I dig my nails into my palms. It's mind-blowing. Can even Max get away with presenting himself as an icon of altruism?

Gordon looks baffled. 'Didn't have to be one or the other,' he says, attempting to disagree. 'All a misunderstanding.'

'Exactly. I was ready to see it in that light and overlook it.'

The Chair of Governors asserts himself. 'We want no more of this nonsense.' He sounds testy. It's unclear whether he's referring to what Max is saying or what he has done. 'You know my opinion of the regime which Fullwood set up. You've always been a prime advocate of it, Mr Truman. It should be clear to you now that it won't do. Mrs Lincoln's tried to curb the worst excesses. Credit where credit's due. But now we must have root and branch change.'

Old prejudices have won. And I have lost again. With Max as a witness. However 'disproportionate' my reaction might have been, it still offers the perfect excuse to attack the school's liberal ethos.

Gordon turns to me. 'Put it on the agenda for the next governors meeting.'

What can I do but acquiesce?

Gordon closes his briefcase with a double decisive snap and

departs, leaving me awkwardly tête-à-tête with Max. It's not what I intend but it's inevitable that I find myself exchanging companionable glances with him. One of those glances which asserts fellow-feeling against a common enemy. It's difficult to regain the distance I'm determined to keep between us.

Max speaks ahead of me. 'It's everything we feared, Isabel, isn't it? I want to assure you there are no hard feelings.' And he holds out his hand to me.

I ignore it.

He covers the rejection with an easy gesture. 'It was bound to happen. Too good a chance for Gordon and his pals to miss.' He shrugs. 'I blame myself.'

The nerve of it comes close to robbing me of speech. I swallow and say, 'Yes, it's thanks to your behaviour that we're in this situation.'

He shakes his head. 'I should have been more patient. More ready to explain.'

'Explain? What is there to explain? Clare complained about you and the governors upheld her complaint. No teacher ought to behave like that with a student and no explanation is going to make it acceptable in my eyes.'

'I agree with you. But you're basing your judgement on Clare's account of what happened. Which you accepted as the truth from the beginning. The kid was crazy about me. She's not an impartial witness.'

'I won't listen to this hair-splitting. You were found guilty. For whatever reason, you've accepted the Final Written Warning. We can only move forward on that basis. There's no point in discussing it.'

'Aren't you forgetting something? The governors didn't dismiss me. There's no love lost between us yet they didn't dismiss me.' He doesn't spell out the implication. 'I'm still your Deputy,

Isabel. We have to work together. I don't see how we can do that if you refuse to discuss what's happened.'

The trouble is, he's right. I meant to have a discussion. One in which I was very much in charge. Warning him about his future conduct. I think I had some wild notion that he'd be remorseful. Wrong-footed, I say, 'We have to discuss how we're going to work together, yes.'

'And to do that we have to be honest.' If I didn't know him so well, I'd think the appeal in his eyes was genuine. 'We came close to it that day when you walked in on me and Dana. When we talked about gender awareness. I thought we were going to work together on it. But you made your mind up there was stuff going on which you had a mission to root out. My inept handling of a few girls who had crushes on me became some sort of paedophile ring.' He shakes his head. 'You'd have had girls coming to you in droves if that was the case. You can't keep something like that quiet, can you?' His voice rises in innocent enquiry.

I don't believe him. I can't believe him because if I did I'd have to accept I'd done incalculable harm on the basis of a sick fantasy. 'We both want to stick to the facts, don't we? There was only one charge. Inappropriate behaviour with Clare Henderson.'

'Fine. Fact one, that was the charge. Fact two, Greville told the governors dismissal was the appropriate punishment. Fact three, they didn't dismiss me. That has to raise a few doubts, doesn't it?'

'Perhaps.'

His eyes narrow. He shakes his head. 'Isabel, I don't want to argue with you. It's tough on both of us. Shouldn't we try to make it as easy as possible? If you want to ignore what's happened, I'm prepared to do that too.'

Now he's being magnanimous. I don't seem able to take charge of the discussion. 'We can ignore the past. As long as you realise you're at risk. In future, your conduct will have to be above suspicion.'

Max smiles a little. 'Above suspicion? With some people's level of suspicion, that's a mountain to climb. There's always prejudice. *Single at thirty-eight? What's wrong with him?* But I'll do my best to overcome it.' The smile widens. 'And I hope you'll help me. Put me right if I get it wrong.'

I don't return the smile. 'I hope you'll listen to me.' I throw it out like a challenge.

'I promise to listen.' He sounds as if he's humouring me.

Stung, I reach for **The Dossier**. 'Reading this should help.'

He takes it and glances through it. He looks up from it with a little shrug. 'Anonymous, I see.'

'No. It came with a list of names. But I've hung on to those.'

'Then I'll read it. I want to learn in any way I can.'

I watch him put it face down on the coffee table. I was crazy to expect remorse. He'd have to admit he was in the wrong. He's the prisoner of his secrets.

He settles back in his chair. 'There's one question I have to ask you. Gordon hasn't persuaded you, has he? You don't believe all his crap about a dangerous regime? You haven't gone over to the enemy?'

I've been tormenting myself with that question. Yet when Max puts it like that I find there's only one answer. 'No, I haven't gone over to the enemy.'

'Brilliant,' he says. 'You don't know how relieved I am to hear you say that. And I hate to admit it but there's some right on Gordon's side. In the past Thomas Paine has been run by men. A male-dominated culture. Naturally, you're determined to change that. You have my total support.' He pauses. Perhaps he's waiting for me to thank him. 'I'm sure you can rely on Jack as well, the way things are between you.' He grins at me. 'It doesn't have to be a secret, does it? Jack seems hyper-sensitive about it. I mentioned it when we were having a drink together the other night and he got quite fierce. Maybe he's afraid folks will think it's just a smart career move on his part.' He laughs.

How has he latched on to my insecurity? 'I don't see that my relationship with Jack is anybody else's business.' As so often, I sound grudging, in contrast to his magnanimity. 'But no, it doesn't have to be a secret.'

'There's a lot of partisan feeling. I'll make it clear it's over and done with as far as I'm concerned. I've no interest in pursuing grievances.' His smile offers forgiveness. 'Attacks from the governors have one benefit. The staff will unite to resist them, just as they did in Will's time. Don't be downhearted, Isabel.' Maybe he's noticed my failure to return his smile. 'We can build up morale again. We'll tackle it at Thursday's staff meeting.'

I glance at my watch, lie that I have another appointment. I can't listen to Max any longer.

Yet when I'm left alone it's as though I can still hear his persuasive re-interpretation. He's always done it. Used the past as raw material to be re-shaped to suit his purposes. *Human kind cannot bear very much reality.* And Max less than most. Deception. Perception. Two or three letters which change everything. I may ask students to tell me exactly what's happened. But I know it's not possible. They can only tell me their perception of what's happened. When does a different perception become deliberate deception? With Max, I hear deception and resist. Yet it is seductive. If I'm prepared to see the past as he sees it there is a way forward where I saw only dead ends. I came to do so much. To make such a difference. I still could, if I'm willing to go along with his pretence.

Outside, the early dusk of November has already darkened the sky and the morning's fog is returning.

Chapter 24

Jack wakes to awareness. First of Isabel, warmth curled against him. Then, with dismay, to the week of disasters rippling outwards from the governors' inconclusive verdict. It's like time has lost its way and gone backwards to April 1981. The same suspicion of Isabel. The same crowd backing Max. Max the martyr-hero, wronged once again. And once again holding out the hand of friendship to the woman who wasn't satisfied with grabbing the job which should have been his. The woman who took a trumped-up accusation to the governors, the school's sworn enemies. Okay, that's the extreme position. The one taken by the likes of Tim Mayhew. Jack's always kept his head down before. Now he's in the firing-line. Publicly identified as Isabel's ally. He supports her, of course he does, but it's uncomfortable. Max is claiming to want to let bygones be bygones. Maybe he's playing a double game. Who's to know with Max? But it can't hurt to play along with him, can it? With so much negativity around it seems crazy to keep the row going. Trouble is, Isabel thinks it's some kind of moral duty to go on suspecting him. She won't listen when Jack points out she's done her best. Which has to absolve her of any further responsibility.

Isabel's stirring, turning on to her back. Propped on one elbow, he gazes down at her, smiling. Tension has etched lines around her mouth. With one loving finger he strokes the curve of her perfect cheekbones. She smiles, and the lines fade a little. He can't make it right for her, only provide the ultimate distraction. He throws back the duvet so he can gaze down at her nakedness. Why does Max want to have it off with kids? If Isabel's right about him, that is. Jack can feel his erection hardening. But he's not impatient. He rolls her nipples between his fingers. Tugs them and hears her little gasps of arousal. She murmurs his name. Her hand stretches out to fondle him. His hand slides down over the smooth skin of her belly. Her breathing quickens as he strokes her. He feels her stiffen. He teases her a little. Makes her murmur, 'Go on, go on.' Then she gives a cry of satisfaction and it's his turn.

A miserable Saturday morning. A November gale rattling the sash windows of Isabel's sitting-room. Splashing rain against the glass in a dozen different patterns. Soaking the fallen leaves until the autumn colours darken to an indeterminate brown. The drowsy warmth of the bed they shared seems remote.

They're sitting on the sofa, Jack's arm stretched along the back behind Isabel. They had to talk, she insisted. So they're going over the same arguments. 'I don't see what good it does,' he says. 'If there's nothing you can do about it, there's no point.'

'There's one thing I can do.'

'What's that?'

'Resign.' And then in response to the disbelief which must be written all over his face, she spells it out. 'Leave. Straight-away. Write to the governors saying I'm outraged by what they've done and I can't stay as Head.'

She doesn't mean it, she's outlining the most extreme position only to rule it out as an option. He keeps the game going by asking, 'You reckon it's the only way?'

'Not the only way. But the best way.'

'How do you make that out?' Isabel, who never gives up. 'Don't you want to stay and fight?'

'I shan't stay, no.' Said with a calm finality.

It's like a punch in the diaphragm. Jack can't find a response. He feels a sort of obligation to say he'll go too. Only it's different for her. She's worked in other schools. For him, teaching is the High School. How would he survive anywhere else? But if he stayed on without her ... He catches himself imagining how it would be.

Breaking free of his thoughts at last he says, 'You mean it, don't you?'

'Yes, Jack, I mean it.'

'You'll apply somewhere else? Carry the Thomas Paine message to another school?'

She grins at him, making a dismissive gesture, as though he doesn't understand. 'No, Jack. Who would want me?'

That's it then. She does mean it. She's giving up. Admitting it's too tough for her. Where's the courage he's always admired? Yet he feels protective too, now she's so vulnerable. He puts his arm around her shoulders. 'Maybe you should let the dust settle. Not do anything in a hurry.'

'No. I'm not going to play other people's games any longer. All my life I've been trying to win on their terms. I never got to make up the rules. No wonder it was so hard to win. I should have seen that years ago. How could I succeed, with the scoring loaded against me?'

'If you go and Max stays, he will have won. When you're so convinced he's abusing his position.' *You're* convinced. Implying he isn't. The nearest he'll come to admitting his doubts. About what Max may have done. And about how inexcusable it is.

'Yes, I'm convinced. Totally convinced.' The look she gives him seems to challenge contradiction. 'But as you've pointed out several times already that's irrelevant if I can't convince the governors.

He tries to get under her skin. So she'll change her mind. 'Without you everything will slip back into the old ways.'

'I guess so. I can't afford to bother about that. I can't change the system as long as I'm prepared to be part of it.'

'You have changed things.'

'A bit. Nothing like enough. Because I had to be careful. Never say what I really thought in case I lost my place on the greasy pole. I've done my absolute best as part of the system. And failed.' Isabel's eyes widen, eyebrows lifting. 'Rather spectacularly. You were right, Jack. I was never going to win.'

He cuddles her against him. 'You were right though.' He feels generous. 'Right to want to stop Max.'

'Right end. Unrealistic means.' Isabel leans into his embrace. 'I believed in him for too long.'

He draws away from a long kiss to say, 'He fools everyone.'

'Including himself. His safety depends on fooling us. He invented another Max, because the truth was too dangerous. His secret rules his life. He can never be open because society doesn't allow him to feel the way he feels.'

She's made her mind up. He's a paedophile. Which makes the sympathy in her voice even more surprising. 'It sounds like you're sorry for him.'

'I was dazzled by Max when I met him. Convinced I could never compete. Appointing me instead of him had to be the governors' prejudice. He'd done such a brilliant job as Acting Head. Max the hero. And then he was so generous in his response to me. Max the saint. All my stuff. I spent ages trying to make the real person match my inflated expectations. Finally I've got over my disappointment. I can feel some compassion. Acknowledge what we have in common: hiding the truth.'

'You hide the truth? You're the most straightforward person I know.'

'Am I, Jack? I know how it feels when it seems unsafe to be yourself. Maybe that's why Max was afraid I'd see through him. And me being a woman made it worse. Women are natural people-watchers in a way men seldom are. We study faces in case they signal disapproval. We listen, trying to work out the subtext. Bred into us by years of subservience.'

'I notice the way things look.' He's a painter, after all. 'But I don't leap to conclusions the way you do.'

She grins. 'Okay, you're observant too. You observe how things look. I work out what they mean. Which makes me dangerous. I understand why he wanted to get rid of me.'

'Wasn't it the other way round? You wanting to get rid of Max?'

'I sometimes see it as Max tempting me. Teasing me with glimpses of his sexuality. Leading me on to set up a confrontation he knew I'd never win.'

'Conspiracy?' It's too devious to convince Jack. 'Cock-up, more likely.'

'Maybe. I had taken his job though, hadn't I? I was ambitious. Determined to be a Headteacher. Why not me, as much as any man?'

He kisses her, a bit amused by her vehemence. 'Why not? Gender doesn't make any difference nowadays.'

'No? A man wouldn't worry who knew he was having an affair with his Deputy. People might be indifferent. Admiring. Jealous. But not contemptuous.'

'That's your fear, not the reality.'

'It's what they want. Evidence I'm not Superwoman. Human after all. As the woman in charge seems not to be. So it confuses them. And diminishes my authority.'

It confuses Jack sometimes. But there's titillation in it too. His boss yielding to his will when his lovemaking becomes masterful. 'It can be a nice confusion.'

She captures his wandering hand. 'Men are allowed to have views. Will's approach to education infuriated the governors but they took it seriously. If I argued the case for feminism they'd laugh at me. So I couldn't be myself any more than Max can.'

'Now you understand all this, why do you need to leave? You can allow for it. Work with it.'

'Working with it means bending myself to fit.'

'You're not worried about Thomas Paine High?'

'I can't let myself worry. Or my overdeveloped sense of duty will keep me there.' She leans closer to kiss him again.

'You must wish you'd never taken the job.'

'No way. I met you, didn't I? And I have so much to thank you for. So much joy I never expected.'

'Was it unexpected?'

'Utterly. All those weeks when I wondered why everything was so awkward between us. And then that evening coming away from Malcolm's, you kissed me, and I realised what the problem was. I was crazy about you.'

Jack holds her close, murmuring, 'And now?'

'Still crazy about you, eleven months later. While you're kissing me I'd agree to anything you asked.'

'Only while I'm kissing you?'

'Come on, I'm allowed to have a mind of my own.'

'It's one of the many reasons why I love you. You always have the courage of your convictions.'

'The courage of my perceptions. I had to accept there was no absolute truth for me to discover. Only the way it seemed to me.' She lifts his arm to kiss the inside of his wrist. 'Which wasn't the way it seemed to you, was it?'

He starts to insist it was.

'No, I love you most of all because you sided with me, despite your doubts.' She smiles at him. 'Backed me when I took on Will Fullwood's mantle and ruled out any compromise.'

'But you always said—'

'Yes. And the governors were uncompromising. Condemning the school. Loathing Max. But they opted for compromise.'

'What will you do?'

'Discover the truth about myself. Who I want to be, not who I imagine I want to be. It must be possible.' She shakes her head. 'Other people, like Max, will remain a mystery. There's no way I shall ever see the world through their eyes.' She strokes his cheek. 'I can't even see it through your eyes, Jack. Or know what you're really thinking.'

'I'm thinking I'll always love you.'

She looks troubled. 'Always?'

Permanence. For the first time, he pictures it. Him and Isabel. A partnership. Not what he'd imagined for himself. Two kids. He gets on with them. But they're not his kids. He loves her though. So he reassures her. 'Always,' he says. 'For always.'

'Darling Jack. But it wouldn't do, would it?'

He knows she's testing so he teases her. 'This morning in bed it did very well, didn't it?'

'In bed you are brilliant. The perfect lover. So clever at knowing exactly what delights me. And so generous in giving it to me. I'll always want to make love with you.'

'That's all right then.'

'No. I wish it was. But it isn't. It's another part of the game. Pleasing men. My fault. Not yours. I'm not ready for an equal relationship. Until I am, I have to stay on my own.'

'Okay, not for always then. Nothing that ties you down.

Carrying on as long as we're both enjoying it and then separating with no hard feelings.'

Her only response is a smile. He's not quite sure if the smile means she's agreeing so he kisses her. He can't believe she's serious about ending the relationship. Or about resigning. If she is, well, he's always managed to change her mind before. There's no hint of holding back in her response. Which ought to be good news. Except it could be because she no longer fears the persuasion of his kisses.

The phone's interfering warble comes between them. Isabel never leaves it to the answer-phone now. It might be Laura from Oxford, after waiting her turn for the communal phone. Irritated by the interruption, Jack listens to one side of the conversation, trying to work out how long it will last.

'Yes.' Formal. Half enquiring.

Not Laura then. Good. That would have gone on a bit.

Isabel says yes once or twice more. And then, 'No!' A decisive angry negative. Someone trying to sell her something. Any moment she'll slam the phone down.

But she goes on listening and answering in monosyllables for what seems like a long time.

At last she says, 'Yes, thank you,' in a way that sounds final. She attempts to put the receiver back in its cradle. She fumbles it and has to have another try. Her hand goes to her mouth and she gives a long shudder. 'Max,' she says.

'Phoning you here?' He's ready to be indignant on her behalf.

'That was the police. From Derbyshire. He's dead.' She repeats it, as though she can't take it in. 'Max is dead. Killed in a climbing accident. He went out on his own. Early this morning. He'd left a contact number with the pub where he was staying. My phone number.'

He steps towards her and grips both her arms. 'Max is dead?' he says, his voice cracking in disbelief.

She avoids his gaze, bowing her head to look down at the carpet. 'Yes, dead.' Her voice is toneless. 'Why, Jack, why?'

There's no answer he can give her. Shouldn't there be some meaning in a death? Something to make sense of a life cut short? Possibilities jumble together. Max is dead. But which Max? The pervert who abuses kids, driven by self-loathing? Or the innocent victim who despaired of proving a negative?

As though Jack's spoken his thoughts aloud, Isabel looks up at him and says, 'What have I done?' Her face is a distorted mask of doubt.

He hunts for some words of comfort. He finds none. His hands still rest on her arms but as the silence grows between them it feels like he's moving away from her. It's her responsibility. Her fault. When Max left her phone number he put the blame on her, fair and square.

And she's accepting it. Jack doesn't stop to think it through. It's something ten times more powerful than logic which makes him fold her in his arms and hold her hard against him.

It's from the safety of his embrace that she murmurs, 'I shall never know the truth now.'